She felt the warmth of his body at her back...

"I've been trying to forget Paris," Pierce said after a minute.

"You and Humphrey Bogart?" Brianne replied dryly.

"What? Oh. Oh!" He chuckled, then his eyes narrowed. "Local gossip says that there's a move to involve you with your stepfather's brand-new business partner, a sort of family merger."

She lost all color, but she didn't blink an eyelash. "Really?"

"Don't prevaricate," he said impatiently. "I know everything that goes on in this town."

"I can take care of myself." She straightened her shoulders.

"At nineteen?"

"Twenty," she corrected. "I had a birthday last week."

He made a rough sound. "Honey, you're fighting city hall when you tangle with your stepfather, much less with his shady partners."

"Something you know from experience?"

He smiled at Brianne. "I didn't say *I* couldn't win. I said *you* couldn't."

"Nobody tops Diana Palmer...I love her stories."
—Jayne Ann Krentz

DIANA PALMER

Once in Paris

MIRA

MIRA

ISBN 1-55166-470-4

ONCE IN PARIS

Copyright © 1998 by Diana Palmer.

Printed in U.S.A.

To all the wonderful people at MIRA Books, with love.

Chapter One

A woman in red, very blond and chic, stood before the Mona Lisa with a much taller, dark man and made a sharp comment in French. The man laughed. They seemed inclined to linger, but there was a very long line of tourists impatient to see the da Vinci masterpiece in the Louvre, and very vocal about having to wait so long for their turn. One of the visitors had a flash cameras aimed at the timeless masterpiece, which had been placed behind layers of bulletproof glass, until a guard spotted him.

Brianne Martin, from her vantage point on a nearby bench, found the visitors as interesting as the works of art. In her shorts and tank top, with her green eyes sparkling, her blond hair in a French braid and a backpack slung over one thin shoulder, she looked what she was—a student. She was almost nineteen, a pupil at an exclusive girls' school on the Left Bank in Paris. She didn't mix well with most of the other students, because her background was not one of wealth and power.

She came from middle-class parents, and only her mother's second marriage to international oil magnate Kurt Brauer had given Brianne the opportunity to sample this luxurious life-style. Not that it was by choice. Kurt Brauer didn't like his stepdaughter, and now that his new wife Eve was pregnant, he wanted Brianne out of the way. A boarding school in Paris seemed the ideal choice.

It had hurt that her mother hadn't protested.

"You'll enjoy it, dear," Eve had said hopefully, smiling. "And you'll have plenty of money to spend, won't that be a change? Your father never made more than minimum wage. He really had no inclination to better himself."

Comments like that made the strained relationship between Brianne and her petite, blond mother worse. Eve was a sweet but selfish creature, always with an eye to the main chance. She'd gone after Brauer like a soldier on campaign, complete with frilly battle plan. To Brianne's astonishment, her mother was married and pregnant within five months of her adored father's death. From their nice but small apartment in Atlanta, the Martin women had been transplanted to a villa in Nassau.

Kurt Brauer was wealthy, although Brianne had never been able to discover the exact source of his wealth. He seemed to be involved in oil exploration, but strange, dangerous-looking men came and went at the Nassau office he infrequently occupied. He had a home in Nassau and beach houses in Barcelona and on the Riviera, and a yacht to sail between them. Chauffeur-driven limousines and meals that cost three figures were commonplace to him. Eve was in her element, rich for the first time in her life. Brianne was miserable. Very quickly Kurt sized her up as a threat and got her out of the way.

She looked around the Louvre with great interest, as always. It had been her favorite haunt since she'd arrived in Paris, and she was in love with the old converted palace. It had only just gone through a major renovation. Although some of the changes were not to her liking—especially those gigantic modern-looking pyramids—she loved the exhibits, and she was young enough not to mind showing her enthusiasm for new places and experiences. What she lacked in sophistication she made up for with spirited enjoyment.

A man caught her eye. He was staring at one of the Italian paintings, but not with much enthusiasm. In fact, he didn't seem to see it. His eyes were dark and quiet and his face was heavily lined, as if he were in pain.

There was something very familiar about him. He had thick, dark wavy hair with threads of silver in it. He was a big man, broad in the shoulders and narrow-hipped. She noticed that he was holding a cigar in one hand, even though it wasn't lit. Perhaps he knew better than to smoke in here with all these exquisite treasures but couldn't do without something in his hand. She often picked at her fingernails, sometimes tearing them off at the quick when she was upset. Maybe the cigar kept him from biting his nails.

The thought amused her and she smiled. He looked very prosperous. He was wearing a cream-striped sport coat with white slacks and a beige shirt. No tie. He had a thin gold watch on his right wrist and a wedding ring on his left ring finger. He was holding the cigar in his left hand, so presumably he was left-handed.

He turned, and she got a glimpse of a broad, darkly tanned face. His mouth was firm and thin and wide, and his nose had a crook in it. There was a faint cleft in his chin. He had heavy dark eyebrows over large black eyes. He looked fascinating. He also looked familiar. She couldn't quite remember...oh, *yes.* Her stepfather had given a party after the wedding for some business associates, and this man had been there. He was something big in construction. Hutton. That was it. L. Pierce Hutton. He headed up Hutton Construction Corporation, which specialized in building transatlantic oil drilling platforms and also high-rise, high-tech buildings. He was an architect of some note, especially in ecological circles, and conservative politicians didn't like him because he opposed slipshod conservation methods. Yes. She remembered him. His wife had just died. That was three months ago, but he didn't look as if he'd done much healing.

She approached him, drawn by the look of him. He was still staring at the painting as if he'd like to set a match to it.

"It's very famous. Don't you like it?" she asked at his side, fascinated by his height. She only came to his shoulder, and she was fairly tall.

He looked down at her with narrow, cold eyes. *"Je ne parle pas anglais,"* he said in a voice that chilled.

"Yes, you do speak English," she countered. "You don't remember me, I know, but you were at the reception when my mother married Kurt Brauer in Nassau."

"My condolences to your mother," he said in English. "What do you want?"

Her pale green eyes searched his dark ones. "I wanted to say that I'm sorry about your wife. Nobody even mentioned her at the reception. I suppose they were afraid. People are, aren't they, when you lose someone. They try to pretend it hasn't happened or they get red in the face and mutter something under their breath. That's how it was when my father died," she recalled somberly. "I only wanted someone to put their arms around me and let me cry." She managed a smile. "That never occurs to most people, I guess."

He hadn't thawed a bit. His eyes swept over her face and lingered on her straight, freckled nose. "What are you doing in France? Is Brauer working out of Paris now?"

She shook her head. "My mother's pregnant,"

she said. "I'm in the way, so they sent me over here to school."

His eyebrows jerked together. "Then why aren't you in it?"

She made a face. "I'm cutting home economics. I don't want to learn how to sew and make pillows. I want to learn how to do accounts and balance spreadsheets."

He made a sound in his throat. "At your age?"

"I'm almost nineteen," she informed him. "I'm great in math. I make straight A's." She grinned at him. "Someday I'll come and pester you for a job, when I get my degree. I swear, I'm going to escape from this ruffled prison one day and get into university."

He actually smiled, even if it was reluctantly. "Then I wish you luck."

She glanced down the way toward the Mona Lisa, where the line was still just as long, and the murmurs were louder and gruffer. "They're all impatient to see it, and then they're shocked that it's so small and behind so much glass," she confided. "I've been eavesdropping. They all expect to see some huge painting. I imagine they're disappointed to have waited so long in line, and not to find it covering a whole wall."

"Life is full of disappointments."

She turned back to him and searched his eyes. "I'm really sorry about your wife, Mr. Hutton. They said you were married for ten years and devoted to each other. It must be hell."

He closed up like a sensitive plant. "I don't talk about private things—"

"Yes, I know," she interrupted. "It needs time, that's all. But you shouldn't be alone. She wouldn't want that."

His jaw twitched, as if he was exercising a lot of restraint to keep his expression under control. "Miss…?"

"Martin. Brianne Martin."

"You'll find as you get older that it's best not to be so outspoken with strangers," he continued.

"I know. I always rush in where angels fear to tread." Her pale eyes were smiling gently as she looked up at him. "You're a strong man. You must be, to have accomplished so much in life already, when you're not even forty yet. Everybody has bad times, and dark places. But there's always a little light, even at midnight." She held up a hand when he started to speak again. "I won't say another word. Do you think he's exactly in proportion?" she wondered, nodding toward the explicit painting of a man and a woman that he'd been looking through. "He seems a bit, well, stunted, don't you think, for his size? And she's exaggerated, but then, the artist was something of a connoisseur of plump nudes." She let out a long sigh. "What I wouldn't give to have her attributes," she added. "I'm going to be two walnuts for the rest of my life." She checked her watch, unaware of his start and the strange, reluctant smile that touched his eyes. "Gosh, I'll be late for math class, and that's the one I don't want to cut! Goodbye, Mr. Hutton!"

She ran toward the steps that led down to street level without looking back, her braid flying like her long, thin legs. She was gangly and inelegant. But Hutton had found her a delightful diversion.

She'd thought he was displeased with the painting. He laughed shortly as his eyes fell to the cigar, unlit, in his left hand. He hadn't come here to look at paintings, but to consider a plunge into the Seine after dark. Margo was gone and he'd tried and tried, but he couldn't face the future without her. He wouldn't see her blue eyes light up with laughter, hear her soft, French-accented voice as she teased him about his work. He wouldn't feel her soft body writhing in ecstasy under his in the darkness of their bedroom, hear her pleas, feel her nails biting hungrily into his body as he brought her to fulfillment again and again.

He felt tears sting his eyes and blinked them away. There was a hole in his heart. Nobody had dared approach him since her funeral. He forbade the mention of her name in the quiet, empty mansion in Nassau. At the office, he was tireless, ruthless. They understood. But he was so alone. He had no family, no children, to console him. The greatest pain of all had been Margo's inability to conceive after her tragic miscarriage. It didn't matter. It had never mattered. Margo was everything to him, and he to her. Children would have been wonderful, but they weren't an obsession. He and Margo had lived life to the fullest, always together, always in love, right until the very end. By her bedside, as she wasted away to a pale white skeleton before his anguished eyes, Margo had thought always of him. Was he eating properly, was he getting enough sleep? She even thought of the time afterward, when she wouldn't be there to take care of him.

"You never wear a coat when it snows," she complained weakly, "or use an umbrella in the rain. You don't change your socks when they get wet. I worry so, *mon cher*. You must take care of yourself, *tu comprends?*''

And he'd promised, and wept, and she'd cradled him on her thin breasts and held him while he cried, unashamedly, there in the bedroom they'd shared.

"God!" he cried aloud as the memories rushed at him.

A couple of tourists glanced at him warily, and as if he'd only become aware of where he was, he shook his head as if to clear it, turned and walked down the steps and out into the hot Paris sunshine.

The routine sounds of traffic and horns and conversation restored him to some sense of normality. The noise and pollution in downtown Paris had made a high-strung population even more nervous, but the noise didn't bother him. He clenched his big fist in his pocket, then relaxed and searched for a lighter. He took it out, looked at it there on the stone steps that led to the sidewalk. Margo had given it to him on their tenth wedding anniversary. It was gold-cased, inscribed with his initials. He carried it always. His thumb smoothed over it and the pain hit him right in the heart.

He lit the cigar, puffed on it, felt the smoke choking him for an instant, and then calming him. He took a breath and looked around at the glut of tourists on their way into the Louvre. Having holiday fun, he thought, glaring at them. He was hurting right down to his toes, and they were all smiles and laughter.

He thought then of the girl, Brianne, and what she'd said to him. How odd, to have a total stranger come up out of nowhere and lecture him on the healing of his broken heart. He smiled despite his irritation. She was a nice child. He should have been less curt to her. He remembered that her mother had married Brauer and become pregnant. Brianne had mentioned the painful loss of her father and her mother's immediate remarriage and pregnancy. She'd know about pain, all right. She was in the way, she'd said, so they'd sent her over here. He shook his head. It seemed that everyone had problems of some sort. But that was life. He glanced at the Rolex on his wrist with a rueful smile. He had a meeting with some cabinet ministers in thirty minutes, and in the maddening traffic through the city at this hour he'd be lucky if he was only thirty minutes overdue. He walked to the curb and hailed a cab, resigned to being late.

Brianne sneaked into the building and into her math classroom, grimacing as haughty Emily Jarvis spotted her and began to whisper to her friends. Emily was one of the enemies she'd made in the little time she'd been at this exclusive finishing school. At least there was only another month to go, and she could be sent somewhere else. To college, hopefully. But for now she had to bear this la-di-da finishing school and the highbrow snobbery of Emily and her friends.

She opened her math book and listened to Madame lecture them on advanced algebra. At least this course was fulfilling. And she understood equations, even if she didn't understand meticulous sewing.

After class Emily paused in the hall with her two cohorts flanking her. Emily was from a titled British family that could trace its heritage all the way back to the Tudor court. She was blond and beautiful and wore the most expensive clothes. But she had a mouth like a gutter, and she was the coldest human being Brianne had ever known.

"You skipped class. I told Madame Dubonne," she added with a venomous smile.

"Oh, that's okay, Emily," she replied with an equally sweet smile. "I told her what you've been doing with Dr. Mordeau behind the Chinese screen in art class on Tuesday after class."

Emily's shocked face drew in, but before she could reply, Brianne flashed her a gamine grin and skipped off down the hall. It always seemed to amaze other students that although Brianne looked fragile, almost vulnerable, that look concealed a strong and stubborn spirit and a formidable temper. Students who thought they could pick on Brianne were soon dispossessed of the notion. She hadn't been lying about what she'd said to Madame Dubonne, either. Emily's careless assignation with the school's art professor, Dr. Mordeau, had been overheard by several students, all of whom were disgusted by the couple's lack of discretion. Anyone walking into the studio would have heard what they were doing, even without their silhouettes so visible behind the flimsy screen.

Later that day, Dr. Mordeau went on extended sick leave and Emily wasn't in class the next morning. One of the girls had seen her leave in a chauffeured limousine, suitcases and all, just after breakfast.

After that, school became less of a trial to Brianne, as Emily's former cronies realized their reduced status in the student body and behaved accordingly. Brianne became close friends with a copper-haired girl named Cara Harvey, who was just eighteen, and they spent their free time going to art galleries and museums, of which Paris had more than its share. Brianne wouldn't admit that she'd hoped to find Pierce Hutton at any of them, but she did. The big man fascinated her. He seemed so alone. She'd never felt quite that level of empathy for anyone before. It was a little surprising, but she didn't question it. Not then.

The day of her nineteenth birthday, she went alone to the Louvre in late afternoon to look at the painting she'd found Pierce Hutton staring at. Except for a card from Cara, her birthday had gone by without any notice at all from others. Her mother had ignored it, as she usually did. Her father would have sent roses or a present, but he was dead. She couldn't remember a birthday that was so empty.

The Louvre for once failed to lift her drooping

spirits. She whirled, making the skirt of her ankle-length slip dress flare out. It had a pale green pattern that made her eyes look bigger, and with it she wore a simple white cotton T-shirt and flat slippers. She wore a fanny pack instead of carrying a purse, because it was ever so much more comfortable, and her hair was loose, long, blond, straight and thick. She tossed it impatiently. She'd have loved curly hair, like some of the other girls had. Hers was impossible to curl. It just fell to her waist like a curtain and hung there. She really should have it cut.

It was getting dark and soon she'd have to go back to school. She'd splurge on a cab, she decided, although she wasn't the least afraid of Paris after dark. As she scanned the street, looking for a cab, a small bistro caught her eye. She wanted something to drink. Perhaps she could get a small glass of wine. That would make her feel properly an adult.

She walked into the dark, crowded interior and realized at once that it was more a bar than a bistro, and very exclusive. She didn't have much money in her fanny pack, and this environment looked beyond her pocket. With a faint grimace, she turned to go, when a big hand came out of nowhere and shackled her wrist.

She gasped as she looked up into black eyes that narrowed at her start of surprise.

"Chickening out?" he asked. "Aren't you old enough to drink yet?"

It was L. Pierce Hutton. His voice was deep and crisp, but just a little slurred. A wave of his thick black hair had fallen onto his broad forehead and he was breathing unevenly.

"I'm nineteen today," she faltered.

"Great. You can be my designated driver. Come on."

"But I don't have a car," she protested.

"Neither do I, come to think of it. Well, in that case, we don't need a designated driver."

He led her to a corner table where a square whiskey bottle, half full, sat beside a squat little glass and a taller one with what looked like soda in it. There was a bottle of seltzer beside them and an ashtray where a thick cigar lay smoking.

"I guess you hate cigar smoke," he muttered as he managed to get into the booth without falling across the table. Obviously he'd been there for a while.

"I don't hate it outdoors," she said. "But it

bothers my lungs. I had pneumonia in the winter. I'm still not quite back to normal.''

"Neither am I," he said on a heavy breath. He put out the cigar. "I'm not anywhere near back to normal inside. It's supposed to get better, didn't you say that? Well, you're a damned liar, girl. It doesn't get better. It grows like a cancer in my heart. I miss her." His face contorted. He clenched his fists together on the table. "Oh, dear God, I miss her so!"

She slid close to him. They were in a secluded corner, not visible to the other patrons. She reached up and put her arms around him. It didn't even take much coaxing. In a second, his big arms encircled her slender warmth and crushed it to his chest. His face buried itself hotly in her neck, and his big hands contracted at her shoulder blades. She felt him shudder, felt the wetness of his eyes against her throat. She rocked him as best she could, because he was huge, all the while murmuring soothing nothings in his ear, crooning to him, whispering that everything would be all right, that he was safe.

When she felt him relax, she began to feel uncomfortable and a little embarrassed. He might not appreciate having let her see him so vulnerable.

But apparently he didn't mind. He lifted his head with a rough sound and propped his big hands on her shoulders, looking at her from unashamedly wet eyes.

"You're shocked? American, aren't you, and men don't cry in America. They bury their feelings behind some macho facade and never give way to emotion." He laughed as he dashed away the wetness. "Well, I'm Greek. At least, my father was. My mother was French and I have an Argentinian grandmother. I have a Latin temperament and emotion doesn't embarrass me. I laugh when I'm happy, I cry when I'm sad."

She reached into her pocket and drew out a tissue. She smiled as she wiped his eyes. "So do I," she said. "I like your eyes. They're very, very dark."

"My father's were, and so were my grandfather's. He owned oil tankers." He leaned closer. "I sold them all and bought bulldozers and cranes."

She laughed. "Don't you like oil tankers?"

He shrugged. "I don't like oil spills. So I build oil drilling platforms and make sure they're built properly, so they don't leak.'' He picked up his glass and took a long sip. As an afterthought, he passed it to her. "Try it. It's good Scotch whiskey, imported from Edinburgh. It's very smooth, and it has enough soda to dilute it."

She hesitated. "I've never had hard liquor," she confessed.

"There's a first time for everything," he told her.

She shrugged. "Okay, then, bottoms up." She took a big sip and swallowed it and sat like a statue with her eyes bulging as the impact almost choked her. She let out a harsh breath and gaped into the glass. "Good heavens, rocket fuel!"

"Sacrilege!" he chided. "Child, that's expensive stuff!"

"I'm not a child, I'm nineteen," she informed him. She took another sip. "Say, this isn't so bad."

He took it away from her. "That's enough. I'm not going to be accused of seducing minors."

Her eyebrows rose. "Oh, would you, please?" she asked brightly. "I've never, you see, and I've always wondered what makes women take off their clothes for men. Looking at statues in the Louvre isn't really the best method of sex education, and just between us, Madame Dubonne seems to feel that babies are brought by seabirds with big beaks.''

His own eyebrows rose. ''You're outrageous.''

''I hope so. I've worked hard enough to get that way.'' She searched his dark face quietly. ''Feeling better?''

He shrugged. ''Somewhat. I'm not drunk enough, but I'm numb.''

She put her fingers over his big hand. It was warm and muscular, and there were thick black hairs curling into the cuff of his long-sleeved white shirt. His fingernails were wide and flat and immaculately cleaned and trimmed. She touched them, fascinated.

He looked down, studying her own long, elegant fingers with short nails. ''No paint,'' he mused. ''How about on your toenails?''

She shook her head. ''My feet are too stubby to be elegant. I have useful hands and feet, not pretty ones.''

His hand turned over and caught hers. ''Thank you,'' he said abruptly, as if it irritated him to speak the words.

She knew what he meant. She smiled. ''Sometimes all we need is a little comfort. You're no weakling. You're a tough guy, you'll get through it.''

He shrugged. ''Maybe.''

''Certainly,'' she said firmly. ''Shouldn't you go home now?'' she asked, glancing around. ''There's a very slinky-looking woman over there with platinum hair out of a bottle giving you the eye. She looks like she'd just love to lead you home and make love to you and steal your wallet.''

He leaned toward her. ''I can't make love,'' he said confidentially. ''I'm too drunk.''

''She wouldn't care, I think.''

He smiled lazily. ''Would you?'' he mused. ''Suppose you come home with me, and we'll give it my best shot.''

''Oh, not when you're soused, thanks,'' she replied. ''My first time is going to be fireworks and explosions and the *1812 Overture*. How could I possibly get that from a drunk man?''

He threw his head back and burst out laughing. He had a nice laugh, deep and slow and robust. She wondered if he did everything as wholeheartedly as he grieved.

''Take me home, anyway,'' he said after the laughter passed. ''I'm safe enough with you.'' He hesitated after he'd laid the bills on the table. "But you can't seduce me, either."

She put her hand on her heart. "I promise."

"All right, then." He stood up, weaving a little, and frowned. "I don't even remember coming here. Good God, I think I walked out in the middle of negotiations for a new hotel!"

"They'll still be going on when you get back," she chuckled. "Heave ho, Mr. Hutton. Let's find a cab."

Chapter Two

Pierce Hutton lived in one of the newest, most exclusive hotels in Paris. He fished out his key for her as they passed the doorman, who looked suspicious. So did the desk clerk, who approached them at the elevator.

"Something is wrong, Monsieur Hutton?" he asked pointedly.

"Yes, Henri. I'm very drunk," he replied unsteadily. His big arm tightened around Brianne. "Do you know my business associate's daughter, Brianne? She's in school in Paris. She found me at Chez Georges and brought me home." He grinned. "She saved me from a *femme du nuit* who had her eye on my wallet."

"Ah," Henri said, nodding. He smiled at Brianne. "Do you require assistance, *mademoiselle?*"

"He's rather heavy, but I think I can cope. Will you check on him later, just to make sure?" she added with genuine concern.

The last of Henri's misgivings evaporated. "It will be my pleasure."

She smiled shyly. "*Merci beaucoup.* And please don't reply with more than *il n'ya pas de quoi,*" she added quickly, "because that's the entire extent of my French vocabulary, despite Madame Dubonne's most diligent efforts."

"You are at La Belle Ecole?" he exclaimed. "Why, my cousin is there." He named a girl whom Brianne knew just faintly.

"She has black hair," Brianne recalled. "And she always wears a long sweater, however hot it is," she added with a chuckle.

"*Oui,*" Henri said, shaking his head. "The *enfant* is always cold. Here, let me help you, *mademoiselle,*" he said, and assisted them to the elevator.

Henri helped them into the elevator, which was fortunately empty except for the operator, and instructed the man in rapid French to get Monsieur Hutton into his apartment.

"He will assist you," he assured Brianne. "And we will take excellent care of *monsieur*," he added gently.

She grinned at him. "Then I won't worry."

He nodded, thinking what a kind young woman she seemed. And such glorious blond hair!

She rode up in the elevator with Pierce and the operator, who helped her get him to the apartment, which she unlocked with his key. They maneuvered him into the huge bedroom, done in a black-and-white color scheme that seemed to suit him. The bed was king-size, with four posts that rose like slender wraiths toward the ceiling. They lowered him onto it, and he opened his eyes as he stretched on the black coverlet.

"I feel odd," he murmured.

"I don't doubt it," Brianne mused, thanking the elevator operator, who smiled at her and closed the door behind him.

Pierce's black eyes searched over Brianne's flushed face. "Feel like helping me undress?" he asked.

She colored even more. "Well..."

"There's a first time for everything," he reminded her.

She hesitated. He wasn't in any condition to do it himself. He was very drunk. Probably he wouldn't remember what she looked like in the morning.

She untied his shoes and pulled them off, and his socks with them. He had nice feet. They were long and elegant, and very big. She smiled as she walked around the bed and eased him up into a sitting position. She took off the jacket and then unbuttoned the shirt. He smelled of expensive soap and cologne, and under that shirt was a broad, dark-skinned chest with thick black hair covering it. She touched it accidentally and her hand tingled.

"Margo was a virgin," he said softly. "I had to coax her out of her clothes, and even though she loved me desperately, she fought me at first, because I had to hurt her." He touched Brianne's red face gently. "I don't suppose there are any virgins left these days. Margo and I were always the odd ones out. Very traditional. I didn't make love to her until we were married."

"Can you move your arm…? Yes, that's fine." She didn't want to hear this, but she was a captive audience. She pulled the shirt off and had to fight not to admire the tanned, muscular arms and chest. He didn't look like a man who spent a lot of time behind a desk.

"You're only nineteen," he said on a rough breath. "If you were older, I think I could make love to you. You're very pretty, little one. Your hair excites me. It's so long, and there's so much of it." He took it in both hands and closed his fingers. "Sexy hair."

"Yours is nice, too," she said for the sake of conversation. "Now, I don't think I can..." she added, her hands hesitating at his belt.

"Of course you can," he said quietly. He coaxed her hands to the belt and held them there, helping her, his eyes on her face as she fumbled the buckle loose. He guided her to the fastenings and then deliberately placed her hands under both waistbands. "Now, pull," he coaxed. And he arched his back to help her.

A hundred shocked, outraged, delighted thoughts flooded her mind as the clothing came away from that lithe, powerful body. He was nothing like the painting in the Louvre. He was beautifully made, a work of art in himself, with not a white streak or a bulge or a hint of fat anywhere. Fine hair shaded the most intimate part of him, and she hesitated with the slacks around his knees, with her heart beating her to death as she stared helplessly at where he was most a man.

It was a good thing, he thought dimly, that he was drunk, because her rapt expression would have triggered a raging arousal any other time. As it happened, he was too relaxed to feel desire at all, and for her sake, he was glad. She found him intimidating even in relaxation. He permitted himself a small upturn of the lips as he considered her expression if she saw him in full arousal.

That, of course, would never happen. Margo was dead. He was dead, inside and out. The brief amused light in his eyes went out. He lay back on the pillows with a long sigh.

"Why do people have to die?" he asked wearily. "Why can't they go on forever?"

She broke out of her trance and finished stripping him, before she tugged the coverlet over his hips to spare herself any more embarrassment.

"I wish I knew," she confided. She sat down beside him on the bed. Her hand went to rest on his where it spread over his chest. "Try to get some sleep now. It's the best thing for you."

His eyes opened, searching, haunted. "She was

only thirty-five," he said. "That's no age at all these days."

"I know."

His hand turned and caught hers, smoothing it palm down into the thick hair that covered him. "White knights come in both sexes, it seems," he mused drowsily. "Where's your armor and lance, fair Joan?"

"In my pocket. Want to see?"

He smiled. "You're good for me. You chase the clouds away." He studied her. "But I'm bad for you. A very bad influence."

"It was only a sip of whiskey," she reminded him.

"And a striptease," he added blithely. "I'm sorry about that. If I'd been more sober, I wouldn't have put you in such an embarrassing situation."

"Oh, it wasn't so bad. I'd seen that painting in the Louvre, among others, after all." She cleared her throat. "He really was, uh, stunted, wasn't he?"

He chuckled with pure delight.

"Sorry." She pulled her hand away and got to her feet. "Can I bring you anything before I go?"

He shook his head. It was already beginning to

hurt, despite the stupor. "I'll be all right now. You'd better get back to school. Did you get in trouble for cutting that class?"

She chuckled. "Not a bit. I'll finish next month."

"Then where do you go?"

She looked forlorn for an instant before she disguised it. "Oh, back to Nassau, I guess, for the summer. But next fall, it's university, whatever they say, even if I have to pay for it myself. I'm already a year behind the class I should be in. I'm not waiting any longer."

"I'll pay for it if they won't," he said, surprisingly. "You can pay me back when you have your degree."

"You would...do that for a total stranger?"

He frowned slightly. "Total stranger?" he asked pointedly. "When you've seen me totally nude?"

She couldn't manage a response.

"Which is something of an accomplishment, let me tell you. Until now, Margo was the only woman who ever saw me like that." His eyes became dull again. He winced.

She put her fingers against his cheek in a comforting gesture. "I envy her," she said genuinely.

"It must have meant everything to her, to be loved like that."

"It was mutual," he managed to say through his teeth.

"Yes, I know." She drew her hand away with a little sigh. "I'm sorry I can't stop it from hurting so much."

"You can't imagine how much you've helped," he replied solemnly. "The day I was in the Louvre I was looking for a way to get to her, did you know?"

She shook her head. "I only knew that you seemed totally alone and despondent."

"I was. You eased the pain. Today, it came back, and you were there." He searched her pale eyes. "I won't forget that you pulled me back from the edge. Whatever you need, I'll be around. I have a house of my own in Nassau, not too far from Brauer's. When things get too hot, you can always come visiting."

"It would be nice to have a friend in Nassau," she confessed.

His eyes narrowed. "I don't have a friend. At least, I didn't." He laughed coolly. "You're a damned funny friend for a man my age."

She smiled. "I was going to say the same thing."

"So people will talk. Let them." He caught her hand and brought the palm to his mouth. It was firm and cool against the faint moisture under her fingers. "I'll see you again, Brianne."

"I know." She got to her feet, and her eyes lingered on his broad, dark face. "You have to look ahead, you know," she said gently. "One day, it won't be so hard. You must have things you haven't done that you've always wanted to, designs that you haven't tried yet, projects to complete."

He stretched a little sorely. "For the past two years, I took care of Margo while the cancer ate her alive. It's not easy, learning to live for myself. I don't have anyone to take care of."

She opened her eyes wide. "Don't look at me. I'm independent, I am."

His eyes darkened. "You're a miracle," he said unexpectedly. "Maybe guardian angels really do exist and you're mine. But it's reciprocal. I get to be yours. Pick the college you want. I'll get you in, even if it's Oxford. I have connections everywhere."

Her eyes twinkled. "You don't look like anyone's fairy godfather."

"Appearances can be deceptive. I've never seen a father confessor with long blond hair, either."

She chuckled. "I'm going."

"Go on, then. Thank you," he added.

"It was no trouble. You're worth saving from yourself." She paused at the bedroom door and looked back, a little less bubbly now. "You...will be all right, won't you?" she asked. "I mean, you won't do anything..."

He leaned up on an elbow. "I won't do anything," he promised solemnly.

She made an awkward movement, a little unsure of herself. "Take care of yourself."

"You, too," he replied.

She opened the door, hesitated.

"I know you don't want to go," he said, his voice deep and a little curt. "But you have to."

She looked at him over her shoulder with huge, curious eyes. "I don't understand," she murmured worriedly.

"We've learned more about each other in a lot less time than people usually do," he explained. "It's a kind of bonding that I haven't experienced, either.'' He smiled dryly. ''Don't worry about trying to understand it. Friendship is a rare thing. Just accept it.''

She smiled. ''Okay.''

''Wait a minute. Hand me my slacks.''

''You're going with me?'' she mused, handing them to him.

''Funny girl,'' he muttered darkly. ''I'd fall down the elevator shaft in my present condition. No. I want to give you something.''

''If you try to pay me…!''

''Will you stop flashing those eyes at me?'' he grumbled, pulling a card from his wallet. He tossed it onto the coverlet. ''That has my private number, here in the hotel. If you get in trouble, if you need me, use it.''

She picked it up and lifted her eyes to his. ''I'm sorry I misunderstood.''

''And what exactly would I pay you for, anyway?'' he demanded irritably. ''The sort of woman you're thinking of does a little more than take off a man's pants!''

She gasped.

''Get out,'' he told her. ''And take your evil mind with you, nasty girl.''

"You stop calling me names," she said haughtily. "I don't have an evil mind."

"Ha!"

She put the card in the pocket of her dress and smiled at him. "You must be feeling better, you're growling again. Now, I'm really leaving."

"It's just as well if all you have to offer me are insults."

She glared at him from the door. "Would you like me to go back to Chez Georges and send that woman with the thick lipstick up here to visit your wallet? I'll bet she'd know what to do when she got your pants off."

"Why, you libertine," he accused softly.

"And one of these days, I'll learn what to do, too, then you just look out."

"Brianne."

She turned with the door open. "What?"

His expression was very solemn. "Be careful about tutors for that particular skill. Be very careful."

She tossed back her hair. "Oh, you don't need to worry. I already have someone in mind."

"Really? Who?" he asked curtly.

She stepped out the door and stuck her head around it. "You, when you've had enough time to get over your grief," she said gently. "I think you'll be worth waiting for."

And while he was getting over that shock, she closed the door and left him.

Nassau was filled to bursting with tourists, strolling along the coastline from the new development at Coral Cay all the way into Nassau itself. Colorful jitneys darted through traffic, barely avoiding collisions with mopeds and cars and pedestrians. Brianne wandered through the market at Prince George Wharf, admiring the colorful straw purses and hats and dolls, but all she bought was a new hat. This one was made of crushable hemp with woven purple flowers on the brim. As she paid for it, she grinned at the lady who sold it to her, then moved along to watch an ocean liner from the United States being maneuvered out of the expanded bay. She was sure that she'd never get tired of watching the huge ships come in and out of the port city. Often, too, there were military ships in port, like the United States destroyer down at the end of the pier. Sailors filtered through the tourists on their way back to the ship, pausing to admire a pretty brunette boarding one of the glass-bottom tourist boats.

It was time for lunch, but she wasn't ready to go home. Not that Kurt's villa could be called anyone's home, except perhaps, her mother's and half brother's. The baby, Nicholas, was a year old now and the apple of his mother's eye.

Brianne spent as little time at the villa as she could. Kurt had a business acquaintance staying with them, a Middle Eastern national who was very nearly Pierce's age. He was tall and slender and dark, with scars on one lean cheek that gave him a dangerous look. Brianne hadn't met him before, and now she wished she hadn't come home. Philippe Sabon was said to have a perverted obsession for young, innocent girls. He was some sort of rich state-official in an underdeveloped Arab nation. Sabon's mother was of Arab descent and his father, allegedly, was French but of Turkish ancestry. Very little was known about his shady background. He had millions, they said, but he'd spoken to Brianne of small, ragged beggars in the souks of Baghdad, as if he knew firsthand what their life was like. If it hadn't been for his smarmy reputation, Brianne might have enjoyed his company.

Kurt kept throwing Brianne and Sabon together at every opportunity. He was always nice, but there was something in the way Sabon looked at her that made her very nervous. He wanted Kurt to invest in some project in his homeland of Qawi, which was sandwiched between several other small nations in the Persian Gulf. It was the only nation that had, until now, refused to consider developing its oil potential. Its ruler, an elderly sheikh, was old enough to remember European domination, and he wanted no more of it. Sabon had convinced him that the abject poverty in his nation was too widespread to ignore. Sabon owned his own island, Jameel, just offshore from Qawi. The name, he told Brianne, meant ''beautiful'' in Arabic.

Sabon had apparently talked Kurt into approaching an oil consortium for him, and even investing in this scheme to develop the poor country's oil wealth. As a high minister in that nation—and many said that he'd bought the office—Sabon now had power enough to put through any sort of land deal he chose. He controlled the country's mining rights. He had given Kurt a part interest in these, and Kurt had sent a firm of mining engineers to do a study on the oil-producing potential of the untouched land. The move had been a good one. The engineers found a wealth of un-

tapped gas and petroleum under the hot sands. All
that was needed was more money for equipment
to exploit the resources, because the oil company
was only willing to provide a percentage of the
capital required for drilling, and the national treasury of Qawi itself was apparently off-limits for
such industry. Brianne thought that odd, but Kurt
seemed not to care as long as he held title to half
the mining potential of the country.

Kurt and Sabon had combined their own resources, and Kurt had coaxed an oil consortium
to join in the venture. Kurt now had most of his
fortune committed to the enterprise, which he expected to put him in the billionaire class. He had
to keep Sabon in his hands, however, to realize
that potential. Sabon had already inferred that another rich Middle Eastern friend would be happy
to replace Kurt in the endeavor. Kurt had too
much money tied up to risk backing out now.
He'd noticed Sabon's fascination with Brianne. If
dangling Brianne as bait would keep Sabon in his
power, he was more than willing to provide it,
with or without her permission.

There were stories about Sabon's perverse appetites circulating all over Nassau. The way he'd
looked at Brianne when they were introduced

made her feel as if he'd touched her body under her clothing. He found Brianne's coldness a challenge; she found *him* frightening. There was something in his dark, intent eyes that intimidated her. He was dignified and courteous to a fault; he was charming. But there was something about him that belied his reputation, and Brianne couldn't think what it was. He was like an iceberg in the sense that most of his character was carefully hidden behind a shield of reserve. People said he was perverted, yet Brianne saw nothing about the man that spoke of perversion in any form. He seemed always to be apart from others, always alone. He sought out Brianne and watched her quietly, but there was no hint of disrespect or lewdness in his manner toward her. Perhaps, she mused, it was her inexperience that kept her from seeing the truth about him.

She'd heard that Sabon was an enemy of L. Pierce Hutton, who had publicly denounced Sabon's recent support of a nation that was constantly under sanctions from the world community because of its aggressive political stance. Pierce seemed certain that Sabon was only seeking political support in the region by his public friendship with the other country. He wanted wealth and power and didn't mind what he had to do to obtain it. In that, he had something in common with Kurt Brauer, Brianne mused. Kurt didn't seem to have a conscience or a limit in his search for material wealth. And there was still something very shady about his income. He seemed to do no real work of any sort, although he was connected in some way to oil exploration. But the men who visited him didn't look like oilmen to Brianne. They looked like...well, like killers.

Philippe Sabon's continued presence at the villa, and his unwavering scrutiny, made Brianne very nervous. She spent as much time away from the villa as possible. Her mother thought she was overreacting to an older man's interest in her, and Kurt didn't care what his friend and associate was up to as long as he benefited from it financially. Brianne had no allies in that elegant house on the bay, not one.

Pierce Hutton had come back to the island three months earlier, but Brianne had only seen him once, last night, at a fancy social gathering that Kurt and her mother had taken her to. He was conducting business with a vengeance. He looked much better, but there was still a haunted darkness in his eyes. And he seemed ill at ease when he saw Brianne.

She remembered walking up to him with a smile, only to have him give her a strangely hostile glare and turn his back on her. It had hurt more than anything in recent years. Presumably he only wanted to be friends with her when he was drunk. She'd taken the hint and she'd avoided him all evening. Not one word had passed between them. That had probably been the best thing that could have happened, because Sabon disliked Pierce and Kurt wouldn't do anything to irritate him. Certainly it wasn't likely that Pierce would receive any invitations to the Brauer home while Sabon was in residence.

As she gazed at the crowds at Prince George Wharf, she realized that thoughts of Pierce's hostility had kept her awake most of last night. Silly, she thought, to imagine that he'd meant anything he said while he had half a bottle of Scotch whiskey inside him. She really was naive for someone who'd just turned twenty years old. She remembered her last birthday vividly. She'd spent it with Pierce. This year had no such pleasant associations. Her mother and stepfather had given her a pearl necklace, and her friend Cara Harvey had mailed her a scarf from Portugal, where she was spending the summer with her parents and having a rough time with a Portuguese nobleman who thought she was trying to seduce his younger brother. Except for Cara's gift, it had been a singularly uneventful birthday.

Sabon had wanted to throw her a party on his yacht, but she'd quickly found a reason to go into town. She had visions of being kidnapped and carried off into sexual slavery by that libertine. She'd heard rumors about him that didn't exclude kidnapping.

The wind blew her loosened blond hair around the shoulders of the pink silk tank top she was wearing with white Bermuda shorts and sandals. She wore a fanny pack so she wouldn't have to lug a purse, and she felt young and full of ginger. If it hadn't been for her situation at home, Nassau would have been all she wanted from life. It was so fascinating.

As she watched the big white ocean liner being turned by two tiny tugboats in a bay that seemed far too small for such an operation, she became aware of someone standing just behind her, watching. She turned, and there was Pierce, neat as a pin in white slacks and a yellow knit shirt.

He had his hands in his pockets. His black eyes were still full of storms, but they were oddly intent on her face.

"Hello, Mr. Hutton," she said politely, and with a smile. It was the sort of smile she'd have given the most distant acquaintance. He knew it, too.

His broad shoulders shifted as he glanced past her to the ship. "I've been entertaining a businessman from the States." He nodded toward the ocean liner. "He just left, on that."

She didn't know what to say. She only nodded awkwardly, turned and started back down the pier toward the wharf, her long hair flying away in the breeze. She knew that he wanted nothing to do with her; he'd made that clear at the party. She was willing to oblige him.

"Oh, hell, stop!"

She froze, but she wouldn't turn around. "Yes?" she asked.

All around them, tourists walked past, talking excitedly, gesturing. Nearby, one of the boat owners was singing a West Indian tune, hoping to attract more business with his talent. Brianne was hardly aware of the noise. Her heart was beating so loudly that it shook her.

She felt the warmth of his body at her back.

"I've been trying to forget Paris," he said after a minute.

"You, and Humphrey Bogart," she said dryly.

"What? Oh. Oh!" He chuckled. "I see."

She turned around then and squared her shoulders. "Look, you don't owe me a thing. I don't want rewards or even attention. I'm doing all right. I think Kurt will be more than willing to put me through college just to get me out of his hair."

His eyes narrowed. "That isn't what local gossip says. I hear there's a move to involve you with his brand-new business partner, a sort of family merger."

She lost color, but she didn't blink an eyelash. "Really?"

"Don't prevaricate," he said impatiently. "I know everything that goes on in Nassau."

She felt her blood go cold. Kurt hadn't said any such thing to her, but if it was common knowledge around the island, it might be true. She straightened her shoulders. "I can take care of myself."

"At nineteen?"

"Twenty," she corrected him. "I had a birthday this week."

He made a rough sound. "Okay, maybe you're not such a kid, after all. And maybe you can take care of yourself, in your own league. But, honey, you're fighting city hall when you tangle with Kurt Brauer, much less with Sabon."

"Something you know from experience?"

He cocked an eyebrow and smiled. He didn't want to tell her that he'd once intervened in a shady oil deal that Brauer was making with a terrorist group to provide them with arms in return for making an assault on a rival's oil tanker fleet. That information hadn't gone past his own security chief, Tate Winthrop, a former government operative who'd foiled Brauer's attempted coup. Winthrop was a full-blooded Sioux Indian with a mysterious background and friends in some of the highest offices in Washington, D.C. He had sources that even Pierce didn't.

He smiled at Brianne. "I didn't say *I* couldn't win. I said *you* couldn't. Where are you in such a hurry to go?"

"I thought I'd get on my swimsuit and lie on the beach for a while. Kurt owns the Britanny Bay

Hotel, you know. I can use the facilities there, and I keep a bathing suit in the office.''

''Come home with me. I have a private beach. You can swim there.''

She remembered his attitude the night before and hesitated. ''You don't really want me around.''

''No,'' he agreed at once. ''I don't. But you need someone. I seem to be all you've got right now.''

She flushed with angry pride. ''Thanks a lot!''

''Don't knock it,'' he added heavily, and his eyes were resigned and quiet as he studied her. ''You're all I've got.''

The statement rocked her right down to her feet. He was the most astounding man. He came out with the most profound things at the oddest times.

''I told you,'' he added, ''that I don't have family. I was an only child, and after Margo miscarried, she couldn't conceive again. Except for some cousins in Greece and France and Argentina—all distant—I have no family. And no close friends.'' He stuck his hands in his slacks pockets and stared out over the turquoise water of the bay as he spoke. ''Brianne, do you really think anyone else would have given a damn if I got rolled that night I drank too much?'' he asked ruefully. ''Do you think anyone would have cared if I'd died right there?''

''I would have,'' she said.

''Yes, I know. It doesn't make things any easier. You're too young.''

''You're too old,'' she retorted. She smiled. ''Does it matter, really?''

His black eyes surveyed her with faint amusement. ''I suppose not. Come on. I've got the car.''

Chapter Three

The entrance to Pierce's villa was through a high wrought-iron gate that had to be opened electronically by a device in the Mercedes he drove on the island. The paved driveway was lined by towering casuarina pines with their feathery spines, and flame trees in glorious bloom. Along the sand that flanked the driveway were blooming hibiscus plants and sea grape trees with circular leaves, which slaves were said to have used for plates in the days of pirate ships.

Two huge German shepherds lived in a kennel near the main house.

"King and Tartar," Pierce said, indicating the dogs as they drove past the chain-link fence that contained the animals. "They're let loose at night inside the gates. I wouldn't want to run into them myself."

She smiled. "I guess in your income bracket, you can't afford to take chances."

"I don't. I have a security chief who makes the White House brigade look sloppy." He glanced at her. "I'll have to introduce you one day. He's Sioux."

Her eyebrows rose. "Indian?"

"Indigenous aborigine," he corrected her with a grin. "Don't ever call him an Indian. He speaks five languages fluently and has a degree in law."

"Not your average security chief."

"Not at all. There's still plenty I don't know about him, and he's worked for me for three years." He pulled up in front of the house and stopped. As he helped Brianne out, a middle-aged man with a Mediterranean look came out the door, smiled and replaced Pierce behind the wheel.

"Arthur," Pierce said, waving the man away. "He usually drives me. He'll put the car in the garage. And this is Mary," he added, smiling at the pretty middle-aged black woman who opened the door. "She came with the villa. Nobody, but nobody cooks conch the way she does."

"Nobody except my mama," Mary agreed. "How you doing, miss?"

"I'm fine, thanks," Brianne said, and smiled.

"Any calls?" Pierce asked.

"Only one, from Mr. Winthrop, but he said it wasn't urgent."

"Okay. We'll be at the pool."

"Yes, sir."

Mary closed the big wooden door behind them, and Pierce led Brianne down a cool arched stone walkway that led to a huge swimming pool with a commanding view of the ocean beyond it.

She shaded her eyes with her hand and looked toward a jutting promontory where casuarina pines waved in the breeze and two sailboats lay at anchor.

"It's so peaceful here," she commented.

"That's why I like it."

She turned back to him. He pulled out a cushioned chair at a white wrought-iron table with an umbrella covering it and indicated that she should sit down.

"Do you spend much time in the pool?" she asked curiously.

"Not a lot. I can swim, but I don't care too much for it. I like to sunbathe out here. It helps me think things through." He motioned to Mary, who brought a tray with two tall, milky-looking drinks on it and a plate of small cakes.

Mary put the tray on the table and smiled as she left them by the pool.

"Mary makes good tea cakes," he said, reaching for his drink. "Help yourself."

She reached for one and put it on the saucer Mary had provided. She tasted it with delight.

"How delicious!" she exclaimed.

"Mary says it's the amount of flavoring she uses that gives them such a nice taste."

She reached for her drink and sipped it, surprised to find that it didn't contain any alcohol.

He noticed her expression and chuckled. "I'm not giving alcohol to a minor, even in Nassau," he murmured.

"I'm not exactly a minor," she informed him.

"You're not twenty-one yet," he replied. His dark eyes slid over her youthful figure and up to her pretty face with intense scrutiny as he sat with one big lean hand wrapped around his glass. "You're young. Very young."

"Blame it on a sheltered childhood," she said.

Her gaze slid over him like searching fingertips. "How old are you?" she asked abruptly.

One bushy eyebrow lifted. "Older than you."

She wrinkled her nose. "Much older?"

He shrugged and sipped his drink. "Much older." His dark eyes met hers levelly. "Almost twice your age."

"You don't look it," she said, and meant it. He had the physique of a man ten years younger, and there were only traces of silver at his temples. She smiled at him wistfully. "I guess you haven't given a lot of thought to seducing me?"

Both eyebrows went up. "I beg your pardon?"

His tone would have made a lesser woman falter, but Brianne was made of stouter stuff. "We talked about it in Paris," she reminded him. "Of course, you were pretty drunk at the time, so I can't really expect you to remember too much of our conversation. But I did admit that I was going to wait for you." She grinned wickedly. "And I have, despite the temptation."

He hated himself for asking. "What temptation?"

"There was a very handsome Portuguese nobleman in one of my classes. He was older than the rest of us, very cultured, very correct. All of us were wild about him, but there was a fiancée waiting back home.'' She shook her head. ''Poor Cara.''

''Who's Cara?''

''My best friend. She's from Texas. She went to Portugal this summer to stay with her sister, and guess whose brother her baby sister got involved with?''

''The nobleman's.''

''Bingo. I understand it's been open warfare since her ship docked.'' She shook her head. ''Cara never liked Raoul in the first place,'' she recalled. ''They couldn't get along.''

''But you liked him.''

She nodded and smiled at him. ''Very much. He was nice to me.''

He chuckled deep in his throat, and there was a look in his eyes that didn't make much sense to her.

''Why are you laughing?'' she asked.

He gave her a complicated look. ''Do you think I'm nice?'' he asked softly.

She looked stunned. ''Nice? You? Good Lord, you're a barracuda!''

The laughter grew, deep and rich. ''Well, you're honest.''

"I try to be." She looked down into her glass with a sigh. "Philippe Sabon's after me, you know," she said with visible discomfort. "He wanted to throw a birthday party for me on his yacht, and my stepfather was all for it. I refused, and now he's not speaking to me. But I heard the two of them talking, and it made me nervous."

He didn't have to ask why Sabon was interested in her. He already knew. He spun the ice around in his glass before he took another sip.

"According to what I've heard, Sabon has a yen for virgins," he said curtly. "I won't tell you what he's said to do with them. But he isn't doing it to you."

His concern made her feel warm inside. She smiled. "Thanks. Could you loan me your security chief for a few days to make sure of it?" she added half-jokingly.

"I'll take care of it myself," he said, and he didn't smile. His eyes narrowed on her young face. "You can hang out over here until he leaves. I understand that he's facing the threat of a military coup by a poor neighboring country with no oil. They want his."

"So does my stepfather," she informed him. "He's all but bankrupted himself putting money into developing the oil fields over there, and he's attracted other investors to help him. If the military coup succeeds, he'll be standing on the street corner selling pencils out of a cup.''

''Or diving for conch,'' he added mockingly.

''That isn't likely. He can't swim.''

''He's made a bad bargain there,'' Pierce murmured thoughtfully. ''A real deal with the devil.'' His dark eyes narrowed as they slid over her. ''What are you supposed to be, collateral?''

She flushed. ''Over my dead body.''

He didn't reply to that. He was thinking, and his thoughts weren't pleasant. ''How did you end up with Brauer for a stepfather?'' he asked after a minute.

''My mother is beautiful,'' she said simply. ''I'm just a poor carbon copy of her. She was selling jewelry in an exclusive shop and he was buying a present for a friend. She said it was love at first sight.'' She shrugged. ''I don't know. Anyway, my father had just died a few months earlier and she was lonely. But not lonely enough to become a rich man's mistress,'' she added with a faint smile. ''It was marriage or nothing, so he married her.'' She toyed with her glass. ''They have a new son and he's the whole world for Mother.''

''Is Brauer good to her?''

''No,'' she said flatly. ''She's afraid of him. I don't know that he's actually hit her, but she's very nervous around him. Now that she has the baby to think about, she never argues with him like she used to when they were first married.''

''Does she talk to you about him?''

She shook her head. ''Kurt makes sure that I never have much time alone with her.'' She met his eyes. ''I didn't like him from the beginning, but she thought I was resentful because it was so soon after Dad's death.''

''Brauer is nobody's idea of a white knight,'' he murmured curtly.

She studied him. ''You know something about him, don't you.''

''I know that he's devious and underhanded and that he'll do absolutely anything to make money, and he does,'' he said flatly. ''We've been rivals for some time now. I cost him a lot of money a few years ago, and he's never forgotten. If he has an enemies list, I'm at the very top of it.''

"Can I ask how you cost him money?" she wondered aloud.

He was reluctant to tell her, but in the end, he decided that she needed to know the truth about her stepfather. "He was trying to make a deal with a terrorist group to attack an oil platform and cause an environmental disaster."

"Why?" she asked, aghast.

"I've never been quite sure," he told her. "Kurt plays a close hand, and his business dealings are kept under the table. All I know is that an enemy of Kurt's was making some threats. Kurt reasoned that by making the man look criminally careless about damaging the global ecology, he could give him enough bad publicity to bring him down. And it might have succeeded."

"You stopped it?"

"Tate Winthrop did," he said with a faint smile. "My security chief has contacts everywhere, and we soured the deal. Brauer never knew how it was done, but I know he suspects that I was behind it."

"Are you in competition with him?"

He chuckled as he finished his drink. "Not really. I'm in the oil business, of course, but I deal primarily in the construction of oil platforms. Kurt has an interest in an oil shipping firm. Still, he's got a few scores to settle with me, and I've heard some veiled threats that I don't like about my newest site. I can't afford an environmental disaster. I've spent too much money building this platform with adequate safeguards to prevent any wholesale leaks. So I've sent Winthrop and some of his men out to my new platform to stand guard while it goes into operation. Just in case.''

"Where is it?"

"In the Caspian Sea," he said. "It's brimming over with oil, but most drillers won't put a lot of money into extracting it because of the dicey situation in the Middle East. It would have to be piped through hostile territory or tanked around. But we're working on a deal, and with any luck, we may strike a bargain that's mutually beneficial."

"It sounds very complicated."

"It is. We're very sensitive to environmental issues. I don't want to cause an oil spill. And not because it's bad publicity. I have no patience with people who are willing to sacrifice the planet on the altar of profit margins."

She smiled at him. "No wonder I like you."

He smiled back. She was bright and she seemed

to sparkle. He liked her, too. It wouldn't do to let that feeling get out of hand, of course. He had to try to think of her as a child.

"You aren't eating the tea cakes," he pointed out. "Don't you like sweets?"

"Very much. But I'm not really hungry," she confessed. "I've been worried about Mr. Sabon."

"You can stop worrying. I'll deal with Sabon."

"He's very rich," she said worriedly. "He owns a whole island somewhere off the coast of his native country in the Middle East. It's called Jameel."

"I own two islands," he countered with a chuckle. "One's off the coast of South Carolina, and I own one here in the Bahamian chain."

"Really?" She was impressed. "Are they inhabited?"

He shook his head. "Not inhabited or developed. I'm leaving them both as wildlife habitats." He smiled at her delighted expression. "I'll take you to them one day and show them to you."

Her heart skipped and she sighed with open pleasure. "I'd like that a lot."

He searched her face with quiet, thoughtful eyes. His expression became somber. "So would

I.'' He put his empty glass down on the table. ''Tell me about your father. What did he do?''

''He was a loan officer in a bank,'' she said. ''He wasn't handsome or terribly intelligent, but he was kindhearted and he loved me.'' Her eyes grew sad with the memories of him. ''Mother never had time for me, even when she was at home. She worked a six-day week at the jewelers, and she always seemed to feel that Dad didn't give her the life-style she deserved. He was a failure in her eyes, and she never stopped telling him so.'' She grimaced. ''One day he went to work and we got a phone call just after lunch. They said he'd started toward an office to talk to one of the vice presidents and he just folded up. He died right there of a heart attack. Nothing they did brought him back.''

''I'm sorry. It must have been rough.''

''It was. Mother didn't really even mourn. And just three months later, there was Kurt, and suddenly I didn't have a family I belonged in anymore.''

A long silence fell between them. Then he said, ''I never had a family at all. My parents died when I was in grammar school, in a plane crash. I went to live with my father's father in America.

He had a small oil transport fleet and a smaller construction company. My first job was helping to put up buildings. I learned it from the ground up, the hard way. Grandfather never pampered me, but he loved me. He was Greek, very old-world even after becoming a naturalized American citizen." He chuckled at the memory of the gruff old man. "I adored him, rude manners and all."

"But your last name doesn't sound Greek," she said.

"It was Pevros, before he changed it to Hutton, after a wealthy family he'd read about in the States," he replied. "He wanted to be American all the way. I still have French citizenship, but I could qualify as an American citizen, having spent half my life in New England."

"You said your grandfather had a small construction company," she murmured. "But yours is enormous and international."

His broad shoulders rose and fell. "I had a sort of sixth sense about mergers that paid off big. Once I got the hang of it, there was no stopping me. I sold the oil tankers and parlayed the proceeds into an enterprise that became the core company of an empire." His eyes narrowed as he studied her. "Margo's father had a chain of building supply companies in Europe," he recalled. "The merger led to a marriage and ten of the happiest years of my life." His face seemed to harden to stone. "I thought she was immortal."

Impulsively, she laid her hand over his big one on the table. "I still miss my dad," she said softly. "I can only imagine how it must be for you."

His hand stiffened. Then it relaxed and turned, enveloping hers in its warm, strong grasp. "That empathy of yours saved me," he said, searching her eyes quietly. "If you hadn't taken me home to my hotel that night in Paris, I really don't know where I would have ended up."

"I do," she murmured dryly. "You'd have ended up with that industrial-strength blonde, being rolled for your wallet!"

He chuckled. "I probably would have. I was too drunk to care what happened to me." His eyes softened. "I'm glad you were there."

Her fingers curled trustingly into his. "I'm glad I was there, too."

His eyes grew slowly darker as they stared intently into hers. His thumb began a lazy stroking motion against her palm. She felt the sensation all through her body, as if he was touching her bare skin instead of just her hand.

He saw the reaction and deliberately enlarged the area of her palm that he was stroking. He hadn't wanted women in his life since Margo's death, and he certainly shouldn't be encouraging this green little innocent. But she made him feel kingly when she looked at him with those soft, drowning eyes, when she trembled from the merest touch of his hand. Any man could be forgiven for being tempted.

Her breath was choking her. She looked at him with an ache that made her sick all over. "I don't suppose you'd like to stop that?" she asked unsteadily.

"Why?" he asked softly.

"Because I'm getting this awful ache in a place I can't tell you about," she whispered tightly.

His hand tightened around her soft fingers. He wasn't thinking about right and wrong anymore. He had an ache of his own, and he needed something to numb it before it doubled him over.

"Suppose I told you that I have a similar ache?" he asked huskily, holding her gaze with steady, hot black eyes.

"In a...similar place?" she asked outrageously.

"Tell me where yours is," he murmured wickedly.

"Just south of my navel," she said bluntly, and her mouth felt bone dry. "And my breasts hurt," she added huskily.

His eyes fell to them with keen, sharp interest and he saw the peaked nipples under her thin top. His intake of breath was audible.

"Nobody ever looked at me there, or touched me there," she whispered when she saw where his eyes were riveted. "I've saved it all up."

He felt as if the world were crashing down on his head. He had to stop looking at her, thinking of her, wanting her. He'd put her right out of his mind until he'd come to Nassau. Then he'd seen her again, at her stepfather's, and all the wicked, forbidden longings had surfaced again at his first sight of her after the months of absence.

His fingers edged between hers in a sensual caress. "I'm thirty-seven," he bit off.

"So what?" she asked breathlessly.

"So you aren't even legal yet."

"Excuses, excuses," she muttered huskily. Her lips parted as the sensual caress of his fingers threatened to stop her heart. "For God's sake, can't you just do something? Anything!"

His eyes narrowed to slits as he looked at her. "With Mary right in the house and Arthur likely to come looking for me any second?"

She groaned aloud.

He made a rough sound under his breath and glared at her. He jerked his hand back and stood up, turning his back to her while he fought to stop himself from reaching for her, right over the table.

He jammed his hands hard into his pockets and grimaced when he saw how it outlined the raging, highly visible arousal he couldn't help.

Margo was the only woman who'd ever been able to do this to him instantly. It seemed that the long abstinence was making him careless, and vulnerable. He had to get this wide-eyed innocent out of his life.

She was already inside the house by the time he turned around, heading right toward the front door.

He went after her, noticing when he joined her at the curb that she wouldn't look at him.

"Sorry," she said through her teeth. She was clutching her purse as if she expected it to make a break for freedom. "I don't honestly know what came over me. Maybe it's some tropical virus that makes your mouth independent of your brain.''

He chuckled in spite of himself. "Not quite. But it seems to be contagious.''

She wouldn't look at him. "Don't make fun of me, please.''

"I don't know what else to do," he said bluntly. "I'm not seducing children this week. Sorry.''

She glared up at him. "I was trying to seduce *you*," she pointed out. "With no success whatsoever, I might add. I guess I'll have to find some sort of school where they teach seduction and take lessons.''

He burst out laughing. "You shameless hussy!''

"Thanks. I'll file that compliment along with all the others.''

"It wasn't a compliment.''

"If you don't do it, he will," she said, suddenly serious. "I'll throw myself in Nassau harbor right in front of the Prince George Wharf before I'll let Sabon touch me!''

"What do I have to do with him?" he asked, genuinely puzzled.

"He likes virgins. Virgins!''

"Ah," he murmured. "I begin to see the light. If you become suddenly experienced, he'll lose interest, you think?"

"Yes, I do. And if you'd cooperate, I'd be right off the endangered species list. But, oh no, you can't make one little sacrifice for my whole future! Excuse me for asking you to risk your body in bed with me!"

His eyebrows levered up as he stared down at her. "Careful," he said softly. "You're walking on broken glass."

"I'd like to create some," she muttered. She looked away from him and sighed loudly. "Well, I'll go to the casino over on Paradise Island tonight. Surely there's some man desperate enough to give me what I need...."

He jerked her around and held her bruisingly by one arm. His black eyes blazed down at her. "Don't you dare," he said in a voice that sent chills down her spine.

"Well, you won't!" she protested.

"Maybe I will," he murmured. He was disturbed, and he looked it. He felt Margo's loss keenly, still, and even to think of sleeping with another woman seemed like adultery. But Brianne was young and sweet and loving, and it wouldn't be any hardship to give her what she wanted. On the other hand, she was painfully young and impressionable. If it hadn't been for the specter of Philippe Sabon lurking somewhere in the shadows, he wouldn't even be considering this harebrained proposition in the first place.

"You just hold your horses," he said shortly. "Don't lead with your head."

"Advice, advice," she muttered. "Why don't you just back me up against a wall and give it your best?"

He dropped her arm. "You incredible child!"

"I'm not a child, thank you."

"You're outrageous," he continued.

"Totally. It comes from living among idiots." She stared at him with quiet, soft eyes. "I'll wear you down," she promised. "Day by day."

He stared at her with mixed emotions. "Whatever happened to virginal terror?"

"I don't know. I'll ask someone."

"Aren't you afraid of the first time?"

"With someone like you? Are you crazy?"

He laughed in spite of himself. His eyes twinkled with humor. "All those expectations. I'm getting older. What if I can't live up to your expectations?"

"Oh, but you can," she said with solemnity. "You want to. You just think I'm too young. I'm not, you know. I grew up around people older than me, and I've always been more mature than my own age group."

"I'm not making you any promises," he assured her. "I said I'd think about it."

She shrugged. "Take your time. No rush. But if that lobo wolf comes looking for me, I'm coming after you, and I don't care what time it is."

"How is he supposed to know, at your age, that you're still virginal?" he asked reasonably.

She glowered at him. "Because, unknown to me, Kurt had a private detective following me from the day I went off to school," she muttered. "I was watched like a hawk, and two months ago Kurt demanded that I have a physical to make sure that I hadn't caught some virus he said I'd been exposed to." She shivered at the thought of what the doctor had done to her. "Part of the physical included a gynecological exam," she added. "I had no idea that the doctor was going to do that, until I was in the examination room and the nurse had me on my back." She let out a breath. "I yelled the place down, but the doctor had the information Kurt wanted."

"No reputable doctor..." Pierce began furiously.

"He wasn't a reputable doctor," she returned. "He was barred from practice in the States and came down here to run some sort of clinic."

"I see."

"I never connected it until Sabon started turning up at the house at all hours and watching me like a hawk." She lifted her gaze to his hard face. "I'm not scared of much," she said, "but that man gives me the shivering willies."

"Don't feel bad. He has that effect on some men."

She lifted her eyebrows. "On you?"

He chuckled. "I was a drill rigger for a couple of years." He held out his big hands and showed her his knuckles, replete with tiny white scars.

She pursed her lips. "Tough guy, huh?"

"Yes," he said simply. "And I'm not afraid of much, either."

She searched his eyes. "What scares you?"

He leaned close to her, so that his eyes filled the world. "Sex-crazed virgins," he whispered.

He looked and sounded so wicked that she burst into helpless laughter. "I asked for that one," she murmured through her chuckles.

He laughed with her. He'd never known anyone like Brianne. She was changing him, changing his life, his world. She made the sun come out again, brought back the rainbows. He didn't dare consider the implications of what he was feeling. He turned away and went to find Arthur to tell him to bring the car around, so that he could drive them back into Nassau.

In the weeks that followed, Brianne became Pierce's shadow. To her stepfather's dismay, she kept a mile away from his friend Philippe Sabon and spent so much time with Pierce that rumors began to abound. They were seen together everywhere, fishing and swimming and just sunbathing. Mostly they did the latter at Pierce's house, but occasionally they went to the beach.

The companionship they shared was as rare as the humor that bound them together. Pierce didn't realize how necessary Brianne was beginning to be to him, but the hours he spent alone brooding over Margo were dwindling with time. He looked forward to Brianne's wry insight on the world around them, to her savvy sense of politics. For a young woman, she had a mature outlook. He was impressed with her. More than impressed. He didn't mind her constant presence in his house.

But Kurt did. Things came to a head when Philippe sailed into port on his yacht to see Brianne and she wasn't at home. Worse, his private detective had a very thorough report of where she'd been most recently.

Sabon's rage was all the more intimidating for being quiet. He glowered at Kurt, his black eyes flashing, his lean fists clenched at his side. "You know that your stepdaughter has become special to me," he began. "I have even told you that my plans for her might include marriage. Yet you have permitted her to practically live with Hutton. What must I do to keep her around when I wish to see her, kidnap her?"

Kurt held up a hand, his face worried. "No, you have it all wrong. You have the medical report," he said quickly, wary of his wife's presence somewhere nearby. He didn't want her to hear this. "I assure you, the girl is fastidious, chaste, regardless of the time she spends with Hutton!"

Sabon didn't speak for a moment. His eyes caught every nuance of expression in the other man's face, from the fear that made him pale to the greed that made his eyes hot. Brauer had no idea at all of his real plans, or his true desire. He had made certain of it. The man's cooperation was essential at this point. He had to ensure it any way that he could.

"I know how badly you need my help," he told Kurt coolly. "I have had your financial assets examined most thoroughly. If I should back out now, before the oil is discovered and processed, and replace you with someone else, you would be left destitute, would you not?"

Kurt swallowed. He was in over his head, with no way out. The man knew too much. "Yes, I would," he confessed heavily. He drew out a spotless white handkerchief and wiped his sweaty forehead. "I have no option but to go right through to the end. But this business about involving the United States—I don't know. I don't know if it will work."

Sabon's thin lips pursed thoughtfully. "Of course it will." He studied Brauer. "I have told you that I think a marriage between Brianne and myself might be advantageous for both of us. A...seal on our agreement."

"Marriage." Kurt's greedy eyes glittered as he turned the thought over in his mind. Sabon had millions. He was supposedly one of the wealthiest men in the world. He would certainly take care of his wife's relations. Even if the oil deal fell through, Kurt would have all the money he needed, without having to fall back on his usual means of making money—a tricky enterprise these days, with so many customers who reneged on their promises of payment. He would never have to worry about money again! He smiled from ear to ear. "What a wonderful proposition! Yes, yes, it would be the perfect seal on our bargain!"

Sabon didn't meet his eyes as he bent his head to light one of the small, thin Turkish cigars he liked to smoke. "I thought it might appeal to you."

Kurt almost drooled with pleasure. His future was assured. Now he had to talk to his wife, quickly, to make her understand how important Brianne's acquiescence was in all this. She would back him up. She was the girl's mother, and Brianne was still a minor. She could be made to comply. And so, he thought with cold reason, could her mother.

"And you will handle the chore I require of you in America," Sabon added.

"Of course." Kurt waved a careless hand. "You may consider this done. It will be my pleasure, in fact. Brianne will make you a lovely wife, give you many children!''

Sabon said nothing. The thought of joining their families by marriage had turned the trick. He would have no more worries with Kurt. Briefly he thought of the young, bright Brianne in his arms and the torment almost bent him double. Brauer would sell his stepdaughter, anything he owned, in his headlong search for power. Sabon hid the contempt he felt for the unscrupulous man before him and wished, not for the first time, that he had other options, other means, to accomplish what he must for his country. Although he'd sorted Brauer out, Pierce Hutton would pose as big a threat as the too-close enemy on the borders of Qawi. He had to keep the man at a distance before Hutton learned anything from Brianne that might tempt him to interfere.

By demanding Brianne's company, by dangling the bait of marriage with her before Brauer, he hoped to accomplish that. Sabon gave one regretful thought to Brianne, so desirable and kind, who would suffer at her stepfather's hands because of his proposal. But he couldn't hesitate now, when so much was at stake! He had to think of his people.

Kurt watched him curiously. "You weren't serious about kidnapping her?"

The more Philippe thought of the idea, the more it appealed to him. His dark eyes narrowed thoughtfully. "It would be one way to ensure her...cooperation, would it not?"

Kurt scowled. Brianne was an American citizen, and Hutton was possessive of her. "It could complicate matters," he persisted.

Philippe smiled coolly. "Indeed it could." He said no more, but there was a new and introspective look about him that made Kurt nervous. He had so much riding on this endeavor, almost too much! He simply could not afford to let Philippe double-cross him. And the best way to accomplish that was to get in the first blow. Kurt had half the rights to the long-protected mineral wealth of Sabon's little country. If he could overthrow the government—and what sort of defense was a sick old sheikh with a small army?—he could cut Sabon right out of the loop and deal directly with the oil consortium. He'd have all the wealth he'd ever need, and he could put his shady friends on the payroll to protect his investment. He would never have to resort to arms dealing, his true business, again. The more he thought about it, the better he liked the idea. Sabon was so trusting, really. He thought he held all the aces. He would discover that he had nothing. Nothing at all.

Chapter Four

The minute Philippe left to return to his yacht, Kurt Brauer went immediately to find his wife. She had told him that Brianne and Pierce had gone to Freeport on a shopping trip. She didn't know that the shopping trip had been a last-minute invention, because Brianne had seen Sabon's yacht coming into port and she'd run to Pierce's house to keep out of his way. In fact, she'd stayed there until she was sure that Sabon had sailed away.

Kurt had been impressed by Sabon's threats, and his finances were such that he couldn't afford to back out. He was between the proverbial rock and the hard place, and Brianne was slowly crushing him with her determination to avoid Sabon.

He was upset that she wouldn't help him keep in the good graces of Sabon, and angry that she seemed determined to outflank him. He didn't know if Philippe had been serious about kidnapping her, but he was beginning to think it might be the only way to make her see sense. He spoke firmly to his wife, but he couldn't find Brianne until the next day. He cornered her in the living room of the beach house the minute he saw her and spoke to her about it.

"Philippe went away angry about the way you avoided him. He knows that I can't afford to back out of the deal, and he's talking about new partners. I don't like your refusal to help me entertain him," he said in his faintly accented English as he glared at her, both hands shoved into the pockets of his trousers. "And I especially don't like you hanging around with Hutton. You must know that he and I aren't on good terms."

"He's my friend," Brianne said simply. "And I like him."

"Bosh! He's years too old for you," he said, conveniently forgetting that his friend Sabon was the same age as Pierce. "I don't want you spending so much time with him. It looks bad. Besides," he added uneasily, "Philippe has heard of it, and it made matters even worse. He doesn't approve."

"Philippe doesn't app—" she burst out.

He silenced her with a raised hand. "You don't understand how I'm placed!" he said angrily. "I can't afford to upset him in any way! Everything I have is invested in his country's oil exploration and development. I'm risking all of it!"

"You shouldn't have let him talk you into the investment in the first place," she pointed out.

He glared at her. "I talked him into it," he corrected her, "because I saw the chance to triple my investment. My finances are not what they once were," he said coldly. "If I do nothing, I will lose what little I have left. This is a perfect investment opportunity, absolutely foolproof. But in order to make it work, I must remain friendly with Philippe. I cannot afford to antagonize him—or permit you to do so." He cleared his throat, aware of the building resentment in her young face. "It is time you married," he said harshly. "Philippe has said that he wishes it. It will be the best way to cement our business partnership."

"Marry...him!" she burst out, appalled. "Listen, I am not marrying your friend Philippe! He scares me to death! You must surely have heard the gossip about him, about what he does to young girls!"

He turned and looked at her down his nose. "Your mother is quite happy here, *ja?*" he asked slowly. He smiled. It wasn't a nice smile. "She and the child. You wouldn't want anything to...upset her, now, would you?"

As veiled threats went, it was a masterpiece. She felt her body going numb as she considered what he was hinting at. She knew that her mother was afraid of him and that she was deeply regretting her marriage. Brianne also knew that her mother was vulnerable with the new child. She couldn't really afford to make Kurt madder than he already was, for her mother's sake. But there was no way on earth she could marry that repulsive man, even to save her mother and half brother!

She stood there, defiant but frightened, uneasy, searching for the right words. Pierce could save her. She couldn't tell her stepfather that; her words might inflame him to the point that he would do something desperate to her poor mother.

For almost two years she'd blamed her mother for her hasty marriage and equally hasty pregnancy, but blood was thicker than water. She couldn't cause her only remaining parent to come to harm, regardless of her feelings of betrayal.

"You understand me, Brianne?" Kurt continued slyly. "You will do as I say?"

"Do I have a choice?" she replied quite calmly.

He smiled, not a pleasant smile at all. "No," he returned. "So I think we might discuss plans for the wedding. Your mother will be happy to assist you, I am sure."

"Not today," she said, and searched desperately for an excuse. She squared her shoulders and came up with the perfect one. "I'm meeting a girlfriend for lunch at the Lobster Bar downtown."

"A girlfriend?" He was immediately suspicious. "Who is she?"

Her mind would barely cooperate. "My friend Cara, from school," she invented. "She's on a cruise and will only be in town this afternoon. I haven't see her since graduation."

He hesitated, still not quite trusting her. He pursed his lips and thought for a minute. "Very well. But Philippe has sailed to one of the outer islands and is to arrive back here tomorrow. I will expect cooperation from you.''

"Certainly."

She was pale and not as confident as she sounded, but she forced a smile for him and went to dress.

Brianne's mother, Eve, having left the baby with the live-in nurse, slipped into her room as she was changing into jeans and a green silk shirt that matched her eyes.

"Has he spoken to you?" the older woman asked quickly.

"Yes," Brianne replied. She stared at her mother, seeing the new lines in her pretty, soft face, the new haunted look in her pale eyes. "Indeed he has."

Eve twisted her hands together. "I had no idea that he was going to take it this far, Brianne," she said miserably. "I know you don't like Mr. Sabon. I know what people say about him. But he's very rich and powerful—''

"And you think money is the most important thing in the world," she replied with cold eyes.

Her mother averted her gaze quickly. "I didn't

say that. He could give you anything you wanted, though. And it would make Kurt happy.''

''Making your husband happy isn't my main goal in life, Mother,'' Brianne said with an unfamiliar iciness in her tone. ''And if you think I'm going to marry that man to keep Kurt Brauer happy, you are sadly misinformed.''

Her mother looked horrified. ''You…you didn't say that to him?'' she asked with real fear.

''Of course not!'' she replied quickly. ''Mother, I'm not a fool. He did make certain threats about you, and the baby,'' she added reluctantly. She and Eve had never been close. At times like this, it was sad, because they could have confided in each other, comforted each other. Eve had always lied about her age. Brianne's very presence, not to mention her age, was a visible contradiction. Like many pretty women, she had a hard time accepting the advance of her years.

Eve made a helpless gesture with one perfectly manicured hand. The older woman looked vaguely hunted. ''Kurt has a very bad temper,'' she remarked. ''I haven't seen it often, of course,'' she said with a wary glance at her daughter. ''But we argued over you, quite badly.

That was one reason I agreed when he wanted to send you to school in France. Things haven't been quite calm here for some time, and especially not since he got mixed up with Mr. Sabon.'' She brushed back a strand of color-tinted blond hair. Her green eyes pleaded with those of her daughter. ''Couldn't you pretend to agree to marry him, just until I can think of something, anything, to do? There's Nicholas, the baby, to consider. I really couldn't bear it if Kurt...well, if he fought me for custody, Brianne. You know I'd lose. I haven't any money of my own. Please! If you won't do it for my sake, do it for Nicholas's! You must know what sort of life he'd have without me.''

The sad thing was, she did. Nicholas would grow up at the mercy of a man who had none. She frowned worriedly as she finished buttoning her blouse over her small breasts. She turned and stared at her mother with sad eyes. ''You used to say that all you needed to be happy was a lot of money. Do you still feel that way?''

The older woman paled. ''I was tired of being poor,'' she replied bitterly. ''Of having nothing and working all hours. Your father had no ambition at all!''

"No, but he had a kind heart and a generous soul," Brianne replied quietly. "He would never have raised a hand to you." Her face hardened as she looked at the woman who'd raised her but never loved her or cared what happened to her. Certainly Eve hadn't treated her as she treated the baby, cuddling him and kissing him and rushing to satisfy his every whim. It was a painful reminder that she hadn't been really wanted, or loved.

"You repaid my father's love and loyalty by leaping into Kurt Brauer's arms barely a month after his funeral," Brianne said, thinking aloud. "You can't imagine how I felt about that."

Her mother's face was a study in shock. She put a hand to her throat. "Why...Brianne," she said huskily. "You never...you never said a word."

"What would have been the use?" Brianne's face was as sad as her voice. "You didn't care about my feelings, or my grief. You wouldn't wait and risk losing Kurt and all his money."

"How can you speak to me in such a way?" Eve asked huskily. "You're my own child!"

"Am I?" she asked with real pain. She searched her mother's brittle, beautiful face. "I don't remember that you ever cuddled me or held me when I cried, or did anything except criticize me and wish me out of the way.''

Eve, for once, didn't have a comeback. She looked confused, unsettled.

''My father loved me,'' she said with icy pride. ''He kissed the hurt places and took me to see art shows and concerts even when he could barely afford it. You did nothing except complain that he was spending time with me that he could have spent working his way to a promotion.''

Eve frowned, searching the face of this stranger in the room with her. ''I didn't realize that you wanted to be with me,'' she said uncomfortably. ''You never seemed to like me very much.''

''Nor did you like me. I wasn't beautiful.'' The words came out much more forcefully than Brianne meant them to, but there were years of pain behind them.

Eve swallowed. She clasped her hands at her waist, which was still a little full despite the baby's age. ''If you had your hair properly styled and used makeup and wore the right kind of clothes...''

''You might love me?'' Brianne asked with a hollow laugh.

Eve actually winced. She took a single step forward with her hand lifted, but it was too late. Years too late. The barely perceptible gesture of conciliation was completely ignored.

Brianne gathered her purse from her bed and snapped it shut. She couldn't think of anything else to say.

"Where are you going?" Eve asked helplessly.

Brianne glanced at her. She didn't dare risk telling her mother the truth. "My friend Cara from school is in town just for the afternoon. I promised to meet her for lunch."

"Oh. Oh, that's fine, then," Eve said. She forced a smile. "Now, don't worry. Everything will be all right here. It's just this business deal upsetting Kurt. He'll be fine once the pressure is off, once he's got what he wants." She was the picture of a stubborn woman rationalizing an untenable situation. "He loves me. He does. He loves the baby, too. He won't do anything to hurt us, no matter what he told you," she added.

"Good. Then I won't have to marry Philippe Sabon to keep you safe, will I?"

The question took all the color out of the older woman's face. She moved forward quickly, almost frantically. "Brianne, you must think carefully about this," her mother said frantically. "You mustn't make any snap decisions!"

"I won't." She turned her purse in her hands, all too aware that she looked like an Amazon next to her pretty little mother. Brianne had nice legs and pretty hair, but she fell far short of Eve's idea of what her daughter should be.

Eve seemed to sense that. She reached out, hesitantly, and for the first time in years, she touched her daughter, touched the long, thick, straight blond hair and felt its clean texture curiously.

"You do have such lovely hair," she said slowly. "My stylist could do wonders for it. And you have the body for couture. I never noticed how elegant you are."

You never noticed me at all until I could help you tuck some more pretty feathers in your nest, Brianne thought resentfully, but she didn't say it. She stepped back and her mother's small hand fell.

She went quickly to open the door and paused to look back at the doll-like face of her mother with sorrow and pity. "I'm only twenty and I know that happiness can't be bought. Why haven't you learned that in almost forty years?"

Her mother's pretty face closed up. "I'm barely

thirty-five,'' she protested with a false laugh. ''And besides, I like nice things.''

''You must. You're going to pay a very high price for yours.''

''It isn't so much to ask, that you marry one of the richest men in the world, Brianne. Think of all I've done for you. Think of what Kurt's done for you,'' she added quickly when she remembered how little she could claim to have contributed to her child's well-being. ''He sent you to a very expensive school in Paris, and he's even supporting you now. You owe him something for that, Brianne,'' she added, trying to regain the upper hand. She smiled that empty, cold, social smile she used to impress Kurt's business associates, a frightening group of people whose exact connection to her husband was something she still couldn't quite figure out. ''I know you'll do the right thing, once you've thought about this.''

Brianne didn't say anything else. It was pointless. The two women had never had much in common, and now they had even less. Her mother wasn't going to let go of Kurt and his money regardless of what it cost her, she'd just said so. She was even willing to sacrifice Brianne to keep it.

But Brianne wasn't going to be sacrificed. She was going to the one person who could rescue her.

Pierce, fortunately for her, was at home. He was on the phone with his security chief, but what he was hearing made him uneasy.

"We had an attempt on the rig last night," Tate Winthrop said in his deep, unaccented voice. "We foiled it," he added, before the explosion he could hear forming on the other end of the line. "But I don't think it will be the last. And I've heard some new rumblings about Sabon's country. They say one of his poor neighbors is stockpiling weapons from a sympathetic nation and is considering an attack to capture the drill rigs in Sabon's first oil fields. He was right about the oil, you know. They've hit paydirt, or so my sources say."

Pierce stretched lazily, and his eyes went to the white beach beyond the confines of the swimming pool where he was lounging alone. He sipped his whiskey sour. "I wonder if letting them prevent the development wouldn't be the best thing," he said after a minute. "Brauer will set up the fields without safeguards or any regard for the ecology if he has his way."

"If they attack and get beaten back, the first thing they'll probably do is set fire to the oil," Tate pointed out.

Pierce whistled softly. "What a disaster that would be. That wouldn't make them any friends in Washington."

"Speaking of Washington," Tate said quietly, "there's a rumor that Brauer is about to try to pull some strings and get the U.S. involved in this."

"You're kidding!"

"I used to work for the CIA—I don't have a sense of humor."

"Sorry."

"Brauer went to school with one of the senators on the foreign affairs committee," he continued. "He's been in touch. I understand he's due in Washington soon to lobby for U.S. aid."

"He wants Uncle Sam to help him build an oil field?" Pierce drawled.

"Not at all. He wants Uncle Sam to protect it while it's being built."

"Sabon is a millionaire and he owns half the country, not to mention its king and most of its ministers. Why can't he protect it himself?"

"He's wealthy. His country isn't. Odd duck,

Sabon," he added. "He has a reputation for perverse sexual habits, but the funny thing about it is that no charges have ever been brought against him, and nobody's ever found any of his discarded lovers."

"Curious."

"Brauer labels him as a money-grubbing assassin, but that isn't the reputation he has among the people in his own country." There was a pause. "Why would a man deliberately picture himself to the world as a debaucher?"

"Beats the hell out of me. I've been wondering why he wanted Brauer as a business partner."

"Nobody else has any clout with the United States," Tate mused. "Think that might have any bearing on it?"

"Very possibly, but he couldn't have picked a more dangerous ally. Brauer's done so many immoral things in his lifetime that he makes Sabon look good."

"I'll drink to that."

The other man sounded offhand, distant. "You sound preoccupied," Pierce said suddenly, because he knew the man's mind wasn't on the subject they were discussing.

"A...personal problem, nothing I can't handle,'' Tate said quietly. ''Look, I'll talk to a few people about Brauer and see who he knows in Washington. If you hear anything new, get back to me.''

''I'll do that. Sabon was in town yesterday, but he's gone now.''

''That was a quick trip. Why was he there?''

Pierce's dark face hardened. ''Brauer has a twenty-year-old stepdaughter. Sabon wants her, apparently.''

''Good God!''

''You know what he'll do with her if he gets her,'' Pierce said coldly. ''She's spirited and smart, but she's no match for a man like Sabon.''

''Want me to come over?''

''I can take care of her,'' he replied. ''I'm not over the hill yet.''

There was a rare, deep chuckle on the other end of the line. ''Nobody who watched you knock Colby Lane to his knees on that drilling platform would ever say you were.''

''Speaking of the devil, how is he?''

''Colby linked up with another group of mercenaries and went to Africa, but I hear he's come home and he's working for Uncle Sam now. He's changed so much lately that I don't know him. That damned woman!''

"It's not her fault that he can't give her up and let her settle with her new husband," Pierce reminded him. "If he will get drunk twice a month and start fights, he can expect someone to knock him around eventually."

"Nobody was game to try it until you came along."

"Not even you?" Pierce chided.

"Oh, he knew better than to pick on me," he said carelessly. "Didn't you notice that big white scar on his jaw?"

"You rogue, you."

"He caught me at a bad time."

"I'd like to see anyone catch you at a good one lately. Speaking of men with chips on their shoulders, we could talk about yours," he added.

"Not today. I've got work to do. Watch your back. Sabon doesn't like you any more than Brauer does, but he's supposedly got more money than Brauer and he's devious. I'd hate to get a call at three in the morning telling me you'd washed up on a beach over at Freeport."

"You won't. Keep in touch."

"Sure."

Pierce hung up and reflected on what he'd learned. It was unwelcome news. The oil business had always been boom or bust. It was more complicated than it looked to an outsider, as well. There were a thousand worries that included oil spills, leaks, explosions, fires and disgruntled employees mad enough to cause accidents. There were funding problems and quarrels over who absorbed which costs, and squabbling between the oil companies footing the bill and the construction outfit building the rigs and pipelines. It was an ever-changing pattern of problems, and Pierce was where the buck stopped.

The newest venture involved building a rig for a consortium in the Caspian Sea, a project beset by legal and political woes. The pipeline was to go through a nation that the U.S. government had sanctions against, and there was a ceiling on the amount of foreign investments that were allowed. The Russians argued that the usual limitations shouldn't apply because the Caspian Sea was landlocked and didn't fall under the legal specifications. The oil companies involved in the project were international, but not above the sanctions that the U.S. had persuaded other nations to honor.

There was ongoing interference from people in Sabon's country. They needed a pipeline in a similar area. The difference was that Sabon had the right contacts, and any enemy of the United States was a friend of his. He didn't bother with sanctions or political correctness; he simply greased palms and did what he liked. He and Brauer had done a bit of that of late, and if Tate Winthrop was right, a major political fracas was shaping up back home. Brauer's friend in the Senate could cause some real trouble for the consortium's project, and therefore for Pierce, who was supplying the equipment and labor to construct it.

He was deep in thought when the gate enclosing the swimming pool opened and Brianne joined him near the changing rooms.

He was sunbathing and he'd long since shed his trunks. Brianne had stared at him and blushed the first time she saw him that way, despite the time in Paris when she'd put him to bed. It had amused him that she was still so innocent. After that once, she accepted his lack of clothing as de rigueur and never commented on it or bothered to avert her eyes from his blatant masculinity. In fact, she seemed to find him as fascinating as she had in Paris.

"You look preoccupied," he commented when she sat down on the lounger beside his and dropped her purse on the nearby table.

"I'm not preoccupied. I'm suicidal." She glanced at him with a rueful smile. "Want to help me tie an anchor around my neck?"

He sat up, serious now. "What's wrong?"

"I've been handed an ultimatum," she said in a colorless tone. She stared at her bare feet in the flimsy white sandals. "Kurt says that either I marry Philippe Sabon or he'll do something drastic to my mother and half brother. He's pretty desperate," she added. "I don't think he's bluffing. He's tied up every penny he has in this oil deal with Philippe. He stands to lose it all without Philippe's cooperation, and he's going to lose that if I don't marry the repulsive Monsieur Sabon."

His face hardened. He hadn't thought that even Brauer would go so far in his pursuit of wealth. He was wrong.

"What do you want to do?" he asked her abruptly.

She glanced at him with a wan smile. "Can't you guess?" She slid her hands over her jeans-clad thighs. "It's now or never."

His black eyes narrowed as they searched over

her slender body with calculation. "Would you care to be more specific?"

"Sure." She stood up and abruptly pulled off her silk blouse. There was nothing under it except her small, pretty breasts. "How's this for specific?" she asked bluntly.

Chapter Five

Pierce had refused to think of Brianne as a woman lately. He hadn't overcome his grief for Margo and he wasn't ready for any intimate involvement, especially with a woman as young and innocent as Brianne.

But the sight of those soft, pretty pink breasts with their hard mauve tips had an immediate and unmistakable effect on him.

Her eyes followed the movement of his body with wide fascination that quickly turned to apprehension. She folded her arms across her breasts, and her brazen demeanor went into eclipse.

"Lost your nerve?" he taunted softly.

She had. It wasn't possible to pretend that she didn't find him intimidating. "Sorry," she said, because his irritation with her was also apparent. "The magazines don't show men like that," she added self-consciously.

"They wouldn't dare." He got to his feet and moved closer to her, slowly taking her hands away from her breasts. They were hard-tipped, just slightly swollen. He looked at their delicate pink contours with pure appreciation.

"I'm...small." She wanted so badly to be sophisticated, but she felt gauche and uncomfortable. He was looking at her as if he liked what he saw, but she was self-conscious about her size.

"You're perfectly formed and not too small," he replied gently. He smiled at her, and it made him less frightening. His black eyes were tender as they traced the stark outline of her breasts. His gaze lifted to her face and his eyes narrowed with faint calculation. "Do they ache?"

She wondered how he knew that. She nodded, a little stiffly.

His head lifted. "Come here and I'll make it stop."

His voice was deep, soft, slow. She was aware of the sun beating down on them through the casuarinas, the sound of the waves on the beach just beyond the privacy fence. She was aware of an airplane roaring overhead. But none of those things really registered as she felt the impact of Pierce's eyes on her body for the first time.

She drew in her breath and took a step toward him. She felt tight, swollen, all over. She'd always found him attractive, but this was beyond her slight experience. It was like being in the grip of a tidal wave. She couldn't help herself.

His big, dark hand lifted slowly, and his fingers traced lightly around just the edges of one small breast. She gasped. He smiled at her reactions, because she was too green to hide them.

His other hand drew her a little closer. His breath sighed out at her forehead as his thumb eased just to the outline of the hard nipple and away again. He felt her stiffen, heard her breathing rustle in her throat.

"The…gate," she said through dry lips.

"No one ever comes through it when I'm sunbathing. It's an unwritten law." He was feeling alive for the first time since Margo's death. It was like rebirth to feel a woman's soft breast under his fingers, feel a woman's shaking heartbeat against his hand, hear her breathing catch in her throat. Brianne smelled of spring flowers, and he thought how exquisite it would be to take the rest of her clothes off and touch her where she'd never been touched.

His own heartbeat raced at the images that claimed his mind. He stopped thinking about her age and inexperience. They didn't matter. Nothing mattered past the heat in his loins.

His fingers went to the waistband of her jeans. He unsnapped them and pulled the zipper down. Her hands caught his, but he expected the faint panic and his head bent as she struggled with his fingers.

"Virginity is hard to give up," he whispered at her lips. "But you'll like the way I take yours. It's going to be slow and sweet, here in the sun." His mouth touched her upper lip and then her lower one as his hands began to move.

She made a sound and he smiled patiently. His head bent and his mouth opened over one hard nipple. He suckled it tenderly, aware of her hands falling away from his, aware of her body arching helplessly, her fingers suddenly tangling in the thick black waves of his hair just at the nape of his strong neck.

He had her jeans down below her hips. She felt

the air on her body and it was welcome, because she was so hot. She couldn't breathe. He was suckling her breast hungrily and it made her body swell and ache.

It wasn't only his mouth now, it was his hand. He probed gently, touched, stroked, in that place that had never known a man's touch. She should be shocked, ashamed, but she wasn't. It was exciting. He touched her and her body felt moist there, open, hungry, empty.

She moved her legs apart for him. Her tiny gasps were barely audible above the shocked beat of her own heart.

She arched backward, opening her body to him, to whatever he wanted to do to it. She was free as she'd never been, wanton and brazen and completely submissive to his ardor.

It occurred to her in one last flash of sanity that he was easing her down onto a big, thick towel in the small patch of grass beside the concrete edge of the pool. She opened her eyes, noticing that they felt heavy and weighted.

He was removing the jeans and the briefs under them. That was nice, because they were far too tight. He put them aside, along with her sandals.

He was slow, patient. He didn't rush or act as

if he were desperate to do more than look at her for several long, breathless seconds. He knelt there, between her long, splayed legs, with his hands on his thighs, just studying her body.

She shivered at the heat in his eyes. He was more potent than she'd dreamed he would be, and a little frightening like that. She'd never seen pictures of an aroused man, but it seemed that he was a lot more endowed than the centerfolds in those magazines she and her friends had passed around in Paris.

She'd expected him to come down on her, to start kissing her body or touching her intimately again. He didn't. He simply watched her as if his mind was detached from his visible desire for her.

"Aren't you going to…to do it?" she whispered.

He smiled slowly. "Do what?"

She swallowed. "Make love to me."

He sighed. His big hands smoothed over her thighs and she shivered with pleasure. "I want to," he said quietly. "I want to, very much. But my conscience would haunt me for the rest of my life."

She grimaced. "Why do you have to have a conscience? You're not taking anything I don't want to give you! Don't you see, if I go back home a virgin, that man...that frightening man...!"

His fingers contracted on her soft flesh. "You're not going back home, Brianne," he replied. "Not now, not ever. You're staying right here."

She was surprised. Awed. "You want me to live with you?" she asked breathlessly.

He nodded. His eyes went to the soft flesh his hand was tracing, to the faint golden hairs on her legs, whose sheen was like floss in the sunlight.

"I'd like that," she said.

"Your stepfather won't," he replied. "And he could probably get some legal support to drag you back."

She looked tormented. "I wouldn't go!"

"He could make you, if he had the law on his side." His fingers grew slowly more caressing. "That being the case, we're going to make a rather hasty trip to Las Vegas."

She stopped breathing. "Nevada?"

"Nevada." He removed his hands and stood, pulling her up beside him. "You really do have the most beautiful, nubile young body," he murmured, lifting his fingers to the hard tips of her breasts. He teased them, enjoying the way she arched to his touch. "And if you were two years older, believe me, I wouldn't hesitate a second. But you're much too young to be any man's mistress. So I'm going to marry you."

All her dreams were coming true. She stared up at him with pure disbelief. "You're kidding."

He shook his head. "No, I'm not. There's no way in hell I'm letting a pervert like Philippe Sabon get his hands on you. This is the only way I can protect you."

"He wouldn't want me if I'd had a lover," she felt obliged to point out.

"You don't know that. And how would you prove it to him?"

She bit her lower lip. "I guess I couldn't, really."

He caught her by the waist and pulled her nude body completely against the warm contours of his, smiling when she felt him against her belly and gasped.

"Don't be intimidated by me," he said gently. "Your body is more elastic than you realize. You can take me, even if you don't think so right now."

She laughed self-consciously. "Care to prove it?" she asked with pure bravado.

"Not until we're married, I don't," he replied dryly.

She searched his broad, dark face curiously. "Is it because I haven't done it before?"

"Yes," he said simply. "I'm old-fashioned. Bodies come cheap, but yours isn't. I don't care what the rest of the world thinks or does. I go my own way. This is it."

"Marriage or nothing, hmmm?" she murmured, happy enough to tease a little. She reached up and touched his broad, hair-covered chest, liking the way the muscles rippled under her fingers. "Okay. If you're sure," she added, and looked worried.

He touched her long, soft hair and tangled his fingers in it. "I'm sure," he said, and he was. But he couldn't explain why.

His hands smoothed down her back to her hips. He drew them gently closer and studied her mouth. "I've touched you like a lover, but I haven't kissed you. I want to."

She linked her arms around his neck, shivering a little with the delicious pleasure of feeling his skin against hers. "Me, too," she murmured, lifting her face.

He bent and brushed his open mouth against her lips. He hesitated. What he felt was suddenly explosive. He scowled, because it was unexpected. He bent again, and this time he nudged her lips apart with his mouth and brushed at it with slow, whispery contacts that made his body contract and harden even more.

She heard the faint intake of his breath and felt his body stiffen against hers. She drew back and looked into his black eyes, seeing the glitter that began to shine in them. There was a faint tremor in his long, powerful legs as well.

Her eyes were curious, possessive as she looked at him. She stepped a little closer and deliberately brushed her thighs softly against his. He bit off a sharp groan, and the hands holding her hips bit into the soft flesh bruisingly hard.

Her lips parted. Why, he was vulnerable! She'd never have expected it, because his control had been absolute as long as he was touching her. She wondered what might happen if she…touched him.

Her fingers went between their bodies, and she spread them against his diaphragm, looking straight up into his eyes as she moved them very slowly down through the arrowing of hair that covered his stomach and his loins.

He clenched his teeth but made no move to stop her. She hesitated briefly, self-conscious about what she was doing.

He drew in a slow breath. "Do you want to touch me?"

She nodded.

He steeled himself not to lose control. His hands covered hers and slowly guided them down until they rested on his body where it was taut and swollen.

She looked down, surprised and awed by the feel of his body in such devastating intimacy. She smiled with mingled curiosity and fascination.

He moved her hands against him, chuckling hollowly at the pleasure that shot through him under her shy, warm little hands.

"Show me how," she said uninhibitedly, looking up at him tenderly.

"And shock you?"

"It's all right," she said. "I expect you're going to shock me eventually."

"I thought I already had."

He placed his big hands over her small ones

and guided them slowly, patiently, explaining what he wanted her to do. His body began to shiver and then to move helplessly. He swallowed. He bit off a harsh moan. His hands became insistent and he trembled. It didn't take long at all. He cried out and his body was helpless, pulsing, open to her eyes as he went over the edge and felt her watching him. The pleasure was overwhelming. He had to lean against a nearby tree for support as the grinding waves of ecstasy convulsed his body. He let her watch, enjoyed her eyes, her shy excitement, her triumph as she realized what had happened to him.

He held her against him, sweaty and shivering in the delicious aftermath. He laughed with glorious delight, his body open to the sun and her eyes, and not one trace of inhibition or embarrassment afterward.

"You're so...uninhibited," she said softly, smiling. "I wish I was."

"Do you?" He got back his breath and then suddenly lifted her clear off the ground and carried her back to the beach towel they'd abandoned minutes before.

He put her down and positioned her, and his mouth found her in a way she'd only read about.

It was the most shocking, startling, overwhelmingly urgent pleasure she'd ever dreamed. She arched and shuddered and sobbed as he brought her to a level of ecstasy she couldn't have conceived of feeling only ten minutes before. It was so unexpected that she went over the edge almost at once. Her back arched and she held him to her, begging, sobbing her pleasure as her slender young body shuddered in the long, sweet convulsions of fulfillment for the first time.

It took her a long time to come back down from the feverish heights. She felt his warm mouth all over her body, tracing, touching, comforting while she trembled and tried to get one complete breath.

He chuckled at her look of unholy shock when he finally lifted his head. "I let you fulfill me," he pointed out.

"Yes, but I didn't...I didn't...I don't think I could...I never even dreamed..." Her eyes sought his. "Is it...well...natural?"

He grinned. "That depends on your definition of natural. If you liked it, it is. If you didn't, it isn't."

She hesitated. "I liked it," she whispered, and flushed.

"So did I," he replied softly. He slid alongside her and drew her to him, holding her in the lazy aftermath. "Not quite sex, but enough for now."

She shifted on the towel, feeling aroused all over again. Her back arched and she moaned softly.

"Again, so soon?" he asked quietly, arching above her.

She opened soft, misty eyes and moved sensuously. "I'm sorry. Maybe I'm not quite normal."

His hand lay gently on her flat belly. "You're completely normal, as well as an unexpected delight," he replied with somber eyes. He moved his hand and touched her very delicately, gently at first, and then deliberately and with some insistence.

She opened her body to his slow probing, staring into his eyes as she realized what he was doing.

His face was somber and very still. "Is it hurting?"

She nodded. "Just...a little," she replied huskily.

He leaned closer, his eyes filling her vision. He probed again and pushed, slowly.

She bit her lower lip, but her eyes never left his. She swallowed because the pain was burning her.

"Do you realize what I'm doing?" he whispered.

"Yes."

He moved closer. "Don't look away," he said huskily. "Don't close your eyes."

Her back arched delicately, increasing the burning pain. She winced.

His hand moved again and his eyes seemed to fill the world. "Do you feel it tearing?" he whispered deeply.

"Yes!"

Her eyes dilated. So did his. It was the most intimate thing he'd ever done with a woman. It was more intimate than sex. His teeth ground together, and he made a sound in his throat just as she arched up to him and sobbed. He felt the barrier give. He felt it!

"Dear God!" he ground out.

She shivered again. Her eyes looked into his with a new knowledge of him. She saw the same expression in his broad face that she knew was in her eyes.

She lifted. This time there was no pain at all,

just the faint discomfort. He pushed, feeling her body open to the slow thrust of his fingers as it hadn't been able to before.

Her long legs parted. She reached up, inviting him.

But he wouldn't accept the invitation. He shook his head slowly and withdrew his hand. She looked down, fascinated.

"When I have you," he whispered quietly, "there won't be a glimmer of pain."

"But...why not now?" she asked.

"Because I didn't want to arouse you to passion and have to hurt you, to give you a memory of sex that was forever linked with pain." He bent and put his mouth softly to her own, smiling against the faint whisper of her breath against it. "Your first experience of me is going to be one long, sweet pleasure."

She lifted herself against him and kissed him with pure possession, seductively sliding against his strong body. "I know," she whispered. "So will yours, of me."

He smiled to himself as he helped her to her feet. It didn't occur to him until much later that, for the first time in two years, he hadn't thought of Margo. He wanted Brianne with a white-hot passion that he hadn't felt since his teens. It wasn't love, but it was certainly enough to build a foundation on. He was going to marry her to protect her from Philippe Sabon, but more than that, he was going to marry her to sate the passion she aroused in him. It was the most powerful emotion he'd felt in years. It felt good. It had been a long time since anything had felt good. He'd been living in the past, in Margo's memory. He had to stop.

Brianne was years too young for him, but when she tired of him and wanted someone younger, they'd do what they had to do. For now, he was going to enjoy her sweet, lithe body and drown in the forgetfulness of blind passion. He didn't consider his motives past that.

They flew to Las Vegas that very afternoon. Several hours later, they were standing together in a wedding chapel. Brianne wore a short white coatdress and a matching hat with a veil, and she carried a posy of white roses. It had been a rushed sort of buying spree, and it had been fun. Pierce had gone with her to pick out the ensemble, scoffing at the idea that it was bad luck for him to see her in her wedding dress before the ceremony. He wore a tuxedo and drew eyes like magnets as they walked from the big black stretch limo into the wedding chapel where he'd arranged for them to be married.

She had a ring, also quickly purchased. It was a Victorian replica, of fourteen-karat gold, a wide band embossed with ivy leaves in an exquisite pattern of yellow gold. The ring was outlined by tiny bands of white gold. It suited Brianne's slender finger and she loved it. But Pierce was still wearing his old wedding ring. She didn't have the nerve to ask him to change it. That, she told herself, was probably a mistake. But she didn't have time to worry about it, because everything happened so quickly.

The minister performed the ceremony with two paid witnesses to attest to it. Pierce lifted Brianne's veil and bent to kiss her with careless tenderness. His face was very somber, and she wondered if he was remembering his first marriage. She was certain that it hadn't been performed someplace like this. She saw the need for a quick ceremony, because if they'd had a formal wedding, Kurt would surely have found some way to stop them from marrying. But she mourned silently for the beautiful long gown she'd always assumed she'd be married in, and for the love that wasn't present on the bridegroom's face. That Pierce liked her, and wanted her, she knew for certain. But would that be enough to keep them together, with all the love on one side and Pierce living with a beautiful ghost?

She looked into his black eyes with faint misgiving.

He tapped the end of her nose. "Stop glowering," he teased. "We're going to be happy."

"Oh, I do hope so," she said fervently.

He sighed. The teasing light went out of his eyes to be replaced by something entirely new as he looked at her in the modern coatdress that showed her long, elegant legs to their best advantage. "You're very young," he said quietly.

"I'll get wrinkles soon enough, right now if you like. I can soak my face in water until it starts to shrivel," she volunteered with a grin.

He chuckled. "Hooligan," he accused. "You're going to run me ragged."

"I promise to do my best," she said.

They shook hands with the minister and his wife and the witnesses, concluded the paperwork and the fee, and went back outside to climb into the black limo.

"We're married," Brianne murmured with a wicked glance at her brand-new husband. "How about taking me to the nearest motel and loving me half to death?"

He only smiled, like an adult indulging a small child. "There's nothing I'd like better," he said carelessly. "But we have to catch the next flight out of here."

Her expression fell. "We aren't having a honeymoon?"

"Brianne, we got married to save you from Sabon," he said seriously. "I enjoyed making love to you by the pool. Someday, maybe I'll do it properly. But this isn't the time. We've got some major complications cropping up that you don't know about yet. I couldn't bear to tell you and spoil our wedding. But the ceremony's over and you have to know."

"Know what?" she asked with a cold premonition.

Chapter Six

Pierce grimaced, as if he didn't want to say it. She stared at him with her heart pounding and her eyes like green saucers.

"All right, I suppose I can't keep it from you any longer," he said heavily. "I phoned Arthur at the beach house while you were changing at the hotel. Your mother called and asked for you. It seems she's had a slight...accident. She'll be all right," he said quickly when her face began to pale. "She told Arthur that she slipped and fell on the steps, but he said she sounded pretty scared and she needed to speak to you urgently. He didn't tell her where we were, only that we'd be back today."

She let out a breath. "I'll bet he hit her," she said miserably. "He made all sorts of threats against her and the baby if I didn't cooperate with his plans. I suppose he'll find out what we've done?"

He nodded. "Sooner or later."

"He said that Philippe was coming back today and he wanted to see me," she told him. She smoothed back her hair. "Why did my mother marry Kurt?" she asked angrily. "Couldn't she see what sort of man he was?"

"Sure she could. He was rich," he added.

She leaned back heavily against the seat. "Will he hurt her any more, do you think? And what about the baby?"

"They're probably safe enough for now. But Sabon's going to be out for blood when he learns what we've done. I've just put you out of his reach for good. He won't take it lying down. He'll be plotting his revenge on both of us, and on anyone connected with you. And probably, so will Kurt."

Her pulse was racing. She put up a hand and brushed back her long hair. "What are we going to do?"

"Well, you're not going home, for a start," he

told her grimly. "We're flying back into Freeport instead of Nassau. I've already phoned the house and told them to have a driver who doubles as my bodyguard to meet us. It wouldn't do for Arthur to pick us up, anyway, under the circumstances. We'll stay in Freeport for the time being, until things die down and I can get my security chief over here with a team."

"You really think Philippe Sabon is a threat, don't you?" she asked worriedly.

He took her hand in his and held it warmly. "I know he is. But nothing's going to happen to you. You're my responsibility now. I'll take care of you."

She gnawed her lower lip. "It's like a nightmare," she said aloud. "This is the 1990s. Things like this aren't supposed to happen! Heavens, I can't have a total stranger trying to force me to marry him!"

"Sabon is filthy rich. He usually gets exactly what he wants. Your stepfather is in hotter water than he realizes." He glanced at Brianne, who was visibly pale. "I think our best bet is to have you live in the States, where my security chief can keep an eye on you. You said once that you wanted to go to college and study math. Do you still?''

She stared at him with carefully concealed horror. He'd just married her. She was daydreaming about living with him, loving him, sleeping in his arms—and he was offering her a college education.

''I hadn't thought about college lately,'' she confessed.

''You're not too old to start,'' he said easily. ''We'll enroll you in a small college near D.C., and under an assumed name, so that Sabon won't be able to find you. But even if he does, Tate Winthrop will be somewhere nearby, or one of his people will be. You'll be watched night and day until this is over.''

''I can't stay with you?'' she asked, carefully avoiding looking directly at him.

He sighed. ''I'd like you to,'' he said bluntly, his expression solemn and intent. ''But that isn't going to be possible after what has happened between us, Brianne.''

She was surprised. ''I don't understand.''

''Don't you?'' He laughed coldly. ''Listen, honey, you're a tasty little banquet and I'm a starving man. All my good intentions won't spare you if we're under the same roof for very long.''

''But I want you,'' she protested.

''Want!'' he scoffed. ''You're a child on fire with the forbidden. You've just discovered sensual pleasure and you want to explore it. I've done my exploring. I have nothing to offer you except a few feverish lovemaking sessions in my bed. I'd break your young heart. You wouldn't be able to let go, and you'd have to. I'm a loner. I don't want a wife.''

''You married me,'' she said, making an accusation of it.

''Yes, to protect you from Sabon,'' he agreed. He studied her. ''You're barely twenty, naive and aching to lay your heart at my feet. Don't. I want you. I could take you and enjoy you and walk away from you the next morning with my heart intact. You couldn't. You're too intense for me, Brianne.''

''You mean if I could just have sex with you and disappear, you'd let me stay,'' she said stiffly.

''That's it in a nutshell,'' he agreed.

''Perhaps I could.''

''Not you,'' he returned immediately. ''You're already halfway in love with me,'' he added, and watched the shock ripple across her features. "Did you think it didn't show?" he asked softly. "You're an open book. You haven't yet acquired the sophistication it takes to hide your feelings."

She took a deep breath and pushed back her hair nervously. She stared out the tinted window of the limousine instead of at him. "So where do we go from here?"

"You go to college and I get on with my new project," he said carelessly.

"You would'nt like to sleep with me?"

"Oh, I'd like it," he said bluntly. "I'd love it. But I could take it in stride and you couldn't. We'll save it until you're a little older."

She turned sad green eyes up to his. "It was a glitzy ceremony in a vulgar place, so you don't consider those vows binding? So now we go our separate ways."

His heavy eyebrows lifted sharply. He'd only heard the first part of her comment. "Vulgar place?"

She turned away. "What would you call it?" she asked quietly.

He hadn't thought about it at all, until she hit him with the reality of their ceremony. It had been a vulgar place, a tawdry little legalized sex operation that made it easy for girls to forget their principles for a quick wedding that could be followed by an even quicker divorce.

He scowled. Brianne, for all her modern outlook, was a throwback to earlier times. She was the sort of girl who would expect to be married in church, in a trailing white gown with bridesmaids and a flower girl. Margo had been given just such a wedding. But Brianne had been hustled into a marriage mill. Despite the reason for their wedding, he could have found a more conventional way to bring it about.

"I'm sorry," he said, and genuinely was. "I was so preoccupied with getting it done that I didn't quite think about the details. You'd rather have been married in church, wouldn't you?"

She didn't look at him. "Were you, the first time?"

"Of course," he replied. "Margo said that she wouldn't feel married if we didn't have a proper service." He saw Brianne wince, and for the first time he realized how badly he'd hurt her.

"Then we did it properly," she said in an amazingly calm and collected tone. "It's a sham marriage to save me from a worse fate. Having it in church would be a sort of sacrilege. I'm sorry

I said anything. I should be grateful to you for what you've done, instead of criticizing how it happened.''

He reached out and took her cold hand in his. "We don't know each other very well," he said, feeling the resistance in her fingers. "I suppose we'll step on each other's feelings a good bit until we become better acquainted."

"No, we won't," she said. "Not with me in the States, and you in Nassau." She turned to him and smiled at him vacantly. "That's the way you want it, too, isn't it? Even if I weren't being pursued by a madman, you'd want me someplace where you didn't have to see me every day."

His eyes began to glitter. "That's right," he told her.

She sighed. "Okay," she said after a minute. "I get the picture. I won't give you any trouble." She pulled the wedding ring off her finger and handed it to him.

He scowled. "Would you like to explain this?"

"Sure," she said. "You're still married to another woman." She gestured toward the wedding band he wore on his big left hand. "That being the case, there's really no point in my wearing a wedding band, too."

He jerked his hand back from hers and glared at her. "I won't take this ring off," he said shortly. "Least of all to placate a child playing at being an adult!"

The whiplash of his voice was all the more potent for being so soft. She shivered with the coldness it intimated.

"Sorry I haven't enough maturity to play the game properly, Mr. Hutton," she said. "But I'll learn soon enough." She averted her eyes and clenched her teeth. "Since I'm not a true wife, I don't see why I can't date other men. That's what you want, anyway, isn't it, for me to find someone else and get out of your life."

"I want you safe from Sabon," he said through his teeth. "At the moment, that's my only concern. As for other men," he added slowly, "if you break your vows to me, you'd better hide where I can't find you."

She gaped at him. "I beg your pardon?"

"You heard me," he said shortly. "We're married, glitzy, vulgar chapel notwithstanding, and no woman is going to cuckold me!"

"Well!"

"It has nothing to do with jealousy," he continued harshly. "Sabon is the reason it has to be a true marriage and not a sham. Otherwise your stepfather will leap at any opportunity to toss you to Sabon as a prospective bride. If he learns that you're out with other men, he won't believe you have a husband.''

"He isn't the only one," she said under her breath.

He glared harder. "I've been honest with you," he said coldly. "Would you have preferred it if I'd seduced you before we flew to the States?''

She wasn't going to touch that line with a ten-foot pole. She took the ring back and placed it on her finger. "You don't think that Philippe might just give up and go home if he knew we were married?'' she asked, avoiding his pointed question.

He hesitated, as if he wanted to pursue the subject they'd been discussing. But he sighed and let her divert him. "No, I don't,'' he said. "I think it will just make him more determined to have you.''

After that Pierce remained silent until they boarded the plane and took their seats. Brianne fell asleep, and then woke with a start. She looked at Pierce. He had a brooding look as he stared toward the front of the plane, where a waitress was bending to take dinners out of the plane's warming ovens. This was one of the few flights that offered meals.

"They're going to serve dinner. Do you want a tray?" he asked.

"Yes."

He opened the arm of her seat and lifted out the intricately folded table for her, smiling at her look of surprise. "Surely you flew home from Paris first class?" he teased.

"Actually, I came home tourist," she murmured. "Brauer has been tight with money for the past year. Just between us, I think he's teetering on the verge of bankruptcy."

"If he is, no wonder he's so itchy to placate Sabon," Pierce replied thoughtfully. "And if he's sunk everything he owns into this development, in hopes of doubling his investment, he's in big trouble."

"Why?"

He put his own tray into position. "Because we're working with a consortium of oil companies on a deal with the Russians to develop that well in the Caspian Sea that I told you about. We're going to run a pipeline right through—"

He mentioned the country, and her eyes widened in surprise.

"The United States has economic sanctions against it," she exclaimed. "No wonder Brauer would be upset—everyone would take sides, and he'd lose money. But aren't you a United States citizen?"

"Brianne, I could be if I wanted to, but I'm not a United States citizen right now," he said, reminding her with a shock of his European birth and nationality.

"I forgot," she said quietly. "You speak such perfect English. You don't even have an accent."

"I told you that my grandfather raised me. He was Greek, but he spoke several languages fluently. He insisted that I learn English to perfection. It was the language of the business world, he used to say, and I do spend a fair amount of time in the States."

She shifted so that the stewardess could put down the meal, and then waited until Pierce had been served before she spread her napkin in her lap and glanced at him. "I guess I don't know much about the politics of other countries."

He smiled. "You should learn. It's easier to get along with people if we have some understanding of their politics, as well as their social and religious beliefs.''

"How many languages do you speak?"

He shrugged. "Only three, fluently." He glanced at her and grinned. "Do you know how an Arab defines an illiterate person?"

"No. How?"

"As someone who speaks only one language."

Surprised, she laughed. "Well, that puts me right on the top of their list."

"I'll teach you Greek," he told her. "It's beautiful."

She knew that French was one of his languages, but she noticed that he didn't offer any instruction in that tongue. Probably because of Margo, she thought sadly, because she'd been French. He probably made love in French. Her eyes went involuntarily to his big, beautifully masculine hands. She remembered their skill on her body, the exquisite sensations he'd taught her to feel, and she caught her breath.

He heard the intake of breath, and his black eyes met hers with a question in them.

She flushed, moving her gaze quickly to her plate.

She wasn't hiding anything from him. He could

read her like a newspaper. He unwrapped his lunch and started to butter his dinner roll. Surprisingly, he felt his body tauten pleasurably with the memory of Brianne's sensuous movements as he caressed her by the pool. She was untried, but eager and passionate. He had a good idea how it would feel to make love to her completely, and he wanted to. But every time he thought of it, he saw Margo's beloved face, and he felt guilty and ashamed for thinking of taking another woman to his bed. It seemed like adultery.

Brianne ate her chicken casserole and smiled appreciatively at the stewardess who paused to pour her a cup of black coffee. She noticed that Pierce took his the same way, without anything added.

"Where are we going to stay in Freeport?" she asked him suddenly.

"I've booked a suite of rooms at one of the hotels." He named it. "And under assumed names. We'll be fine. Meanwhile, I've sent for Winthrop. He'll be along with one or two of his men."

"You really are taking this seriously," she said.

He nodded as he finished a swallow of coffee.

"Your stepfather will be on his way to Washington today, if what we've heard is accurate." He glanced at her. "I've gotten wind of another rumor that I like even less about what they're planning." His black eyes narrowed. "There's a lot at stake here. Sabon's country has a small, poor neighbor, which has dreams of conquest and possession of all that expensive oil that the West is so desperate to buy. The neighboring country had oil, but their reserves have been exhausted. They have no oil in their country anymore. But they have powerful allies and access to state-of-the-art weapons."

"Oh, my goodness," Brianne said. "You don't think they might invade Qawi?"

"Sure they might. Sabon knows that. I think it's why he's lured Brauer into the deal, because he has a friend in the Senate in Washington. Sabon may be using Brauer to appeal to the United States for help. They wouldn't give it to him because he's in their bad books for supporting an American foe during the Gulf War." He finished his chicken with a grim expression. "But if Brauer can bargain for U.S. protection, with some interest in the developing oil fields for bait, Sabon would have the clout he needed to push the deal through with the oil consortium. Failing that, he might be desperate enough to attempt a first strike against the neighbor.''

"Start a war?''

"Yes. Start a war.'' He glanced at her as he wiped his mouth with a napkin.

"This sounds frightening.''

"It is frightening. The Middle East is a tinder-box. All it needs is a spark to throw the whole area into war. There was a close call when Iraq attacked Kuwait and Israel back in the early nineties. This would be even closer. Countries would line up on either side of the conflict, and it has the potential to spread all the way down to the Persian Gulf.'' He sighed. "That would be bad news for those of us who have investments in the Caspian Sea project. And even if the war was confined to Sabon's country and its neighbor, we stand to suffer delays and the threat of armed hostility. If Brauer can't get the States to intervene on his behalf, I think he might pay some of his hired mercenaries to attack our drilling platform and put the blame on the poor nation next to Sabon's, just to stack the odds in their favor. With the Russians involved with us, that could provoke some very unpleasant retaliation on Sabon's behalf against the poor nation. Which could attract U.S. intervention as well. I shudder to think of the possible consequences.''

"Can't you do anything?''

"I'm doing it,'' he said. "I've got Winthrop up to his neck in investigation. He's already stopped one plan dead in the water. I have every confidence that he can stop another, with a little help from some old friends in the intelligence community. It's to their advantage to keep the lid on this thing, you know.''

"I guess so.'' She sipped her coffee and stared at him over the plastic rim of the cup. "It's all very exciting, despite the potential for violence,'' she said after a minute. She laughed. "I've never done anything dangerous,'' she mused. "My whole life has been one long, dull series of routine days. Well, most of it.'' She grinned. "You've been an adventure.''

"So have you,'' he murmured, and he didn't smile. "You've disrupted my life.''

"Good for me,'' she replied. "You needed someone to disrupt it. You were going to seed. You're much too young to wilt on the vine, so to speak.''

His good humor came back. "I wasn't wilting."

"You were so. You were keeling over in bars waiting to be picked up by potential thieves." She pursed her lips and frowned. "Say, what if that blonde eyeing you in Paris was really a CIA agent, after industrial secrets?"

He chuckled. "I don't know any industrial secrets. I run the business, I don't do the actual drilling, and I don't understand the process except from a layman's perspective."

"Yes, but you know how to build a drilling platform. In fact, you patented one idea for platforms that work best in shallow areas, didn't you?"

He was surprised. "I didn't think you knew anything about the oil business."

"I didn't. After I took you back to your hotel in Paris, I decided that if I was going to get mixed up with a man who built oil rigs, I should know something about the oil business."

"How did you know you were going to get mixed up with me?" he pursued. "I had no plans to go to Nassau or look you up."

"Yes, I guessed that. But I knew you had a home in Nassau and I planned to look *you* up!"

she retorted. "I lost my nerve, though. If you hadn't been at that party Kurt took us to, I don't suppose I would have seen you again except by accident."

"I don't know," he replied. He finished his coffee. "I told you that you were too young for me."

"Seventeen years."

"Eighteen."

She grimaced. "You didn't tell me you'd had a birthday."

"No, I didn't, did I."

His cold glance ended any attempt at humor on that subject. She put down her fork and opened her dessert, a chocolate pie. "I don't know what sort of music you like, what kind of books you read, or what you like to do when you aren't working."

He was reluctant to share those intimate details with her. She was trying to worm her way into his life, and he didn't want her to.

But all the same, he found himself speaking when he hadn't planned to. "I like Debussy, Respighi, Puccini, and modern composers like John Williams, Jerry Goldsmith, James Horner, David Arnold and Eric Serra. I read most anything, but

I'm partial to biographies and ancient Greek and Roman history.''

"I like those composers, too," she said. "And I love opera. My favorites are Puccini's—*Turandot* and *Madame Butterfly*."

He didn't want to tell her that those were his two favorites. "What do you like to read?"

"Romances," she said with a grin.

"Because you're still young enough and idealistic enough to believe in happy endings," he said with faint mockery. "I'm old and jaded enough to know they don't exist."

"You had ten wonderful years with a woman you loved who loved you back," she pointed out.

"And she died," he said brutally. "So much for happy endings!"

"Maybe a little happiness is all we can expect in this life," she said thoughtfully. "What if you'd never met Margo at all? Would you have been happier, really?"

He didn't want to answer that. He glanced down at the remains of his chocolate pie with blank eyes.

"You wouldn't," she said for him. "You were very lucky to have had such a special relationship.

You have memories that are better than the daily lives of most people.''

He'd never thought of himself as lucky. Maybe he was. Margo had loved him unselfishly, generously. He looked at Brianne and thought with a start that Margo would have liked her. She was similar to his late wife in many ways, not the least of which was in her empathy and compassion. She was a giving person. She wasn't beautiful, as Margo had been, but she was pretty in her own way.

"Haven't you ever been in love?" he asked curiously.

"Only with you," she said honestly.

His jaw tightened and he turned his eyes back to his coffee cup. It was empty. He looked around for the stewardess and motioned to the cup. She came back with the coffeepot and refilled it. Brianne shook her head with a smile and the stewardess went on down the aisle.

"You're too young to know what love is," Pierce said after a minute. "You're hot for your first affair and you want me. It's desire, nothing more."

She smiled wistfully. "Whatever you say."

He sipped his coffee and scorched his upper lip. He made a face as he put the cup back down.

"You'll meet someone," he said. "Someday, you'll find a man close to your own age, and you'll understand what I mean."

"I'm married," she replied. "I can't go looking for a husband when I've already got one."

"We won't be married forever," he said shortly, looking straight at her. "Once this is over, we'll get a quiet annulment."

Her heart seemed to stop in her chest. So that was what he meant to do—stay married to her, but not intimate with her, until the trouble with Sabon was over. Then an annulment, which would be easy to get since the marriage hadn't been consummated. No wonder he didn't want to go to bed with her. He was already making plans to get her out of his life for good!

Chapter Seven

Brianne toyed with her paper napkin, tracing the embossed logo of the airline with the tip of her fingernail.

"I see," she said when she realized that he was waiting for her to answer him.

"You know it would never work," he continued shortly. "There's too much difference in our ages. We're from different generations. We don't even think the same way."

"And even if we did, there's Margo."

His eyes flashed angrily. "I loved her," he said, his eyes glittering. "I won't cheat on her."

"Pierce, she's gone," she said softly. "She won't ever come back. You may live for another thirty or forty years. Do you really want to live alone for all that time, by yourself, with no one for company?''

''Yes!''

He said it, but he didn't sound convincing to Brianne. It must be very difficult for him, especially when he was alone with the memories that would be as much curse as comfort to him.

''She wouldn't want this,'' she murmured, thinking aloud. ''She wouldn't want you alone and grieving forever.''

''You don't know what the hell you're talking about,'' he replied icily. ''Let it drop. I don't want to talk about it.''

''Whatever you say,'' she returned. ''I don't suppose you'd like to try having sex in the washroom while we're up here, would you?'' she added wickedly, trying to lighten the tone of their disturbing conversation. ''I saw it in a racy movie once, and I've always wondered...''

''Wonder by yourself!'' He returned his tray to the arm of his chair, got up and went storming down the aisle to the bathroom. He went inside and locked the door, leaning his forehead against its cool surface with a rough sigh. Damn the woman! Couldn't she stop getting at him about the past? Didn't she know that it was killing him to remember Margo's face, her breath in his mouth, her hands on him in the darkness? His life was growing more unbearable by the day.

He thought about thirty more years of this agony and his heart threatened to crack inside him.

If only he didn't find Brianne so attractive. He didn't want to think about her, he didn't want to have the temptation of her nearby. If she went away, he'd be safe, with only his memories of Margo. He wouldn't have to fight his hunger for Brianne.

It wasn't just the sight of her that tantalized him, it was these little remarks she made, half-teasing invitations to ravish her in airplane rest rooms. He laughed in spite of himself. She was so uninhibited, despite her innocence. He found her a continual delight. She was the first woman since Margo who could make him feel light-hearted, who could make him laugh. He was an impatient, irritable man most of the time these days, always spoiling for a fight, because anger could lessen the pain of grief. Brianne knocked the fire off his mercurial temper. She made him see the world with her own soft, happy eyes. It was ironic, he thought, that a woman with such tragedy in her own life could be so optimistic and upbeat.

He stared at his face in the mirror and saw the silver peppering the black hair at his temples. There were lines around his eyes, too. He put a hand to the traces of silver and laughed hollowly. Couldn't Brianne look at him and see how old he really was? It surprised him that a woman of her youth and attractiveness could want him. He wondered what she saw in that broad, hard face staring back at him.

Brianne, sitting quietly in her seat, was wondering the same thing. He wasn't particularly handsome, not with hands and feet and a nose that size. Certainly he was a lot older than she was. But she'd never known a man in her whole life who could hold a candle to him. He was just dynamite, and it was killing her that she couldn't find a way to get to his heart.

The stewardess was offering more beverages. Was that champagne she was offering? Well, why not? Pierce had made it clear that he didn't want her, and she was feeling pretty sorry for herself. Maybe a little pick-me-up would be just the thing!

Two glasses of champagne later, Pierce came back to his seat.

Brianne toasted him, sloshing a little of the fizzy liquid onto her dress. "Oops," she said. She leaned toward him. "Sorry. My hand slipped."

He stared at her with wide eyes. "What are you drinking?"

"Champagne."

"You can't have champagne or any other alcoholic beverage," he said shortly. "You're a minor!"

"She gave it to me," she said, indicating the stewardess halfway down the aisle behind them. "Go tell her she's breaking the law. I dare you," she added smugly, and downed another swallow.

"Give me that."

He took the glass away from her and finished the two swallows she'd left in the glass. "Idiot," he muttered, staring at her. "You can't hold liquor. You've got no head for it at all."

"I can learn to drink," she told him haughtily. "I'm married." She had a sudden thought and her eyes twinkled. "So this is why married people drink!" she exclaimed. She gave him a rakish look. "See what you've done to me?"

"I didn't do a thing," he protested.

"You did," she returned. "You said you won't sleep with me!"

Her voice carried and he groaned audibly. "Shut up!" he muttered. He could feel those amused looks, even if he couldn't see them.

"I won't," she replied. "This is not a bad substitute for our wedding night," she told him. "At least it numbs the parts of me that ache."

"You're too damned young to have achy parts," he remarked.

"I have an achy heart." She smiled drowsily. "That was a song. I remember it. Want me to sing it to you?" She did, even when he started shaking his head.

He held up his hand and the stewardess came quickly to their side.

"Bring her some coffee, please," he told the woman. "Strong coffee. Quick!"

"Oh, dear," the stewardess said.

"She doesn't drink," Pierce said. "Not ever. And she's a minor."

The stewardess made a horrible face. "They'll cut off my ears and feed them to the sharks!"

"No, they won't. I'll say I forced you to give it to me," Brianne said helpfully.

"How?" Pierce demanded.

"I'll say I threatened to jump out a window," she replied with a smile.

Pierce looked at the tiny window and back at her. "Oh, they'll believe that in a heartbeat."

"I'll go get that coffee," the stewardess said quickly. "Dear, dear, I am sorry."

"It's all right," Brianne said. "You didn't know that I'm a minor and that I just got married to a man who doesn't even like me. How could you know that he won't even take me to—"

"Brianne!" Pierce growled.

"Paris," she finished with a wicked glance at her furious husband.

"You should take her to Paris," the stewardess told him. "It's beautiful there."

"Coffee," Pierce repeated. "And something to eat. Now."

"Yes, sir, right now."

The stewardess retreated, and Brianne leaned her head back against the seat and stared dreamily at Pierce. "I can't believe you have so many hang-ups," she told him. "You're positively riddled with them."

"I hope your head explodes," he said venomously.

She gaped at him. "Look who's got a temper!" she exclaimed. "I only had a little drink."

"Two little drinks, and look at you!"

"I look very nice," she informed him.

"You look very sauced."

"I'll sober up when we get back on the ground," she promised. "Meanwhile, I'm going to work on ways to seduce you. I really should buy some more books," she added thoughtfully. "Maybe a video or two."

He cleared his throat and turned to search for the stewardess. He looked like a drowning man clutching at a life preserver.

Brianne put a soft hand on his broad, powerfully muscled thigh. He actually jumped.

"You prude," she whispered when he grabbed her hand and pushed it away. "We're married!"

"No, we're not," he shot back. "We went through a paper ceremony. That's all it is, and that's all it's going to be!"

Brianne pouted. "That's no way to treat a brand-new wife," she muttered. "Here I sit dying for love of you, and you won't even let me touch you."

He felt as if his whole body was on fire. She was too intoxicated to realize the effect she was having on him, which was just as well. She had him so hot that all he could think of was how she'd feel in bed. He had to get her sober before he lost control of himself entirely.

The stewardess came back with a cup of coffee and a snack meal, which Pierce took gratefully.

"Here," he told Brianne, putting the cup carefully in her hands. "Now, drink it!"

"Spoilsport," she mumbled irritably. But she drank it. He opened the cellophane-covered snack meal and watched while she nibbled at it, too. The waitress came back with a second cup, and a third. The caffeine jolted her system like a battery cable, helped by the food, which seemed to absorb some of the alcohol in her stomach. She began to feel her head clearing, and it wasn't an altogether welcome trip back to terra firma. She'd said some embarrassing things to Pierce. He looked somber and glum, and she wondered if she'd done some irreparable damage to their tenuous relationship while she was in her cups.

He buried himself in a newspaper he got from the stewardess, and he didn't surface until they landed in Freeport.

Brianne let him lead her down the covered walkway up to the concourse. He scanned the limo drivers for a placard with his name on it. But what he found was one with Brianne's name, badly printed. The man holding it, a scrawny little dark fellow, didn't look like a limo driver to Pierce, who'd seen plenty.

Brianne, unconscious of anything out of the ordinary, went, smiling, toward the little man. "I'm Brianne Martin," she said, forgetting that she was married and her husband was right behind her.

"Miss Martin," the man said in thickly accented English. He smiled and took her arm. "You will come with me?"

"Yes, wait just a minute, though," she protested, and started to turn toward Pierce.

He'd already gathered that something was badly wrong. He moved forward quickly, with the intention of tearing his wife from the man's hard grasp, just as he felt something in the small of his back. Something round and hard.

"You are her bodyguard, yes?" came another voice, deeper, from behind him. "You come along, too, then. We take no chance that you inform the Hutton man."

Pierce was surprised at the comment, and he saw Brianne's head turn. He had just enough time for a covert jerk of his head. Fortunately, she was so attuned to him that she understood at once what he wanted her to do.

"What are you doing with Jack?" she asked sharply, having picked the name out of midair.

"He come along. Not take chance he talk to police," the scrawny man told her. "You cry out, my friend shoot him dead. You understand, lady?"

"Do I ever," she said, scared. "Okay, it's your party. Where are we going, or do I get to ask?"

"You find out. Come."

He led her, with "Jack" and his guard in tow, out to a long black stretch limo waiting in front of the terminal. The two of them were stuffed in, and the two men came right behind, both holding automatic pistols now and sitting facing them in the interior of the long car.

The scrawny man called something to the driver, who nodded, and pulled out into the line of traffic. But he didn't drive out of the airport. He drove, instead, right around to one of the rental hangars that stood apart from the main buildings of the terminal. The limousine pulled up beside a fancy little corporate jet, whose doors stood open and where a ladder was suspended, ready for its cargo.

Pierce and Brianne were hustled inside, again with the two armed men sitting nearby. But there were two more armed men waiting inside, a total of four. Pierce exchanged a helpless glance with her. There was nothing either of them could do beyond accepting the reality of their situation. Against four armed men, they were powerless.

"Where are we going?" Brianne asked again.

Nobody answered her. She sat back in her seat, across the aisle from Pierce, with one of their kidnappers next to her on the aisle, and closed her eyes. She might as well get a little rest while she could. She had a horrible feeling that she knew who was behind this kidnapping.

It reeked of Philippe Sabon's style.

Hours later, they landed on a tiny strip on a small island. Brianne had seen a small city from the air, and she remembered that Sabon had told her about the island he owned in the Persian Gulf, near the small country where he held so much political influence.

There were two old British limousines waiting for them. Brianne was herded into one, Pierce into the other. She barely got a glimpse of his back before she was pushed inside. The cars sped away.

"Where are we?" she asked one of the men, portly and a little less formal than the other two who had kidnapped her.

"Island."

"Yes, but which island?" she persisted.

"Jameel," he replied, confirming her worst suspicions. He laid his head back against the seat and gave her an appraisal that sent cold chills through her body.

He smiled. His teeth looked as if they hadn't been brushed in the past decade, and there was a faint odor of liquor on his breath. "Very pretty," he said.

She glared at him. "If you work for Philippe Sabon, you'd better remember that he makes a bad enemy," she said, taking a chance.

It was a good shot. The man sobered at once.

The taller of the two other men, the one who'd held the gun, said something abrupt and sharp to the man, who murmured in a conciliatory way.

"You not to worry," the tall man, graying at the temples, told Brianne. "Nobody hurt you." He glared at the portly man, who turned his head quickly toward the window, watching the low scrub flora of the island whiz by the tinted windows.

Brianne felt sick to her stomach. The only way her remark would have affected that portly man was if Sabon really was behind this kidnapping. Now she knew that he was, and she would be in his clutches soon. Pierce was as powerless as she, overwhelmed by sheer numbers and automatic weapons. The island was like a prison, from which they couldn't escape. Sabon would have her!

She closed her eyes, fighting against the fear as she remembered what she'd heard about Sabon's perversions. How would she bear it? That man, touching her. As Pierce had once said, she didn't have the experience to fake sophistication. The perversions that Sabon would inflict on her would destroy her as a woman.

She wondered if any of Sabon's men would recognize Pierce. If they did, he didn't stand a chance. They'd either hold him for ransom and then kill him or they'd kill him on the spot. Almost certainly, Sabon wouldn't risk a kidnapping trial involving the United States. Pierce might not be an American citizen, but Brianne was, and Sabon was counting on Kurt's congressional friends to save his oil fields.

That brought forth another unpleasant thought.

When Sabon had finished with her, he couldn't risk releasing her. She stood to vanish, too, perhaps turned loose in the cruel desert of the country adjacent to this island, where Sabon was in power.

She couldn't die like this, in such a sordid way. She had to use her brain. There must be some means of escape, if she were vigilant and kept her eyes open for opportunities.

She wasn't going to let Sabon win without a fight. She might die in the attempt, but death was almost certain regardless of her compliance. As her beloved father had once said, it was better to go out in a blaze of glory than in an insignificant puff of smoke. A blaze it would be, somehow.

Pierce was thinking the same thoughts, with more pessimism than Brianne might ever know. Here, on Sabon's home ground, he had no chance of escape, and neither did she. He couldn't protect her. He thought of her ongoing pleas and could have kicked himself for not giving in to them. Sabon would soil her sexuality in a way that no psychologist could fix. He would degrade and humiliate her. That delightful spontaneity she had about intimacy would be gone forever. He would mourn it. And he would forever blame himself for its loss.

He'd spoken to Winthrop just before their flight home, and Winthrop would land shortly in Freeport to meet him. He relaxed just a little. Tate Winthrop was the best security chief he'd ever had. He could track a butterfly over concrete. He'd find Pierce and Brianne. The question was if he could do it in time.

The old limousines pulled up at an imposing house overlooking a huge body of water—probably the Persian Gulf, if Brianne remembered her geography. There was a lot of sand, and the vegetation was similar to that in the Caribbean, which this certainly wasn't. There was an Arabic flavor to the scene, and the white-garbed servants that came onto the long tiled porch along with uniformed guards looked Arabian to Brianne.

She and Pierce were bound and prodded into the wide, airy house and along a wide hallway to a small room with one high window too small for either of them to escape from. There was a small bedframe with a single rolled-up dirty mattress and no linen, a rattan chair, a small table, a lamp and bare tiles on the floor. There was a bathroom, nothing but a tiny room with a commode and a sink. No facilities for bathing were provided. There was a thin sliver of soap on the cracked oyster-colored porcelain of the sink. The pipes were old and rusted, like the water in the toilet.

"You stay here," the short man told them, sticking his pistol in his belt.

"Could you at least untie us?" Brianne asked wearily, holding out her arms. "What if I need to use the rest room? I can't do it with my hands tied."

The guard spoke in Arabic to the taller, older man, and they seemed to be arguing. The tall one used a harsh word and pointed to the high, iron-barred window, and then to the heavy lock on the door itself, made of thick carved ebony wood. He seemed to be saying, How would they get out?

The short man must have seen that they couldn't. Even if they stood on the chair, they couldn't possibly reach the window, which had iron bars.

"Okay," the first man said. He untied Brianne's hands, but left Pierce bound. The men went out, closing and locking the door behind them.

"Thank God we're alone now...." Brianne

said, running to Pierce to untie him. The knots were heavy and cumbersome. She finished her task and said, "Well, Jack, old boy, where do we go from here?"

Pierce brushed the loosened ropes away and rubbed his wrists. "We stay put until they decide what to do with us," he answered.

She sat down on the chair with a heavy sigh and glanced at her once-clean outfit, now dirt-streaked, and wrinkled beyond mention.

Pierce was wearing slacks and a sports shirt with a white jacket. He didn't look like a millionaire today. He was dressed the way his real chauffeur often dressed, never in uniform.

No wonder they hadn't realized who he was! But Sabon would. The minute he saw his old enemy, he'd know him. He was furious with Pierce as well as Brianne for standing between him and his plans. No doubt he'd find new ways to make them both suffer. It wasn't a pleasant thought.

"Well, this is another fine mess I've gotten you into," she told Pierce with a hint of her old vivacity.

"We'll get out of it," he assured her with a faint smile.

"Think so?" She glanced toward the high window. "If we only had a ladder and a sledge hammer," she said with a sigh.

He was watching her with narrow, speculative dark eyes. His face grew harder by the minute as he contemplated what could happen to her at Philippe Sabon's hands. Her first experience of a man shouldn't be disgusting or frightening. She'd be scarred forever if Sabon had her.

"Dream on."

She glanced at him. "You're leering at me," she murmured and grinned. "There's a bed in here, just in case you can't restrain yourself a minute longer," she said, pointing to it. "I wouldn't mind at all. In fact," she added persuasively, "you'd literally be saving me from a fate worse than death."

"Namely Sabon," he agreed solemnly. His eyes grew narrow and hot. "I can't stand the thought of Sabon as your first lover."

Her heart jumped up into her throat. She felt her breath catch as she met his searching eyes. "Neither can I. So while there's still time, why don't you do something about it? We're married, you know."

His eyebrow jerked and he chuckled softly. "We must be. You haven't stopped reminding me since the ceremony.'' He got up from his chair slowly, glancing idly from corner to corner. There were no surveillance cameras. He hadn't expected that there would be. The house, while beautiful, was old and had no modern fixtures that he'd noticed. He could be certain that no spying eyes would see them.

He took the chair he'd been sitting in and propped it under the door handle so that no one could walk in without making a lot of noise.

Then he turned to Brianne. His expression was one of resignation, but his eyes were smoldering as he considered the delights that lay ahead for both of them.

''Are we really going to do it?'' she asked breathlessly as he approached her.

He took her arms and pulled her up against him with a soft, amused smile. She was incorrigible. ''You look a little nervous,'' he murmured as his hands caressed their way slowly over her taut breasts and down her belly to the fastening of her slacks.

''Who, me? I'm only trembling with sheer anticipation!'' She locked her arms tight around his neck and felt her breath catch at the expression on his face. "Oh, Pierce, I've waited so long for you! It's going to be...heaven!"

He was feeling a similar emotion. Taut with need, he glanced sideways at the bed and hoped it would hold both of them without crashing to the floor. Then he met her excited gaze and, as the zipper gave way, he stopped being concerned about it at all.

Chapter Eight

Brianne met his lips halfway, holding on hungrily as he kissed her.

He drew away a breath, chuckling. "Not so fast, baby," he murmured as he let his slacks fall to the floor. "We're pressed for time, but it doesn't have to be that quick."

Her nails dug into his shoulders. "I'm just making sure you don't let go," she whispered.

"Not a chance," he bit off against her mouth. "Brianne…!"

She'd thought that he was going to be quick, and that she wouldn't be able to enjoy it. She was wrong. The feel of his big, faintly callused hands on her bare skin was like a narcotic. He touched her delicately, tenderly, while his mouth opened and probed at her lips in quick, hard contacts that were violently arousing. She hadn't really expected that she could be so immediately overwhelmed even by Pierce, but she was. He unfastened her tunic and slid her lacy bra aside, then his head bent and his mouth slid onto one soft little breast, his teeth gently catching the nipple and tasting its firmness. She could feel her body swell instantly as he suckled her. It trembled as he found that most intimate part of her and traced around it in an exploration that was at first teasing, and then all but unbearable. She lifted toward him, moaning, because she needed more than this maddening suggestion of pleasure.

She heard her own quick, fluttering breath. Even when he'd made love to her on the island, it had been nothing like this. He used all his skill to arouse her, and it was vast. In the space of heated seconds, she was wild for him, so aroused that she was fighting her briefs and his own with trembling hands to get them out of the way.

"Yes," she choked into his hard mouth. "Yes...please...please...please!"

She tugged his hands back to her bare flesh and held them there as she whispered feverishly what she wanted. He helped her, amazed at his own headlong rush into passion, despite the circumstances. He groaned and lifted her gently onto the bed, sliding alongside her with aching pleasure as the newness and the sweetness of their intimacy made fires inside his starved body. He pinned her hips with his own, his stomach bare against hers, the thick hair tickling as he positioned her, and slowly, delicately entered her for the first time, careful not to hurt her, because he was more potent than he'd been in a long time. He trembled helplessly at the surge of passion the contact aroused in him.

He heard her shocked gasp at her first taste of true intimacy, and he opened his eyes to look straight into hers as he moved hungrily against her.

He couldn't stop, but he had to ask. "The doctor...you asked him to give you something?" he bit off.

"Yes, and he did—" she sobbed.

Her voice broke on a wave of red-hot pleasure before she could add that she'd forgotten to bring the pills to the States with her and that she hadn't yet taken more than one. It would be dangerous. Very dangerous.

The knowledge that she could become pregnant only made the intimacy more poignant. She gripped his shoulders hard enough to leave tiny marks from her short nails in his skin, but he didn't seem to mind. He groaned softly as he moved even closer to her.

He shifted her, and his mouth bit into hers as his body imposed itself on hers, closer and closer and closer, in an intimacy that far exceeded her dreams about him. She could feel the heat and power of him there, in her most secret place. She could feel him throbbing, as her own body throbbed around him, the hot silence broken only by the urgent rush of their breath and the faint sound of their bodies sliding against each other as his rhythm became quick and rough and demanding.

It was like falling into lava, she thought when the explosion of heat rushed up from her loins. She stiffened under the crush of his powerful body and sobbed like a child, her teeth clenched, her whole body convulsing as if with some unknown and frightening fever. Spasms of pleasure so deep they rivaled pain, contractions that went on endlessly, carrying her along, blind and deaf to everything else. She felt his hot breath at her ear. He was whispering something that she couldn't quite hear, his own voice breaking as he convulsed, too, and gave himself to the violence of the ecstasy that they achieved.

He shuddered in the aftermath, still holding her pinned to the bed. There was a film of cold sweat on his chest and abdomen, and on hers. They clung together unsteadily, breathing in strained, spastic jerks.

She still throbbed where they were joined, a pleasure that lingered on even after the cataclysmic passion, and she moved experimentally to enjoy it again.

He stilled her hips with a weary chuckle. "No. There's no time," he whispered, bending to her mouth. He kissed it slowly, softly, as he broke the intimate connection that had joined them so closely.

He refastened his own clothing before he did the same for her. She was so weak that she could barely stand alone, overwhelmed by her first passion. He kissed her eyes with a tenderness he hadn't felt in years, cradling her head in his big, warm hands until she was breathing normally again.

He bent and kissed her tenderly, searching her

eyes with remembered pleasure. She kissed him back, her soft green eyes drowsy with love and fulfillment. She grinned at him irrepressibly and chuckled. "Talk about cheating the hangman," she murmured dryly.

He lifted an eyebrow. "Sabon's loss." He pushed back her damp hair and took a long breath. "I'm sorry it had to be so quick," he murmured. "One day I'll make it up to you."

She pursed her lips and looked him over blatantly. "When? Name a date and a time. I dare you."

He turned away, shrugging it off, but the comment made him feel guilty. His motives had been somewhat unselfish, but now the enormity of what they'd done hit him squarely between the eyes. "You can have the bathroom first," he said quietly, holding the door open for her.

She passed him, confused, but she didn't reply.

He closed the door behind her and went lazily to the chair and pulled it out from the door. He sat down, his legs crossed, his arms folded over his broad chest, outwardly the very picture of bored indifference. Inside, he was churning at the experience he'd just had. He'd never imagined that he and Brianne would come together for the first time in such a staggering passion. He'd have preferred it somewhere else, of course. Not in the beach house, though, because that was where he and Margo...

Margo! He clenched his teeth as he thought of her. He'd betrayed her with Brianne. He'd sworn that he'd never touch another woman as long as he lived, and he'd lied.

No. He'd only done it to spare Brianne the horror of Philippe Sabon as her first lover. Yes, that was why. It had nothing to do with desire or love, it was an act of charity.

He laughed out loud at his own rationale. That—an act of charity! It had been the most explosive fulfillment in years, very nearly equal to the passion he and Margo had shared. He'd thought of nothing except the softness of Brianne's body under his, the shy enticement of her mouth, the sobbing delight of her ecstasy under such terrible circumstances. Her first time, and she'd achieved satisfaction with him. It gave him a feeling of pride on one hand, and then of shame on the other. They were married, of course. A man was certainly permitted to make love to his wife. But it was a sham marriage, contracted only to protect her from Sabon, just as the intimacy

had been to spare her the madman as her first
lover.

Yet, what he felt with her was surely more than
surface desire. He scowled as he remembered his
own pleasure. Over the years, before his marriage,
there had been women. Some were beautiful,
some were very experienced. He'd enjoyed those
encounters. But none of them had compared with
those brief, heated minutes in Brianne's arms. It
puzzled him that he should have had such a reaction to her. Of course, it could have been her
innocence. There was something deliciously primitive about initiating her to passion. And not only
to have initiated her, but to have done it without
fear or pain on her part. He'd given her as much
pleasure as she'd given him.

His thoughts were interrupted by her emer-
gence from the bathroom, her face free of
makeup, her hair unbrushed but tidier in a braid
down her back. She couldn't quite meet his eyes
now, and the fact of her shyness made him feel
protective.

"What do you think they'll do with us?" she
asked, sitting down on the bare bedsprings of the
tiny bed with her hands folded on her thighs.

"Good question," he replied.

"I can't see them letting us go," she added.

He drew in a long breath. "Frankly, neither can I," he agreed, deciding that honesty was best in the long run.

She looked up and searched his eyes briefly before she dropped her gaze back to her legs. "Well, it's been nice knowing you."

He almost missed the faint gleam of mischief in her green eyes as they flashed to his face and fell again.

"It's been nice knowing you, too, Miss Martin," he replied gently.

She drew in a long sigh and looked toward the locked door. "I don't suppose you've got a battering ram in your pocket?"

"If you had a hairpin, I could try picking the lock," he murmured.

She grinned. "Actually, I do have one."

She pulled it out and handed it to him, just as the doorknob rattled and a key turned in the lock. The door opened. Two men came in. One held a small automatic weapon on them while the other rudely pulled hairpins from Brianne's hair and hand.

"No escapes," the shorter man said in thick

English. "Monsieur Sabon arrive tonight." He grinned at Brianne. "You make present for him."

The other man frowned and said something. He looked at Pierce and back at his comrade.

The shorter man looked suddenly worried. The two of them spoke in Arabic. Brianne didn't understand a word, but Pierce was able to understand a few phrases. The men were worried that Sabon wouldn't like having a man in the room with his intended, not even a servant.

The taller man broke off and moved to jerk Pierce up by his arm. "You come with us," he said.

Brianne opened her mouth to protest, but a sharp look from Pierce's black eyes stopped her instantly.

"What are you going to do with Mr. Hutton's bodyguard?" she asked haughtily.

"We put him in room by himself," the shorter man said. "To remove temptation."

"Temptation indeed!" Brianne huffed. "I don't play around with servants!"

The men prodded him out the door at gunpoint and Brianne was left sitting alone in the room.

It was dark when the two men returned with bread and cheese and a glass of red wine. The tall, older one held the weapon in a vaguely threatening way while the shorter one placed the tray on the small table. Brianne glared at the glass.

"I don't drink red wine," she said shortly. "Can't I have water?"

The shorter one looked harassed. "Wine is good for nerves."

"I don't have nerves," she said, glaring at him.

The two men exchanged amused glances. The shorter one took the wine and left, returning shortly with a tall glass of water. He put it in front of her with a flourish.

"I'm Brianne," she said. "Who are you?"

The shorter man was surprised. "Rashid," he told her.

"And you?" she asked the tall one.

"Mufti," he murmured, and seemed embarrassed.

"Have you worked for Philippe Sabon for a long time?"

"Only briefly," Rashid informed her, and his broken English slowly gave way to formal enunciation, as if he hadn't spoken the language in a while but was beginning to remember more of it.

"He has given much to our village—money to buy medicines and food for the poor."

She was surprised, but it occurred to her that even evil men must have a glimmer of good in them somewhere. "His mother was an Arab, wasn't she?" she asked, recalling a glimmer of gossip.

Rashid nodded. "All his family."

"But he has a French name."

Rashid glanced at the tall man, Mufti, and grimaced. "There are things of which I must not speak. Suffice it to say that Monsieur Sabon has the best interests of our country at heart. He is a brave and good man."

"He is a kidnapper," she said firmly.

He shrugged. "Things are not what they seem, *mademoiselle*. We live in perilous times that may see us undone, but we will do what we must to survive. *Inshallah,*" he added, which was Arabic for something like "God willing." He paused, then continued. "We are constantly under threat of invasion by our enemy, who envies us even the small reserves of oil we have only just discovered."

Brianne listened. She'd never questioned where

raw materials came from before, or how they were obtained.

"Miss Martin," Rashid told her, "the Western nations are dependent on petroleum. We have the largest supply in the region. In other times, the West sought to control and exploit the spice production of the Indies, the rubber production of Africa, the tea production of the Far East. Even now, the rain forests are dwindling because the West wants its lumber, and fast food chains want to clear it for lands on which to enlarge the production of beef."

She sat wide-eyed, staring at them with complete shock. These men had seemed like ruffians, thugs. But they knew more about the political reality of the world than she'd ever learned.

"You are very young," Mufti told her. "And you know very little of the ugliness of commerce or the evilness of man."

"I know some," she argued. She stared at them curiously. "You both seem to be intelligent men. Why do you work for Philippe Sabon?"

"I have four children," Rashid said. "One of them has a form of cancer that is killing him. Monsieur Sabon pays for him to have expensive treatment in France."

"And I lost my family and my home when bombs fell while my wife prepared the meal for our two little ones." Mufti's voice broke. He got a firmer grip on the weapon. "Monsieur Sabon heard of my loss from one of my cousins in the village on the mainland. Only recently, he came to find me and offered me work." Mufti shifted, as if something about his situation bothered him. Odd, he seemed rather old to have small children. His hair was graying. In fact, he looked much the age Brianne's father would have been, had he lived.

"Rashid, we talk too much." Mufti gestured with his weapon toward the door. "We should go."

Brianne felt less threatened than ever before as she looked at the lean, dark faces and saw the harsh lines in them. Her life had been relatively carefree; at least she hadn't had to learn to use a gun and fight in wars. The lives these men had led showed in their faces, older than they should have seemed. She thought of Mufti's wife and children dying in a hail of bombs. She had to remember that there were two sides to every story, and she felt sorry for the man.

"I'm sorry. About your family, I mean," Brianne told Mufti.

He looked sheepish and uncomfortable. "As if you had anything to do with it, Miss Martin," he said kindly. "It is a sad world in which we live. People are driven by circumstances and misfortune and necessity to do many indecent things. I regret your capture. But it was a necessity." He hesitated at the door. "Monsieur Sabon will not harm you," he added surprisingly. "It was not for any immoral purpose that you were brought here."

They nodded politely and left, locking the door behind them. Now, whatever in the world did that mean? She wondered about it long after darkness fell.

There were voices outside the door. She heard a familiar one and caught her breath as she recognized it. Sabon!

She got off the mattress and went to sit in the chair, stiff-backed and unyielding. She was still there when the door was unlocked and Philippe Sabon walked in. He tossed a harsh command to his two men and closed the door.

Brianne stared at his lean, scarred dark face and narrow black eyes with real fear.

He waved a hand impatiently. "No, no," he said quickly, "I have not come for that. It was convenient to let everyone think that I intended you for a depraved appetite, then not too many eyebrows would be raised when you vanished. It would be assumed that I took you for...nefarious purposes."

"I b-beg your pardon?" she stammered.

He sat down on the mattress and crossed his long, elegant legs while he lit one of the small Turkish cigars he liked.

"I'm not such a monster that I enjoy ravishing innocents," he told her calmly. "Although I do find you attractive, and if you were willing, and I were still whole, I might be tempted."

Her eyes asked the question her lips couldn't form. He laughed coldly. "You have no idea, have you?" He leaned forward. "Since you will not leave this place for some time to come, I can answer the question you fear to ask me. I stood on a land mine in Palestine on a business trip; a leftover horror from one of many conflicts in this great region. The wounds were so terrible that I ceased to be a man," he added harshly. "Hence the fiction that I have perverse appetites." He made a distasteful gesture. "It was kinder than the gossip I would have attracted had the truth been known.''

''I'm sorry,'' she said, and she was, in spite of her overwhelming relief that she didn't have to worry about her own seduction now and his curious statement that she would never leave the island. ''It must be...terrible for you.''

''Terrible.'' He savored the word as he stared blankly at the tip of his small cigar. ''Yes. It was...terrible.'' His eyes lifted to her face and remained for a time, as if he were searching for mockery or sarcasm or amusement. He found none of these in that quiet, gentle face. He grimaced. ''A woman like you can make a man ashamed of his baser instincts. If I had met someone like you before this, I might have been very different. As it is, the well-being of my people is all I have to substitute for any other pleasures I might lack in my life.''

''What are you going to do with Mr. Hutton's bodyguard and me?''

He shrugged. ''Those decisions will have to be made later. Hutton will surely come looking for you, and that could cause me some problems. You see, your stepfather and I have concocted a way to provoke your so-protective government into sending troops to protect our oil fields while we open them to drilling in the near future.''

"Kurt?''

He nodded. He got up and paced the room, making a grimace of distaste at her surroundings. "This is uncomfortable, I know, but it was hastily arranged. I will try to improve your surroundings when I can." He turned back to her. "Kurt has sent in a band of mercenaries to attack us, before our enemies rush to do the same thing and without pretence. We will then blame the attack on the government presently hostile to yours, and plead for American intervention to stop them before they realize how weak we are right now as a nation and rush over our borders. Kurt has a friend in the Senate who has persuasive powers, and I think that your government will not need much excuse to launch an attack against our mutual enemy.''

Brianne stood up. "You mustn't," she said earnestly. "You could start a world war!''

He shrugged again and puffed on his cigar. "Better that than let the oil fields be captured by our enemies before we can start exploiting them for the benefit of our people. Believe me, it has not been easy persuading the sheikh that the oil our country possesses must be drawn out of the earth to save our economy from collapse. He believes that it is wrong to depend on the West, even for the development of our potential wealth. I have argued long and hard to convince him that the benefit to our people will be worth the foreign interest here.''

''Benefit to your people...?''

He glared at her. ''You have an interesting picture of me. I am a monster, yes? A vicious, perverted man who enjoys nothing more than despoiling women and making himself richer!''

She made an impotent gesture with her hands.

''My grandmother's village, the place where I was born, is a wasteland of poverty, of malnutrition and disease and ignorance. All around us, the oil-producing nations are counting their wealth while we stand at the door knocking, to be turned away by servants richer than we are.''

She was utterly speechless for a few seconds. ''But there is foreign aid....''

He smiled wearily. ''How naive you are,'' he said. ''How naive and trusting. You live in the decadent West. You have plenty to eat and drink, clothes to wear, cars to drive you, airplanes to fly you anyplace you want to go. You have no idea how most of the rest of the world lives, Miss Martin.'' He puffed on his cigar. ''You might find a month in my country enlightening. Unlike the metropolitan cities of our neighbors, here in Qawi you can live in a mud hut with no indoor facilities, draw water from a sandy well, kill and dress whatever small animal you can catch to cook over an open fire, spin wool to make thread to weave cloth to make your own clothing, and watch your babies starve to death or die of dysentery and fever for lack of medicine. We have no Europeans here, and no modern cities.'' He nodded at her look of consternation. ''You seem stunned.''

''It sounds primitive.''

''It is primitive,'' he said shortly. ''Primitive and hopeless and useless! Without money there is no hope of educating my people. Without education, there is only poverty forever.''

She was at a loss to make suggestions. Astonished at what he was telling her, at the warped picture she had of him and the world he lived in, she was absolutely without the ability to debate him.

''And now we face the problem of what to do with you while Kurt bargains for me in America,'' he continued.

She looked around her worriedly. "Are you going to keep me here? But, why, if you don't want me for, well, for nefarious purposes?"

He sighed. "I brought you here to ensure Kurt's cooperation with the fiction that I wanted to marry you and bring our families into an alliance," he said honestly. "He was most anxious to agree to my plan, which appealed to his unbridled greed. But I understand that his wife tried to talk him into backing out of the deal. He dealt with her in a way that brings no respect from me. I have no patience with men who hit their women, whatever the reason." He held up a hand. "She is not much hurt. I made sure of it."

Brianne's first thought was for her mother's safety. So she was relieved to hear Sabon's reassurance that Eve was all right. For now.

She jerked her mind back to the present. "You mean, I'm here so that Kurt won't try to go against you."

"Exactly," he replied. He smiled coolly. "Of course, he thinks I have...other plans for you, and it was convenient to let him believe so." His eyes briefly sparkled with humor. "I believe your mother actually threatened to leave him if you are harmed. Surprising, no, such concern in such a mercenary woman?''

She caught her breath. ''How do you know so much about my mother?''

''I have spies everywhere.'' He studied her soft features with real regret. ''You are no conventional beauty, but you have a quality of compassion that is so rare as to be precious. I look at you and grieve for the loss of the man I once was. I would have cherished you.''

Her breathing suspended at the statement, so unexpected, and so sincere. He seemed so vulnerable then, so tormented, that her heart ached for him.

He saw that expression cross her oval face and he winced. ''Child, the sight of you hurts me,'' he said hoarsely, and he turned away. ''I never meant to involve you in this, in any way. Kidnapping was the last thing on my mind, but it was as much for your sake as mine that I brought you here. Kurt is unpredictable, and his temper has become unmanageable. I would not have you hurt for the world,'' he added huskily, glancing at her.

Unexpectedly touched by his attitude, she got up out of her chair and moved toward him. He was nothing like the monster she'd made of him

Get 2 Books FREE!

**MIRA BOOKS,
the brightest stars
in women's
fiction™, presents**

The Best of the Best™

**Superb collector's editions of
the very best novels by the
world's best-known authors!**

FREE BOOKS!
To introduce you to "The Best
of the Best" we'll send you 2
books ABSOLUTELY FREE!"

FREE GIFT!
Get a stylish picture frame
absolutely free!

BEST BOOKS!
"The Best of the Best" brings
you the best books by the
world's hottest authors!

2 FREE BOOKS!

▲ To get your 2 free
books, affix this peel-off
sticker to the reply card
and mail it today!

Get 2

HOW TO GET YOUR
2 FREE BOOKS AND FREE GIFT

1. Peel off FREE BOOK seal from front cover. Place it in space provided at right. This automatically entitles you to receive two free books and a lovely picture frame decorated with celestial designs.

2. Send back this card and you'll get 2 "The Best of the Best™" novels. These books have a combined cover price of $11.00 or more but they are yours to keep absolutely free.

3. There's no catch. You're under no obligation to buy anything. We charge nothing – ZERO – for your first shipment. And you don't have to make any minimum number of purchases – not even one!

4. We call this line "The Best of the Best" because each month you'll receive the best books by the world's hottest authors. These are authors whose names show up time and time again on all the major bestseller lists and whose books sell out as soon as they hit the stores. You'll love getting them conveniently delivered to your home…and you'll love our discount prices!

5. We hope that after receiving your free books you'll want to remain a subscriber. But the choice is yours – to continue or cancel, anytime at all! why not take us up on our invitation, with no risk of any kind. You'll be glad you did!

6. And remember…we'll send you a stylish picture frame ABSOLUTELY FREE, just for giving "The Best of the Best" a try!

SPECIAL FREE GIFT!

We'll send you this lovely picture frame, decorated with celestial designs, absolutely FREE, simply for accepting our no-risk offer!

The Best of the Best™—Here's How it Works

Accepting free books places you under no obligation to buy anything. You may keep the books and gift and return the shipping statement marked "cancel." If you do not cancel, about a month later we will send you 3 additional novels and bill you just $4.24 each, plus 25¢ delivery per book and applicable sales tax, if any.* That's the complete price — and compared to cover prices of $5.50 each — quite a bargain! You may cancel at any time, but if you choose to continue, every month we'll send you 3 more books, which you may either purchase at the discount price...or return to us and cancel your subscription.
*Terms and prices subject to change without notice. Sales tax applicable in N.Y.

If offer card is missing write to: The Best of the Best, 3010 Walden Ave., P.O. Box 1867, Buffalo, NY 14240-1867

BUSINESS REPLY MAIL
FIRST-CLASS MAIL   PERMIT NO. 717   BUFFALO NY

POSTAGE WILL BE PAID BY ADDRESSEE

THE BEST OF THE BEST
3010 WALDEN AVE
PO BOX 1867
BUFFALO NY 14240-9952

NO POSTAGE
NECESSARY
IF MAILED
IN THE
UNITED STATES

in her mind. He was nothing like the man the world saw and hated. Hesitantly, she touched his arm, no longer afraid. She felt pity for him.

He looked down at the soft hand on the expensive material of his sleeve with astonishment. His black eyes, so different from Pierce's, so foreign, met hers.

He reached toward her in a moment of suspended time, hesitantly like a young boy alone for the first time with a girl. His lean hands gently touched her upper arms. "You will...permit?" he asked, slowly drawing her toward him.

She let him draw her into his arms and hold her. It was the most incredible experience of her life, there in the room where she was a prisoner, to stand in the circle of that man's arms and let him hold her. That was all he did. He made no move toward intimacy or violence. He touched her hair as if it fascinated him, and she could hear his breath sigh out roughly at her ear. For an instant, she felt his cheek against the top of her head and heard a soft groan pass his lips. A shiver ran the length of his tall, lean body. They called him a monster. A criminal. A beast. He trembled in her arms.

"Can't they do anything for you?" she asked quietly.

He swallowed. "Nothing." His voice broke on the word. His hands cradled her head, and after a minute, they framed her face and lifted it to his eyes. They were wet. He was unashamed of his reaction as he studied her in a painful silence. He clenched his teeth as he saw the stuff of dreams so close that he could breathe it in through his nostrils, and so far away that it might have been a distant star.

Her fingers reached up to his cheek and touched it lightly. "I'm sorry," she said.

He didn't blink. "All I had left were memory and dreams." He managed a faint smile. "Now I will have the look in your eyes as well." He moved away and took her hands, palms up, to his lips. "Thank you," he said huskily, and dropped them at once.

He moved away to the door and stood there for a minute, gathering his self-control. "You will not be harmed, ever, by me or anyone close to me," he said, glancing back at her. "I give you my word. And if you ever need help, for any reason, I am yours to command."

She stared at him with faint wonder. "Why?"

One of his shoulders moved almost impercep-
tibly. "Perhaps because you have a heart more
fragile than any I have ever known, a heart that
can pity a monster like me."

"You aren't a monster," she said.

His eyes hardened. "Yes, I am," he replied.
"And I never realized it until today."

She drew in a long breath. "Mr. Sabon, what
about Jack?"

"Philippe," he corrected her quietly. "Who is
Jack?"

"Mr. Hutton's bodyguard," she said, hoping
against hope that he wouldn't find out who
"Jack" was. "He was brought in with me. They
put him someplace else."

"So Hutton sent a bodyguard with you," he
mused. "He must think me a great threat to your
virtue."

"Yes, he does," she agreed at once.

His laugh was hollow. "There was a time," he
said gently, "when that threat would have been a
very real one. With hair and skin like that, you
would truly have been 'white gold' to a man like
me. Perhaps it is fortunate for you that I went to
Palestine that day."

"What is 'white gold'?" she asked, diverted.

''There was once a flourishing slave trade in this part of the world, where a white woman would bring her weight in gold.'' He chuckled. ''You would have brought a very nice price.''

While she was working out a reply, he glanced at his watch. ''I have business to conduct. You will have everything you need,'' he promised as he turned back toward the door. He paused and glanced at her again, with a soft, curious smile. ''Mufti and Rashid speak highly of you. You are not what any of us expected you to be.''

Her shoulders rose and fell. ''Neither are all of you,'' she replied. ''I suppose we all think in stereotypes until we know something about the people behind the politics.''

He nodded. ''This is true. And I am indeed sorry for your confinement. But too much is at stake to risk letting you go.''

He knocked on the door. It was opened and he left with his two men.

Brianne gnawed on her lower lip while she cursed silently at her inability to sway him from this maniacal course. It seemed perfectly logical to him, to start a war in order to save his country from conquest. But it was her country he expected to fight it for him! She had to stop this. She had to get to Washington, to stop Kurt from what he was planning, to tell someone what Sabon was planning!

But first she had to escape, she and Pierce. How would they get away? And despite his courtesy to her, what might Sabon do to Pierce when he found out who he had in his power? Surely he'd use Pierce's capture to his advantage! He could hold him for ransom if nothing else. Here, in this poor place, a rich Westerner would be in the greatest danger.

She paced the floor, turning plans over and over in her mind. She couldn't scale the wall or break through iron bars. That left the door, and the men were guarding it. Could she play on their emotions, weaken them and then overpower them? Of course, she thought, amused at her own nerve. She could weaken them with pity and then knock them out, two big strong men with loaded automatic weapons. Despite their regard for her, they probably wouldn't hesitate to shoot her if she threatened their boss's plans.

She sat back down again, perplexed by Sabon's strange behavior. She recalled being so afraid of him, so repulsed by the man she thought he was. Now her own sympathy for him put those mem-

ories aside. As long as she lived, she would remember tears in that man's eyes as she let him
hold her.

She got a sudden picture of herself with a sign
around her neck offering hugs to the madman two
countries over, and she laughed softly to herself.
She was getting Stockholm Syndrome—identify-
ing with her captors. Pierce would laugh himself
sick.

Pierce. She wondered what they were doing to
Pierce. She flushed, remembering their earlier encounter. Wouldn't he feel terrible when he realized what he'd done, that there was no threat from
Sabon at all and Brianne wasn't on the pill. He
might have made her pregnant. That would play
hell with his own plans, because he'd said that he
wanted to be alone, and did not want a permanent
relationship with Brianne. Things were very complicated and she had no idea how to resolve them.

Right now, she had to think only of escape.
Later, when she was safely at home again, she
could worry about the things she didn't have time
to consider right now.

Chapter Nine

Tate Winthrop had just gotten off the phone with one of the men in his personal network of "interested observers" of the world situation. His wide, chiseled mouth pulled into a thoughtful expression as he stared out the window of his luxurious Washington, D.C. apartment at the city's night skyline. It glittered like diamonds and sapphires and rubies. It was beautiful, he mused, but a far cry from the natural colors of a South Dakota sunset near the Pine Ridge Sioux Reservation where he'd grown up.

He studied the face of a young, dark-eyed blond woman in the simple wood frame on his desk. He hid the photo of Cecily whenever she came over for supper, which she did occasionally when the Smithsonian could spare her. He couldn't let her know the depth of his feelings for her. She was a forensic anthropologist, and she often worked with the FBI to examine skeletal remains. It was a grisly profession for a sensitive young woman, but it had been her dream to escape her stepfather's clutches and get an education. Tate had made that possible for her. She had no idea how much she owed him, and he wanted to keep it that way. He felt responsible for her, but he'd never permitted even the slightest intimacy between them. He was Sioux and she was white. He wanted no mixing of blood, no child of two separate races growing up without a true identity. Except for that, he might easily have given in to his feelings for her, he mused as he studied the delicate features of her face in the photograph. Cecily Peterson wasn't beautiful. She was pretty and slender, and she had courage and spirit and a keen, cutting wit. If he had a weakness at all, Cecily was it. And just lately, she'd bothered him more than ever before.

Pierce Hutton's phone call had come at an opportune time. It would get him away from Cecily while he refortified his defenses against her. He had to do that periodically. Sometimes it was agony not to just reach for her and have done with it. A man of lesser scruples and willpower would have, years ago.

He smoothed long, dark fingers over the desk and pondered how to proceed. Pierce had wanted him to bring two men and meet him in Freeport. Now a contact in Freeport reported that Pierce's plane had landed, but Pierce had never shown up at the hotel where he was registered under an alias. Neither had the young woman who was supposed to be accompanying him.

That meant that Pierce had been snatched. And Tate had a fairly good idea who'd snatched him. Philippe Sabon and Kurt Brauer were up to something, and Pierce had landed himself right in the way.

He got to his feet, tall and lean and powerful in the light from the window, stretching his six-foot frame to unknot the muscles in his long back. He smoothed a hand over his long, thick black braid. It was silly not to cut his hair, since he lived in a white world, but he still harbored some faint superstitions and beliefs that had been handed down in his family for generations. He believed in talismans, and his long hair was powerful medicine. The only time he'd cut it, he'd been shot in the chest and almost died while working for a secret government agency overseas. Since then, it was occasionally trimmed and nothing more.

He went to the closet and pulled out a small case with some items he was going to need. Then he phoned two of his best men and told them where to meet him. His heart raced at the thought of what lay ahead. Small surges of adrenaline kept him alive during the monotony of security work. This might be dangerous, but it was also going to be fun.

Pierce Hutton, locked in a much smaller room than Brianne's, tried unsuccessfully to pick the lock with a paper clip he'd found in a table drawer. There was some rust inside the old lock, and it wouldn't budge. He dropped the twisted paper clip to the floor with a muffled curse and threw his shoulder against the door. It didn't budge. The damned thing must have steel right through it, because it made his arm sore. He looked up, only to find another of those high barred windows that seemed to be everywhere in this fortress.

He wondered how Brianne was, and what they

were doing to her. He'd never been so angry or felt so helpless. He couldn't bear the thought of her being hurt, but he had no way to prevent it. His eyes flashed as he remembered the things he'd heard about Sabon. If the man hurt Brianne, he'd pay for it. Pierce would hunt him down if it took the rest of his life!

He heard a noise outside the door and then the sound of voices. He moved closer, putting his ear to the thick, heavy surface.

He recognized the voice, even though he'd heard it infrequently. It was Sabon!

"Can't afford to let them go, not yet," he was telling someone.

"You don't mean to kill the child!" one man exclaimed in English.

"Good God, no!" came the sharp reply. "I mean to kill no one. But we cannot risk letting them free before we achieve our goal. The Americans must come to protect us. It would not endear us to them to find that we had kidnapped one of their citizens, regardless of the reason!"

"That is so, but can we not move her to a better place?"

There was a pause. "We will take her, and the bodyguard, to the mainland and place them in the old fortress. It is not so modern as this, but they will have more room. You have heard nothing of Hutton?''

''Nothing. Apparently he is still in the western United States.''

''Then let us hope he remains there until Kurt has concluded our business in Washington. Damn their media, it will be all over the news and Hutton will know then. But perhaps it will be too late for him to prevent it. He is surely in the country on a limited basis. Besides, he has enemies there, and he is no more an American citizen than I am. Kurt has joint German and American citizenship. That is to work to our advantage, I think. Come, let us see if Kurt's well-armed friends have arrived.''

Pierce scowled, reflecting on what he'd heard. Sabon hadn't sounded like a man obsessed with a young woman at all. There had been some alarming hints of aggression in that quick rhetoric, and if Kurt was in the States, why was he there? What plan was unfolding?

Pierce cursed silently at his helplessness. Something big was brewing here and he was as helpless as a cat in a sack. He only hoped that Winthrop noticed his absence and came after him in time. He had it in him to feel sorry for these poor men when his security chief arrived. Winthrop wouldn't be gentle with them.

In the hours that followed, there was a lot of movement outside Brianne's door. She didn't see her captors again, but she heard all sorts of noises. Marching feet. Mechanical sounds, like guns being cocked. Loud voices. There were a lot of men in the corridor for several minutes, and then they were marching away. Outside, she heard sounds like those of aircraft. Not airplanes. Helicopters, perhaps?

She remembered what Philippe Sabon had told her about his plans to garner American intervention, and she shivered. He really meant to attack his own people and blame it on a neighboring country. Did Kurt know that? Was he part of it? And what about Brianne's mother and little Nicholas, where did they fit into this insanity? Kurt couldn't be so desperate that he'd help Sabon start a war!

Incensed by her lack of sight in here, she propped the chair upside down on the bedsprings and stood on it, trying to get high enough to see out the window. But all she could manage to see was the blades of a helicopter go by. This was interesting. Surely it was part of the assault, and it was ready to start. She couldn't warn anybody. She couldn't even help herself. Surely Sabon wouldn't kill his own people. He must mean to fake an attack, for the benefit of any foreigners who might be in residence.

The mainland was several miles away. But the sound of bombs and missiles carried a fair distance, so when Brianne heard explosions a few minutes later, she knew what they must be. It was too late to prevent this. If only she could get out of here in time to warn someone back home, before Kurt spoke to his senator.

She stood, frozen, as she put the pieces of the puzzle together. Kurt was already in the States, Sabon had said. He knew the attack was coming. He was going to be "conveniently" in Washington when he was informed of it. He'd tell his senator friend, who'd tell some colleagues, and—

No, wait! They'd have to have a hearing and appoint a committee, just as they always did before sending troops anywhere. She breathed a sigh of relief. There wasn't going to be any danger. What was she thinking! The Americans weren't like some other nations. They deliberated before they acted. Poor Kurt! And poor Mr. Sabon, too. This was all for nothing.

She got off the bed, turned the chair back over and sat down on it. She didn't need to worry about a war. Her own situation, and Pierce's, seemed of paramount importance now. She only hoped they hadn't discovered his identity. His situation was a lot more precarious than her own.

She wondered if he was thinking about her, after their torrid interlude. She didn't dare tell him the truth about Sabon just yet. When he found out that Sabon was incapable, he'd be furious that he'd gone to such lengths to protect Brianne. Worse, if he found out that she hadn't taken her birth control pills for two days, he'd be livid. The threat of pregnancy was a very real one, because she was halfway between her monthlies—the best time for it to happen. She let herself dream about a little boy with Pierce's dark, wavy hair and black eyes. But it was a sad dream, because he'd hate both of them. He was still in love with his dead wife. She winced as she recalled something from their intimacy that she hadn't wanted to remember. Just as he began to relax from the strain and delight of satisfaction, he'd whispered a name. But it hadn't been Brianne's. She heard the words echo over and over in her mind. "Margo, darling."

She closed her eyes, trying to blot out the memory of all that passion she'd thought they were sharing. She'd only been a substitute for his beautiful ghost, and she hadn't known it until it was all over, and she was about to whisper how much she loved him. She was glad she hadn't. It would only have made a bad situation worse. He didn't love her.

She wrapped her arms protectively around her chest and refused to think about it anymore, for fear of going quietly mad in the lonely room. She'd face all the unpleasantness later, when she had the time. Right now, she had to think up some way to get out of here! Even if Sabon hadn't a chance of attracting American troops here, his mercenaries could miss their target and accidentally bomb the house she and Pierce were held in. Or some of his countrymen, unaware of the real identity of their attackers, might fight back and cause a greater tragedy. While she sympathized with Sabon's position, she thought his approach to a solution was dead wrong. He had tunnel vision. He only saw his own role in this, not the greater picture. World War III could easily start over such a misguided attempt to protect a small, poor nation. He wasn't considering any other country except his own. Perhaps he had good intentions, but they were being lost in his mania. Presumably the elderly sheikh who ruled this country was being kept in the dark about Philippe's plans. Poor old man. Perhaps he was being held captive, just as she was.

She heard a sound at the window. It came again. The room was viciously hot as the sun came up and spilled down, making shadowy bar patterns on the tiled floor. There was no glass at the window, only those iron bars. Suddenly a small projectile whizzed down and landed at her feet. She bent over the paper-wrapped stone and opened what appeared to be part of an envelope.

"Distract them" was printed in block letters, in English.

She crumpled the paper in her hand and stood up, pursing her lips as she considered the meaning of the note and the intent behind the words. Her eyes began to twinkle. Well, well, rescue was at hand and needed a helping hand, hmmm?

She took a deep breath, started worrying her hair and looking as if she couldn't get her breath at all. She grabbed her throat, contracting it a little to make her face look very red.

"Oh…!" she cried out hoarsely. "Oh…I can't…breathe…my heart!"

She clutched her chest and fell to the floor, giving a very good impression of someone having a heart attack. At her age it would have been unusual, to say the least, but the guard had been told specifically by Monsieur Sabon himself to keep her safe. So when he heard her he went running down the hall to her room, key in hand.

He almost made it. A shadow stepped out from the wall and put a steely arm to his throat. He went down instantly and was helped to stay there by another sharp punch.

The keys were extracted. A hand motioned to two other shadowy figures in totally black garb, right down to the face masks and combat boots. The other invaders went methodically down the hall, guns in hand, checking each door along the way.

Brianne was standing when the door opened. All she could see was a pair of black eyes in a face mask, but in a leaner face than Pierce's.

"Are you the cavalry?" she asked hopefully.

"Yes, and I don't mean Custer's," he replied,

giving a smug grin at his little joke and showing a flash of his perfect white teeth. "Miss Martin, I presume."

"Mrs. Hutton, actually, but I'm sure he'll find a solution for that momentarily. Do you know where he is? Is he all right?" she asked.

Stunned by the news of his boss's marriage but not showing it, Tate Winthrop took her arm impersonally and drew her out the door. "We're about to find out. Stay just behind me, please."

"Roger, wilco," she said with an extended thumb.

He showed another flash of perfect teeth before he turned back, automatic weapon in hand, to advance down the wide corridor.

A soft birdcall came around the corner and Tate stopped, listening. He made a similar call back. He started walking again.

Just as they rounded the corner, three men came running at them, men in camouflage dress with weapons firing.

Brianne's breath stopped in her throat. She'd never expected this sort of danger, but apparently the man in front of her had. He fired two short bursts from the weapon in his hand.

"Don't look at them," he said in a soft, deep voice as he herded her beside him down the hall.

She tried not to look at the bodies on the floor, but she couldn't help it. One glimpse was enough to make her stomach heave. She swallowed, and swallowed again, giving way to silent tears. Those men hadn't been Arabs. They were fair. Some of Sabon's invaders, no doubt, and bloodthirsty enough to kill anything that moved. Her opinion of her host changed at once. Men like that weren't going to fake any invasion; they were going to do it for real, casualties and innocent victims and all.

Tate felt her arm tense in his grasp, but he couldn't stop to reassure her. He kept walking, his eyes everywhere. It had been crazy to do this with only two men. Even so, they stood a better chance than a large armed force did of breaching the security here. He hoped they could grab Pierce and get out without any more gunplay. It attracted unwanted attention.

"I wish I could tell you where they've taken Pierce. I don't know," she said, shaken but moving right along beside him.

"My men have found him," he assured her. "The door is giving some trouble. The lock's rusted."

"Can't they just shoot it open?"

He glanced at her with another flash of white teeth. "A steel door? West German manufacture, just like old Saddam's bomb shelters. Choice engineering, except for the iron lock's rust."

"Oh, dear."

"One of my men once served time for bank robbery," he murmured. "There isn't a lock made, rusty or otherwise, that he can't crack, given time." He looked around them with keen scrutiny. "We're lucky those gunshots didn't bring company. They're too busy on the mainland to bother with us right now, but that won't last long. Sabon will be on his way back any minute, once he's assured himself that things are going according to plan."

"He said he only wanted to protect his country's oil fields from a poor neighbor, that his people are starving and he wants to make life better for them."

"And you believed him." He sighed. "What a utopia we'd have if everyone told the truth." He rounded another corner, tensed, and then relaxed. Two men were hurrying toward him with Pierce right alongside.

Brianne started to go toward him, but her rescuer held her back.

"Hurry!" he called to the others. "We've got about two minutes to clear the building before the communications center goes up!"

"What?" Brianne gasped.

"I mined the communications equipment." He drew her along.

"We've got to get back to the States, pronto," Pierce called, falling into a dead run beside them. "Brauer's already there."

"Yes, he is," Brianne panted as she ran, "and this attack is being made by Kurt's hired mercenaries, not the neighboring country! They're going to blame it on the neighbor to give Kurt an excuse to draw American troops in here."

"Good God!" Pierce exploded.

"Well, maybe we have time to stop Kurt from getting to his senator friend," Brianne added breathlessly. "There'll have to be committee meetings and congressional hearings and public hearings before they even think of sending troops...."

"What planet did you say she came from?" Tate asked Pierce.

"What in the world do you mean?" she exclaimed as she gasped for breath at the pace they were going toward the front entrance.

"You do know that covert operations in several secret government departments act immediately in case of aggression that affects American interests?" he persisted. "In other words, ground troops can be here and in the thick of battle by morning, without congressional knowledge or approval."

Her heart jumped, and not due to the speed of her legs. "You're kidding!"

"I'm not." He went out the door just behind her. A huge helicopter was waiting for them, military-looking and armed to the teeth. It looked as if a dozen people could sit in it without crowding one another.

"Inside!" Tate yelled.

Pierce caught Brianne's arms to lift her in beside him. The other men followed suit. Tate tapped the pilot on the helmet, and they took off. Seconds later, they were being subjected to a veritable hail of bullets.

"I believe Sabon's people have just discovered that you're missing." Tate looked at his watch. "Six, five, four…"

"Why is he counting?" Brianne asked Pierce.

The answer came in an explosion of impressive proportions.

"He won't be calling for reinforcements right away," Tate murmured with a grin.

"Where did you leave the plane?" Pierce asked.

"Not at the airport—" came the dry reply. "I knew it would be a primary target. I left it—" He broke off, and his good mood vanished as he looked over the pilot's shoulder and listened to a sudden burst of Arabic that even Pierce couldn't grasp.

The pilot murmured something grimly.

"We have to put down at the next port and hope for a miracle, I'm afraid," Tate told them somberly. "Sabon's hired guerrillas blew up the airport and didn't stop there. They found the strip where I left the plane and blew it up, too."

"Smart boys," Pierce murmured.

"They should be, I helped train at least two of them," Tate said grimly. "We all started out in government service together." He looked down at the land below. "Sometimes I'm sorry I left it. Like right now." He rapped on the pilot's helmet and gave him a sharp command in Arabic before he turned back to his companions. "We've got to get out of this chopper before we cost Hamid his life. He can fly it over the border and he'll be safe, since he's a citizen. We won't be," he added with a rueful grin. "They don't like foreigners."

Brianne couldn't blame them now. She'd learned a lot about this part of the world in a very short time.

"How do we get home?" Pierce asked easily.

"We hop on a freighter," Tate replied. "Most of them will take passengers if the price is right."

"I hid my wallet in the jet coming over here, so they wouldn't find out who I was right away. It will turn up one day, but not in time to help us," Pierce said.

"No problem," Tate said. "I brought plenty of cash." He leaned across the seat and stuffed a wad of bills into the man's flight suit. He did the same with the two uniformed men beside him. None of the three had taken off their masks.

"Since they're masked and they haven't spoken, you won't know them again," Tate said, explaining the masks.

"Would we know them if they weren't masked?" Brianne had to ask.

"That depends on how much attention you pay

to the pictures on the walls in the post office,'' Tate returned dryly.

Brianne looked at the men with new interest, wide-eyed. "Really?" she asked.

"Now, don't do that," Pierce murmured disgustedly. "You're supposed to look scared."

"I am?" She sat back in her seat and contorted her features. "Is that better?" she asked politely.

They both started laughing.

"You are the damnedest woman," Pierce said with pure disgust.

"Amen to that," Tate agreed. He checked his gun and pulled an automatic pistol from his jacket. He checked to make sure the safety was on and there wasn't a round chambered before he extended it, butt first, to Pierce. "Remember how to use that?"

Pierce nodded. He checked the safety himself and stuck the gun in his own pocket.

Brianne was getting uneasier by the minute. She remembered the two men her companion had shot and the way they'd looked there on the tiled floor, so vulnerable and helpless and pitiful. Her eyes went slowly around the interior of the helicopter and she saw what she'd missed at first. These were killers. They knew how to use those guns and they wouldn't hesitate if threatened. Pierce had a knowledge of firearms that had surely come of using one himself, perhaps in some conflict or during some time of danger in his past.

She felt young and gauche. She wrapped her arms around herself for comfort and averted her eyes to the pilot. He was starting to bring the chopper down near what looked like a seaport, but he wasn't landing anywhere near it. There was a lot of sand and a lot of people down there, all of whom looked, as they neared the ground, very Arabic. They wouldn't blend in, she and Pierce and whoever their rescuer was.

When the chopper landed, their rescuer pulled a big duffel bag from under one of the seats and jumped down beside Pierce and Brianne and the others. The two men who'd accompanied him were wished well and released. The pilot took off with a cursory wave.

"What do we do now?" Brianne asked worriedly.

"We blend in," said their rescuer, and he pulled off the mask that concealed his entire head.

Brianne saw at once that he could have blended in, better than she and Pierce. The man was darker than either of them and he had rough features rather than handsome ones. He had deep-set black eyes with a faint almond shape to them, heavy brows, a broad, straight nose and a wide, chiseled mouth. His cheekbones were high, and his chin square. His thick black hair was in a straight braid behind him that reached below his shoulder blades. It didn't take much imagination to divine his identity.

"Mr. Winthrop, I presume," Brianne murmured with a dry smile.

The tall man lifted an eyebrow. "My reputation precedes me, I gather?"

"He only said that you ate scorpions," she pointed toward Pierce.

"Rattlesnakes, too, but only when they try to bite him," Pierce said with a grin. He extended a hand. "Thanks for coming after us. I don't think Sabon intended to let us go for quite a while."

Tate returned the firm handshake. "This is what you pay me for," he reminded the other man. "Hell of a shame to waste money by letting me sit on my thumbs all the time."

"How did you find us?"

Tate grinned at him. "I could tell you..."

"But you'd have to shoot him," Brianne said for him.

"I really would have to shoot him," Tate assured her. "I took an oath."

"He took several," Pierce murmured, "but he only uses them when it suits him." He sobered. "If Brauer gets to the right people in Washington before we do, it's going to mean an explosion of epic proportions in this part of the world. The whole Arab contingent will go to war."

"I brought a phone." Tate opened the duffel bag and produced the instrument. But when he tried to use it, nothing happened.

He turned it over and exposed the battery. There was no battery. He said something in an unfamiliar-sounding language.

"We can find a phone...." Pierce began.

"Not here. There's not a telephone. Only the wireless on the freighters, and I don't have my codes with me. I need a land line." Tate let out an angry breath.

"What happened to the battery?" Pierce asked.

"Our pilot has a small black-market operation on the side," he said irritably. "I never thought he'd stoop low enough to rob me. I should have carried a spare. I usually do. But not this time."

He shook his head and glanced at Pierce. "You should fire me."

Pierce chuckled. "Get us home first, then I'll think about it."

"I'm serious."

"So am I." Pierce clamped a huge hand on the other man's broad shoulder. "Anybody can get caught up in circumstances. You had a battery pack stolen. I got kidnapped." He shrugged. "We're even."

"Okay." Tate dug deeper in the duffel bag and tossed two roomy black garments at Pierce and Brianne. "I didn't have time to worry much about sizes, but they're voluminous. They should work all right. And wind these around your heads— especially yours," he told Brianne, glaring at her wealth of pale hair that reminded him so much of Cecily's. "You stick out like a sore thumb here."

She shrugged into the large garment. "That's no way to talk about 'white gold.'"

Tate frowned. "What?"

"White gold," she repeated. She looked at Pierce, who was faintly amused. "That's what Mr. Sabon thinks of me. He said I'd have brought quite a price in earlier times in the slave trade."

"Did he really?" Pierce asked with eyes that

grew colder by the minute. "I gather that you found him less repulsive than before?"

She frowned slightly at his tone. "I felt rather sorry for him, if you must know."

His eyes looked like black splinters of heat. "How interesting. Then we married for no real purpose, I gather?"

She'd almost forgotten that. They had married to save her from Sabon, who'd turned out to be no threat to her or any other woman, and they'd consummated the relationship for the same reason. Annulment was strictly out now unless they both wanted to lie about the intimacy of their relationship. It would take a divorce, and that would take time.

She looked into Pierce's black eyes and blushed, seeing all over again the heat and passion of his expression in that most intimate of encounters.

He averted his own gaze. He didn't want to remember. He was going to put the whole episode behind him. They'd go home, stop Brauer and his little plot, and then they'd get a divorce, quietly, and Brianne would go to college. It would be easy. Right now, he had to put first things first.

"We need to move," Pierce told his security chief.

All three of them wore the flowing garments and turbans. In the guise, Brianne looked amazingly like a young boy. Her skin was very fair, but Arabs had mixed complexions. She wouldn't stand out too much, especially in the company of Pierce and Tate, both of whom were darker than she.

They made their way slowly into the main part of Qawi's small capital city, trying to blend in with the populace. It would have been impossible in a small village, where everyone knew his neighbor. But this was a port city, and there were always crowds from other parts of the Middle East moving along the docks. They didn't attract much attention once they were near the moored ships. The one thing Brianne did notice was the poverty. Philippe had been right when he said that his country had none of the modern appearance of other Middle Eastern countries.

They wandered down the row of disreputable freighters until Tate saw one that he recognized.

"I know this tub, and its captain," he said quietly. "Stay here. I'll go aboard and see if he's willing to give us berths."

"Can you trust him?" Pierce asked.

Tate shrugged. "You can't trust anyone this far from home, but he's honest enough if he's paid well. I won't be long."

He went aboard the ship, holding on to the rope lines as he passed crewmen coming down the gangplank.

"So that's the elusive Mr. Winthrop," Brianne said. It was the first chance she and Pierce had been given to talk since their confinement. She was uncomfortable with him now.

"Yes. He's impressive, isn't he?"

She nodded. She couldn't quite look at him. She was confused and embarrassed, even a little shy.

He moved in front of her and tilted her face up to his. The expression in her green eyes made him feel guilty. He remembered that he'd called her by his late wife's name, and so must she. It was there, in the faint accusation that shadowed her gaze.

"I'm sorry," he said quietly. "I wanted to spare you Sabon. But I'd already told you that it was too soon for me."

"Two years," she replied. "Most people would start to heal by then."

"She was my life," he said through his teeth, dropping his hand.

"I know that. She still is." She moved away from him. "I didn't learn anything that I didn't already know, except that now I'm not raw material for a virginal sacrifice anymore," she added coldly.

He hated knowing that. He'd done what he had to; he'd protected her from Sabon. She acted as if he'd hurt her deliberately.

"Wasn't the point of the thing to spare you Sabon's advances?" he asked.

"Yes, and you did," she agreed, refusing to tell him the truth about any of it. She kept her back to him, her arms folded defensively over her chest. "No harm done."

That's what she thought. He looked at her and ached all over. For a brief encounter, it was devastating. He'd thought of nothing else since they'd taken him from her cell. He wanted her.

The thought shocked him. Yes. He wanted her! But how could he, when his heart still belonged to Margo?

She wasn't looking at him. Her gaze had gone to the freighter, a rusted old hulk with several foreign-looking men aboard. It was a dangerous

step they were taking, to trust their safety to the
captain of that ship. But if they didn't go on the
freighter, sooner or later their identities would be
discovered and Sabon would have them back in
his clutches. She wasn't really afraid for herself,
because she knew too much about Sabon. But she
was afraid for Pierce and his friend. Their treatment would be unpleasant, especially after Winthrop had shot some of Sabon's mercenaries.
Their friends would want revenge.

She wondered what they'd do if they were re-
captured, and decided that she'd face each minute
by itself, slowly, and not try to swallow the entire
situation in a gulp. Most of all, she couldn't give
in to fear. Only courage would see them through
the rest of this ordeal. She had to be strong, for
everyone's sake. That included not arguing with
Pierce about something he couldn't help. He'd
been gallant, doing something he hadn't really
wanted to do, for what he thought was for her
sake. She knew that to him, it must have felt like
adultery. How could she blame him because he
couldn't return her love? It wasn't his fault that
he loved Margo and still considered himself
bound to her by invisible bonds. It wasn't fair to

make him feel guilty because of something he couldn't help.

She turned back to him, her eyes wide and sad and apologetic. "I'm sorry," she said before she lost her nerve. "You did what you could to protect me, and I'm grateful."

He was surprised at her change of attitude. He stared down at her intently, curiously.

She forced a smile to her lips. "There's absolutely nothing to worry about now," she assured him. "I'm on the pill, and thanks to you, Philippe Sabon won't ever be a threat to me again. We don't owe each other a thing. We're quits."

That was only half true, but why bother him with something that might never happen? If it did...well, she could lose herself somewhere in the world and he'd never have to know.

"Quits?" he asked, and his voice had roughened.

"We'll get out of this," she said with conviction. "When we do, I'll go away to college and you can get a quiet divorce. No one even has to know that we were ever married."

This was moving too fast. He wanted to slow down, to look back, to think about this muddle they were in. She was running for the border and he hadn't even looked at the evidence yet. He scowled and searched for the right words to express what he was feeling.

But before he could speak, there was a movement aboard the ship and he saw Tate Winthrop coming down the gangplank, grinning from ear to ear.

"Comrades," he told his companions, "we have friends in the strangest places, it seems!"

He gestured over his shoulder at the man coming down the gangplank. It was a tall, strangely familiar man. When he got closer, Brianne recognized him. It was Mufti, one of her captors!

Chapter Ten

Mufti grinned at Brianne. "You are surprised, yes?"

"I am surprised, yes!" she parroted. "What are you doing here?"

"I am spying for the government of Salid," he told her, with a flash of yellowed teeth.

"That's the neighboring country that this attack is going to be blamed on," Tate informed her. "We have to get Mufti out because he's just become our star witness." He didn't tell her the rest of the story, that Mufti had been captured and almost assassinated by one of Tate's men before he threw himself on their mercy and told them who he was and why he was in the compound.

His story, easily verified with the appropriate authorities in Salid via shortwave, panned out and Mufti became an unexpected ally. Tate had sent him ahead to find the captain of this boat and make the travel arrangements.

Tate spotted the captain coming quickly down the gangplank. He excused himself and went to meet the man. There was a brief conversation and the captain ran back up onto the ship, shouting orders and waving his hands.

"He just had a shortwave call. Sabon's mercenaries are on their way here," Tate said quickly. "The captain says he can't possibly sail today, anyway. He'll wait for us tomorrow, but we have to find a place to lie low for the night."

"Where?" Pierce asked, glowering as he looked around them at the busy port. "Even in this garb, we're not going to look like natives. We can't just book into a hotel and blend in."

"That wasn't what I had in mind," Tate told him. He motioned to his companions. "Mufti has relatives near here, in a tiny village that's off the beaten track. I've got an idea."

Two hours later, Brianne was sweating and calling Tate vicious names in her mind as she toiled to milk a cow in a makeshift stable of adobe and straw a few miles out of town in a village that looked as if it had remained unchanged since the first century A.D. The men were busily pitching hay and cleaning stalls. Mufti, his graying hair covered by the same wound cloth as his companions, was carrying sacks of grain from a dilapidated truck into the stable. They weren't getting paid for all this labor, but they were going to have a place to sleep—on the clean hay in the loft.

Brianne's derriere was still smarting from the camel ride to this isolated village where Mufti had led them. It was the last place Sabon and his men would think to find them. No doubt he was still scouring the seaport, looking for them. All they had to do was stay hidden for the night and sneak back into town and onto the boat in the morning.

Presuming that they weren't discovered first.

As Brianne struggled with her first attempt at milking, Sabon's quiet words about the plight of his people came back to her. She looked around at the primitive way the people in these outlying areas lived and felt guilty for her silk dresses and leather sandals back home. The poorest family in America lived ten times better than this, she thought. The women looked much older than their chronological ages. The wear and tear on them from this sort of existence was obvious.

The men were stooped and malnourished, and most of the young women were bearing babies on their backs as they went about their chores. The lack of proper clothing was painfully obvious. Some of the young children had the trademark bloated little bellies that denoted lack of adequate food. The older ones drew water from a deep well with a metal pail, which, according to one of the women—Mufti translated for them—had been a gift from the West. This village had its own metal pail and didn't have to use the animal skin bag that most villages did.

Brianne marveled at the pleasure such a trivial thing gave to these poor people. She marveled as well at their acceptance of the lives they led. No one seemed to complain or blame anyone for the poverty that was so obvious. Nor did they seem to mind that just across the border in a rich neighboring country was a city modern enough to compete with any in Europe. Many villagers had gone there, she learned, only to return with crushed hopes of finding prosperity. People who lived under primitive conditions had no computer or literacy skills to better themselves in a city. The very lack of education defeated them in the end, just as Sabon had said.

The village was composed of Muslims, and the simple sincerity of their daily prayers was touching to her. Time seemed to slow down, almost to stop. She could imagine people having lived here in this same manner a thousand, two thousand years before. She felt a connection from past to present, as if she were touching history.

"You look very pensive," Pierce said as he paused with a sack of grain over one shoulder.

"I was looking at the past," she replied with a faint smile. "Isn't it amazing how little change there's been? These people have nothing, yet they seem to be happy in spite of their lack of worldly possessions."

"Their sense of values hasn't been distorted by materialism," he replied. He lifted his head and looked around them. "Clean air, no time clocks dictating a use for every minute of the day, no real crime, no drugs or blatant violence." He met her eyes and smiled. "There's a lot to be said for living close to nature in small groups where everyone knows everyone else."

"There's a lot of disease, though, and a real lack of health care and educational facilities."

He scowled. "Where did you learn that?"

"From Philippe Sabon," she replied. "He said that education was the only hope these people have to escape the poverty."

"He's right." His eyes narrowed. "I hope you haven't let him influence you."

"He may be misguided, and he's dead wrong in the way he's going about it, but I think he does care about his people and wants to help them."

He stared at her intently. "Why aren't you afraid of him?"

She picked at a loose strand of fiber in the basket she was holding. "He isn't what he seems," she said finally. "And I'd bet even money that a good bit of what's going on here is Kurt's doing."

"Your stepfather?" He moved a step closer, towering over her. "Why do you think that?"

She searched his black eyes. "Mr. Sabon could have done anything to me, or to you. But he gave orders that we weren't to be harmed. He told me that the attack on his people was supposed to be a mock one. But those were real bombs and bullets, weren't they?"

"Yes," Pierce replied coldly. "Mufti's cousin said that the body count was terrible."

She grimaced. "Dear Lord!"

Pierce was still puzzled. "Do you mean that Sabon didn't know it was going to be for real?"

"That's exactly what I mean. At least, that's what he said, and I think he was sincere. His grandmother was born in this country and lived here all her life. He has relatives here. Mufti will tell you about the things he's done for his people that the outside world doesn't know about. Does it make sense that he'd kill so many of his countrymen, even to trick another country into sending protection for his oil wells?"

That was a question Pierce didn't want to face. His picture of the monster Sabon was changing before his eyes. "No," he said finally.

"What if Kurt hired the mercenaries and sent them in himself, on Philippe's order but with different instructions than he told Philippe he was giving them?"

Pierce's brow furrowed. "Kurt will be lucky if he lives to tell about it, if that was the case."

She nodded. "Exactly. But Kurt's in Washington. He has Philippe in a very tricky spot. He can say anything he likes to his senator friend. Philippe can't defend himself. Suppose Kurt tells them in Washington that Philippe is a madman who's trying to start a war with his neighbors?

Suppose he tells them that Philippe is behind a military coup here and is trying to take over the government and set himself up as dictator?''

Pierce's eyes widened. ''Good God, Kurt's not that crazy!''

''He stands to lose everything he owns already,'' she replied. ''Philippe has made some veiled threats about backing out of the deal. Kurt may be looking for a way to cut Philippe out of the loop and take over the oil wells for himself. If he can provoke intervention by accusing Philippe of leading a military coup here, he could claim that with his partner Philippe discredited, he owns the mineral rights outright. The government would be in too much turmoil to assert itself. Kurt could walk right in, take his place with the oil consortium, and clean up. Philippe would be in prison or dead. And Kurt would be rich.''

Pierce ran a hand through his wavy black hair. ''Brianne, that's a lot of ifs.''

''I know. But it makes sense, doesn't it?''

''It makes too damned much sense.'' He whistled through his teeth. ''God Almighty, what a mess!''

''For everyone, if we don't get back in time to stop it,'' she told him. ''And if the mercenaries are Kurt's, and he's dictating their actions, they won't take any prisoners. If they find us, they'll kill us all, and Philippe will be blamed for it.''

He was more worried at that moment than he could ever remember being. Brianne was very astute for someone of her tender years, and she made sense. He'd placed Sabon behind everything. But Sabon had too much to lose by killing his own people. Kurt wouldn't hesitate. His past record spoke for itself. He was unscrupulous and he had no sense of honor or morality.

''He'll kill Philippe, too,'' Brianne added suddenly.

''He'll have to. He knows too much.'' Pierce stuck his fists on his hips and stared into space, thinking. ''We can't get out of here tonight. Even by boat, it's going to take a while to reach Miami. Kurt will probably have some of his mercenaries waiting there, expecting us, even if they don't discover how we're going to get to the States. They'll be watching the airports and the marinas.''

''Can't your Mr. Winthrop steal a plane?''

He smiled gently. ''If there was one to steal, yes. There isn't exactly a major airport around here.''

She looked around them and nodded resignedly. "Mufti knows more about this than anybody. Mufti can put Kurt in jail, if we can get him back to D.C. alive to tell his story."

"We'll do it," Pierce told her. "Somehow."

She drew her eyes down to his broad chest and wished that she could curl up in those hard arms and let him cradle her while she slept. She was sleepy and worn-out from the ordeal of the past two days.

"Tired?" he asked.

She nodded. "But I can make it." She bit her lower lip. "Pierce, I don't suppose we could tell Philippe?"

"How would we get to him?" he asked reasonably, irritated by her protective attitude toward their captor. "Besides, he kidnapped us."

"I guess so. But he was doing what he thought would save his country."

"That doesn't make him innocent."

She stared into her basket. "He could have killed us. He didn't."

He moved closer. His big, lean hand tilted her face up to his and he looked straight into her eyes. "Tell me what changed your mind about him."

She sighed. "I can't. But something terrible

happened to him. He isn't what he seems. If you knew, you'd feel the same pity for him that I do.''

He didn't like her having secrets from him, especially secrets that involved another man. He was jealous. He would never have believed himself capable of such an emotion, but there it was.

His eyes went over her lithe young body. He remembered how sweet it had been to look at her and touch her back in Nassau by the pool. He remembered the secret sounds of her voice in ecstasy as he moved against her sensually in the room where they'd been held captive. He wanted her again, wanted her with every cell of his body.

She was feeling something similar. The scent of him was familiar, arousing. She forgot her resentments, her unhappiness at being Margo's stand-in. She forgot everything except the pleasure he could give her. She wanted it. She moved a little closer, so that they were almost touching, so that she could feel the heat from his body.

''These people are Muslim,'' he whispered huskily, stiffening at the proximity that was making his head spin. ''They don't accept suggestive behavior in public.''

She stared at his mouth. Her breathing was quick and ragged. ''I know that.''

"Then why are you looking at my mouth?"

"Because I want to kiss you," she said in a soft, shaky tone.

He didn't answer her. He was on fire, and he hadn't even touched her. He clenched his fists. "We can't."

"We're married," she said miserably.

"I know that, but we won't be alone, even tonight," he said through his teeth. "There isn't any way in hell that I can have you here."

She felt the heat pulsing in her lower body, like a living thing. She shivered with the memory of the pleasure they'd shared and wanted it until it was like a sickness.

"Damn," she whispered brokenly.

"And double damn," he agreed fervently. His eyes narrowed, glittered. "I want you, too. I ache to have you!"

It was the first time he'd admitted it so blatantly. She didn't even care about his reasons. It was enough that he shared the hunger that was consuming her.

He drew in a harsh breath and averted his gaze to the horizon. "You're very young, Brianne," he said after a minute. "Even under the circumstances, our first time together was good. It's natural that you want to explore the newness of it. But this isn't the time."

She closed her eyes and drank in the scent of him, the faint cologne that still clung to him, the smell of camel and leather that overlaid it from their ride into the desert.

"Are you listening?" he asked when he saw that she wasn't looking at him.

He looked at her with aching passion.

Her eyes opened, as green as spring buds, soft with tenderness. "I wish we were back in Paris," she said absently.

He laughed faintly in spite of himself. "I was too drunk to have done you any good," he reminded her.

"You were vulnerable," she replied. "You needed me. You haven't been that way since. I'm alternately a responsibility and a nuisance, and maybe once I was a convenience. But I can't get close to you at all."

His jaw tautened. "We've already had this conversation."

She let out a soft breath. "Yes, I know. You don't want to get involved with me. Once we escape from here, I'll go to college and you'll get on with your business." She searched his black eyes quietly. "But before you send me away, I want a whole night with you."

His body corded as if it had been starched. He thought of that, of having her in a big, soft bed, with all the lights blazing. "That would only make things worse," he said curtly.

"They couldn't be worse than they already are, Pierce," she replied. She lowered her eyes, breaking the spell, and moved away. "I want to be a whole wife before I'm a divorcee," she said flatly. "One brief encounter isn't enough to live on."

He hated the memory of that. It had been, like all his dealings with Brianne, villainous. He'd cheated her of a proper wedding and a proper wedding night, not to mention permitting her to be kidnapped and risking her life.

"It wasn't meant to be memorable," he said shortly. "I was sparing you Sabon."

"So you were." She thought about poor Philippe, who could have nothing with a woman, and it made her sad. Even her cursory encounters with Pierce were more than Philippe would ever be able to enjoy.

"You'd better finish your chores," he said. "The rest of us are going to start building a new wall with the adobe bricks the men made earlier in the week."

"Right up your alley, Mr. Hutton," she said with a forced smile. "Construction."

He nodded. "But not in a place of my choosing," he murmured as he turned away.

She watched him walk away with her heart in her eyes. She was going to have to get used to that view of him. Pretty soon, it would be the last one she'd get, perhaps for the rest of her life.

When they finally finished their labors, they had a scanty meal of bread and goat's milk cheese, which was surprisingly good. Then they all sat around the fire and talked of the day's labor. The villagers' language was musical and soothing to Brianne's ears, even though she couldn't understand a word of it. She was sleepy and her nerves were all but worn-out. She dozed a little.

"She's tired," Tate said, smiling at the picture she made curled up at Pierce's side. "And you look pretty drawn yourself. Why don't you take her on to bed and get her settled? I want to ask our hosts some questions about this so-called coup. My Arabic is a little rusty in this dialect, so I'll need Mufti to translate. We'll be along later."

"Watch your back," Pierce cautioned. "I trust Mufti, but we may have enemies that we don't even know about."

Tate grinned. "If there are any here, I'll find them," he said.

"I don't doubt it."

Pierce bent and lifted Brianne into his arms, answering the good-natured teasing that accompanied the action. He smiled and nodded toward the group as he carried Brianne the short distance to the hay-filled stable and into the last stall, which was packed with fresh straw and two large woven blankets that would serve as pallets.

He laid her down, noting that her arms didn't fall away when she was resting on one of the blankets.

Her eyes opened and looked up into his in the faint flickering light of the oil lamp that had been placed in the stall to light their way.

He felt the barest pressure of her fingers in the hair at the nape of his neck, heard her breathing go ragged, felt her hunger as if it were tangible. His face tightened. He reached up for the lamp and, looking down at her, deliberately blew it out.

She heard the rustle of straw as he replaced it

on a nearby shelf, and the rustle of fabric as he came down beside her.

His big, lean hands smoothed the garment she was wearing up around her hips, and paused on the waistband of her briefs as he slowly searched for her mouth and covered it with his.

He moved over her. She could feel him wanting her. Her legs parted to admit the warm weight of him. She arched as his mouth nuzzled aside the top of her robe and found its way to her soft breast. He suckled her, enjoying her husky moans in the darkness of the stall.

There might be very little time. He didn't dare risk a leisurely loving, regardless of his hunger for it. He roused her quickly, every caress intended to kindle fires. Her body arched up to him as he increased the suction of his mouth, as his hands smoothed up her soft thighs and found her most secret places.

She whimpered. He lifted his head and moved to find her mouth and silence it. While he kissed her with slow, fierce intent, he moved his own garment aside and, catching her upper thigh, brought her hips into sudden, stark contact with his own.

While she caught her breath, he shifted and began to enter her with exquisite care. She was new to this, and despite their earlier intimacy, he had to stop and rouse her carefully before she could accept all of him without discomfort.

The faint noises they made as they moved against each other seemed very loud in the silence. She clung to him, shivering a little as each movement of his hips brought them even closer together. He shifted again, and she gasped at the swell of hot pleasure that stabbed into her.

"There?" he asked quietly.

"Y-yes," she bit off.

He felt her nails biting into him as he moved again, deeper this time, dragging his hips against hers so that the contact was intensified, prolonged.

She sobbed, biting her lip to keep back the sharp cry.

His mouth brushed her open lips as he began to increase the slow, powerful rhythm of his body. He drew her leg over his hips and smoothed it there with teasing caresses, and still the rhythm built on itself.

She was gasping in his ear. She could feel him in every cell. It was beautiful. They were like puzzle pieces locking together, smooth and soft and tender. It wasn't even like sex. It was so exquisite to be intimate with him. She arched her back and hated the darkness that hid them from each other. She wanted to look at him.

Her sensual movements delighted him. She slid her arms around him and moved on her own, intensifying the silken thrusts with her own sinuous motion.

He laughed, deep in his throat, at the sensations she caused. He stilled over her for an instant and caught his breath as her body teased him.

She felt the tension and hesitated.

"No, don't stop," he whispered huskily. "It makes me throb all over when you do that. Do it again."

She followed his lead, like warm silk where she touched him. Her hands smoothed up under the fabric of his own robe until they found his hair-roughened chest and began to caress it hungrily.

He paused long enough to push her own robe up under her arms so that he had access to her soft, bare breasts. He made a banquet of them while his body caressed hers in the heated silence of the stable.

She loved the sensuality of feeling his skin against hers, his hair-roughened chest dragging with exquisite abrasion against the very tips of her breasts.

She lifted to prolong the contact, aware of the heat that was growing, the throbbing fullness that threatened to explode inside her. She grasped his shoulders and held on as the slow thrusts began to build a terrible, sweet tension in her limbs. She gasped as the pleasure grew to a throbbing heat and then a silken orgy of sensation that grew ever sweeter, ever more deliciously provocative.

It became urgent so quickly. From lazy sensuality to fierce passion, the movements became desperate in seconds. He caught her head in his big hands and brought his mouth down hotly on her lips as he drove against her blindly.

She wrapped her silken legs around his and followed his quick movements with countermovements of her own, helping him, demanding, pleading for an end to the exquisite pain of unbearable pleasure.

She moaned harshly under his mouth as she felt herself going over some dark, sweet precipice. She sobbed, arching, shivering as the tension snapped and she convulsed all over.

He felt her body give itself completely with a sense of wonder. Only then did he permit his own body to achieve satisfaction within hers. He arched down into her silken flesh with a harsh groan and gloried in the anguished spasms that racked him above her. It seemed never to stop. He sobbed as the pleasure grew and fed upon itself, as it washed over him like red fire, like red silk, like red waves of throbbing heat.

"Oh, Pierce," she whispered at his ear as she felt him in that most intimate of contacts, burying her face in his throat as she savored the helpless motions of his big body and felt the surge of heat that left him exhausted and shivering above her.

He couldn't get his breath, couldn't speak, couldn't think. He collapsed against her and fought for enough air to make his lungs work. He couldn't remember a time when he'd enjoyed a woman's body so intensely, so thoroughly, with such incredible possession that he felt her in the cells of his skin. He was sated to the roots of his thick hair. Under him, she was soft and warm, and he felt her skin slide against his when he moved helplessly against her to enjoy the echoes of pleasure that lingered even after the release.

She lifted to the movements of his hips and sighed sharply at the delicious sensations her sensitized body felt.

He rolled slowly onto his back, drawing her along, still joined intimately to him. He smoothed her body down on his, catching her hips and pulling her even closer.

She gasped and her nails bit into the hard muscles of his upper arms.

He arched sinuously and shivered with pleasure. "I love the way you feel like this," he said gruffly. "You fit me like a warm silk glove, so that when I move, I feel you all around me."

She hid her face in his hairy chest. "It was uncomfortable at first," she whispered.

"You'll adjust to me, but I'll always have to be careful with you when I'm this aroused." His hands pressed softly against her hips. "Dear God, Brianne, I'm sated all the way up and down and I still want you."

"Can you, again?" she whispered.

"I don't think so." He arched his body, waiting, but his body was too tired to cooperate. He laughed softly. "But I wish I could. It was good, wasn't it?"

"Oh, yes."

His fingers smoothed up and down her back in long, lazy caresses. "You contract inside, all around me, when you climax, did you know? It makes the pleasure all that much greater for me.''

She shivered at the blunt description. Intimacy was still new to her, and a little embarrassing. She was feeling some guilt as well, because she hadn't taken her pill in days and he didn't know that she could already be pregnant.

His long legs moved apart and he slid them over hers. In the intimate position they were sharing, the contact was suddenly even deeper than before and she gasped as she felt the increased pressure of him there.

His hands settled on her hips and he began to move her body against him with a lazy tenderness that had explosive results.

He felt her body begin to tauten, to shiver, to move helplessly with him.

''Baby,'' he whispered urgently into her ear. His breathing was suddenly ragged. ''Baby, do you feel it?''

She cried out softly, because something was happening, something that hadn't happened before. She caught at his arms, feeling his legs contract around hers, feeling his body become insistent under her.

"No," she sobbed, gasping. The pleasure was frightening. Frightening!

She must have said it aloud, because he was whispering tenderly to her, his lips soothing at her forehead. "Don't be afraid, baby," he whispered. "Let it happen. Give yourself to it. Feel it take you. Surrender to it."

She couldn't get close enough. She couldn't... Her body felt as if it had been corded in every muscle and drawn over a rack. She was too weak, she wouldn't be able to reach that impossibly high pinnacle of pleasure. It was so harsh, so demanding, that it drained her of strength and breath. It was so deeply consuming that it almost made her sick. She groaned piteously and shivered.

"You can't imagine how it's going to feel," he whispered, his voice deep, throbbing as he moved under her. "You can't...imagine!"

It caught her unexpectedly, a hot wave of pleasure that had the impact of a body blow. She cried out helplessly as the spasms convulsed her in his arms. She felt him moving, turning, lifting. She was against the blanket now and he was above her, her thighs in his hands, his body driving into hers in the darkness. She could hear his harsh breathing, feel the rigid clenching of his muscles as his fingers became painful on her hips and suddenly crushed them. She heard his hoarse groans, felt him throb and throb and shiver as the pleasure overwhelmed him.

She whispered to him, something wicked, something unexpected and stark. She felt him convulse again as the words heightened his pleasure to near oblivion.

His head dropped to her breasts and he shivered one last time as he slid down against her in heavy exhaustion, her hips still clenched in his hard fingers.

Several minutes passed before his grip loosened. ''You'll have bruises here,'' he said apologetically.

She moved experimentally, swollen with passion and its fulfillment, languid in the aftermath. ''I don't mind. Pierce...is sex always like this?'' she asked, dazed.

He hesitated. He lifted himself carefully away from her and sat up with audible attempts to catch his breath. He pulled down his robes and then carefully rearranged her own there in the hot darkness.

''Pierce?'' she asked in a whisper, aware that something was wrong.

He smoothed the fabric over her almost impersonally. Then he lay back down beside her, with
his hands under his head, and stared into the
blackness of the ceiling, hating himself.

"Did I do something wrong?" she asked uneasily.

He drew in a long, harsh breath. "No. I did."

"What?"

He shifted impatiently. "Try to sleep, Brianne.
We've got a long day ahead of us tomorrow."

She lay beside him unmoving as she registered
the forced carelessness of his tone, at odds with
the tension she sensed in him.

As she came slowly back to the reality of their
situation she thought she understood what was
wrong with him. She was standing in for Margo
again, and now he realized that it wasn't Margo
and he was feeling guilty. She was his wife, but
he was still married to Margo. He'd just committed adultery, for the second time. He'd been un-
faithful to his dead wife. If Brianne hadn't been
so tired and so disillusioned, she'd have cried hys-
terically. Would she never learn that she had no
place in Pierce's life except like this, as a substitute for the woman he'd lost?

She wondered if it might not have been better

if she'd never gotten to know him at all. If she hadn't spoken to him that day in Paris, none of this would ever have happened. She'd have been single and heart whole. Perhaps she'd have ended up married to Philippe Sabon, that poor shell of a man who was so alone in the world. He had nothing to give her, but at least he still had a whole heart—something Pierce hadn't.

She heard the hay rustle next to her as Pierce changed positions.

"It wasn't sex," he said abruptly. And all at once, he got to his feet and left the stable.

Chapter Eleven

Pierce didn't come back right away, and Brianne, exhausted from his fierce lovemaking and still puzzled by his odd behavior, fell asleep.

When she woke, she was sore in unexpected places and alone in the stable. She got to her feet, wrapped the turban around her hair and went out to look for her companions.

Pierce came to join her when she stepped outside the stable, his expression impassive, his eyes giving away nothing. Only when she looked closely could she see the telltale lines that denoted lack of sleep. He was back in his shell again, she thought, and regretting his lapse with her. Nothing had changed; at least on his part.

"We're going overland to the next port," he told her quietly. "It's too dangerous to try going back the way we came. Mufti's cousin says that Sabon's house has been captured and Sabon himself is on the run from his own mercenaries. They're playing havoc in the streets."

"Oh, good grief!" she exclaimed, thinking of the treachery of her stepfather. She hoped Sabon would get away.

"It looks very much as if your theory was correct. I believe your stepfather has sold out his partner and hopes to take over the oil project here," he replied. "We'd better get going while there's still time."

Even in the battered old vehicle Mufti's in-laws drove, it took a long time to get to the next small port because they had to make frequent stops and detours along the way to make sure they weren't being followed. Fortunately, the farther they went from the capital city of the small country, the less turmoil they encountered. The civil uprising hadn't yet spread this far. The island where Sabon's house was located was apparently now captured territory, according to gossip that Mufti gleaned on their way.

The next port was larger than the one they'd

started at. Only one thing in the dirty little harbor was familiar, and that was the rusted old tub that they'd booked passage on the day before.

Tate Winthrop met the captain and finalized the arrangements. They went onboard in a flurry of confusion after someone set off firecrackers on the docks to simulate an armed attack. Tensions were running high, because news of the military coup had reached even here. The government, one of Tate's contacts had said, was on the verge of collapse. The old regime was on the run and the mercenaries had taken over the capital. They had the oil consortium's executives under close guard, along with the supervisors and the men on the drilling rigs. All communications with the outside world had been cut off or crippled. Kurt was literally taking over the small country and nobody knew it except the people who were involved in it.

The refugees were hustled down into the cargo hold and concealed there by the captain, given food and water and assurances that they would soon be in international waters and safe from reprisals. Mufti left the three foreigners down in the hold and merged with the other sailors on deck, with the captain's help.

Brianne held her breath until the ship slipped her moorings and set out to sea. Right up until the last minute, she'd been certain that they were going to be stopped. She spared a worry for Philippe, who must be feeling very betrayed at the moment.

She hoped that she and her companions would make it out alive, to tell their story to the appropriate people before Kurt completed his military coup.

"There's another hitch," Tate told them once they were settled on sacks of grain in the hold with their few provisions—some bread and cheese and several small bottles of water from Tate's survival pack.

"What now?" Pierce asked with resignation. He needed a shave rather badly, and was looking more and more like a mercenary himself.

"The captain can only take us as far as St. Martin," he said. "He's been offered a king's ransom to transport some cargo for a foreign national he's to meet there. We can't match the other offer because the man making it is his brother-in-law."

"So we'll be stranded in St. Martin," Brianne said heavily. "While my stepfather destroys Philippe's country and blames it on him in Washington."

Tate smiled at her. "Hopefully we can book passage on another freighter."

"With what?" Pierce asked irritably. "My wallet is on Sabon's jet. I haven't got a dime."

"Neither have I," Tate said. "But if I can get to a bank, we'll have the funds."

"Why not just fly home?" Brianne asked.

"Because by now the mercenaries know we've escaped, and they'll be looking for us, even here," Tate said. "We have to sneak back into the States."

"It amazes me that Kurt was able to get away with so much," Brianne remarked.

"Pierce told me what you'd suspected about your stepfather," Tate said as they ate cheese and bread later. "You're remarkably astute for a non-politician."

"I know Kurt," she replied with a rueful smile. "And he called Philippe Sabon a monster. Imagine that."

"Sabon must be feeling pretty stupid right about now," Pierce agreed.

"How right you are, Hutton" came a deep,

faintly amused voice from the hatch that led down a corridor to the rest of the ship.

Three pairs of startled eyes met those of a tall, robed Arab. The deep scars down one side of his lean, dark face stretched as he smiled at his own folly.

He joined the others without inhibition and produced a goatskin from under his long robe. He tossed it to Pierce. "Wine," he said. "Being a Muslim, I'm not permitted spirits, but don't let my inhibitions restrain you."

"Is the poison in the wine or on the mouth of the bag?" Pierce murmured with an icy glare.

Philippe Sabon held up a hand. "I'm not that stupid," he asserted. "Besides," he sighed, reaching for a bit of bread and cheese, "I expect to spend weeks trying to explain my part in all this when we regain the government here."

"How do you plan to do that?" Pierce asked.

Sabon gave him a wry glance. "I sent my most loyal men over the border with the sheikh, the minute Kurt's mercenaries started slaughtering my household," he said, and the amusement left his face. "Dozens of my people lie dead in the streets, when I gave strict orders that the bullets were to be blanks and the explosives of the Hollywood variety.'' He glanced at Brianne. ''Your stepfather has a malicious nature, and I have been the world's biggest fool for putting myself and my country in his hands. I actually believed him when he promised the attack would be a sham.''

''You were willing to start a war to provoke American intervention,'' Brianne reminded him.

''I was willing to simulate one,'' he corrected her. His shoulders rose and fell heavily. ''I watched a child starve once, with food in its hands,'' he said quietly, staring at the bit of cheese and bread left in his fingers. ''There had been no grain for some time, and our supplies were stopped at the border. Sanctions, you understand,'' he added bitterly, ''because my government had publicly supported an enemy of the United States in the last conflict on this region. We were able to beg rations from a nation friendly to us, but by the time they came, some of the children were starved beyond help. They died trying to eat.'' He let the cheese and bread fall into his lap. ''How tired I am of rich industrial nations who dictate policy and turn blind eyes to the poor.''

Pierce scowled at the other man, aware of equal

confusion from his security chief. "What are you doing here?"

The Arab's eyebrows lifted. "Escaping execution by Brauer's cutthroats, of course."

"You're filthy rich," Pierce reminded him. "You could have bought a ship and sailed out of here."

Sabon laughed. "The mercenaries have my house," he reminded them.

"So?" Pierce persisted.

Sabon shook his head. "The gossip must have reached you at some point that I do not trust banks."

"You're kidding me," Pierce replied.

"Sadly, I am not." Sabon helped himself to a small plastic bottle of water. "My pocket money bought me a passage on this vessel. If I can make it to neutral territory, I have every hope that I can organize a revolt among my own people with my men who escaped as a core of support, and with some borrowed capital."

"Borrowed from whom?"

Sabon fixed Pierce with a wordless stare.

"You are out of your mind," Pierce told him flatly. "You can't expect me to lend you money after all you've done…you kidnapped us, for God's sake!''

"I kidnapped Brianne and a man who was presumed to be her bodyguard,'' Sabon corrected him. ''It was not until the escape that I knew who had been occupying my other storeroom. Which reminds me…'' He reached into his robe, extracted Pierce's eelskin wallet and tossed it to him.

Astonished, Pierce checked it and discovered nothing missing, not his credit cards or his cash, and there were several hundred dollars in the billfold.

"My pilot found it wedged in a seat on my private jet.'' He frowned. ''I suppose they've blown it up by now. Ah, well.'' He took a sip of water. ''I've persuaded the captain of this vessel to drop me off at St. Martin on the way to the States. If you'll make me a loan of fifty thousand dollars or so, I can reclaim my country, and my wealth, from Kurt's hired assassins.''

Pierce threw up his hands. ''You must have been hit in the head,'' he exclaimed angrily. ''I'm not loaning you a dime!''

"Yes, you are.''

"Why?''

Sabon picked the bread and cheese tidbits from his robe and ate them, washing them down with water. "Because I can connect the attack on your Caspian Sea drilling platform with Kurt. These same mercenaries were responsible for your problems and the deaths of several of your workers. I can tell you who they are."

"You helped hire them for this massacre!" Pierce asserted.

"I did not. Kurt hired them and assured me that my instructions would be followed to the letter. I was willing to give him a free hand so long as he was of use to me. He had friends among the oil consortium, you see, and they were much more likely to listen to a wealthy man with connections in the oil business than a poor Arab."

"Poor Arab, the devil!" Tate Winthrop scoffed.

"My wealth is only counted in millions among my own people," he returned. "You must remember that our inflation rate at present is something like eight hundred percent. Surely you don't think Kurt Brauer would waste his time on an unknown Arab with a thin wallet in a starving nation unless he thought he could profit largely by it?"

Pierce got up and paced the floor. "I don't understand. There were rumors that you had millions, if not billions, that you were seen in all the most exclusive resorts, even in gambling palaces."

"Excellent rumors, were they not?" Sabon took another sip of water. "I started them myself."

"You did?"

"I needed to appear wealthy to interest Kurt in helping to develop my oil fields and keep my enemies at bay," Sabon said with a shrug. "I should have known that I couldn't trust such a man." He frowned. "I assume that he's in Washington right now telling the world that I've attempted a bloody military coup in my own country?"

"You knew?" Brianne asked, astonished.

He nodded. "It was the most logical step he could have taken." He smiled. "And it will, if you'll excuse the pun, blow right up in his face."

Pierce sat back down on a bale of grain. "Could you explain that?"

"The United States will find news of Brauer's covert dealings very interesting," he said. "And I can provide them with information they don't have about his forthcoming plans to set fire to certain oil fields and blame a nation very hostile to the Americans.''

''Why would he do such a thing?'' Brianne asked, aghast.

''To start more wars, of course. He's an arms dealer. Didn't you know?'' Sabon asked his companions. ''That's how I connected with him in the first place.''

''He deals in oil,'' Tate Winthrop said slowly.

''He deals in oil only so that he has access to sensitive information about the countries in which the oil is found,'' Sabon told him. ''By manipulating certain events, he can sell arms at a huge profit and still have the aura of respectability. He lost heavily when a war was recently averted. Now he hopes to recoup his losses by a threatened military coup and clean up by arming the neighboring nations. It was his real plan all along, but I had no knowledge of it. I thought his interest in developing the oil wealth of my country was sincere, because I knew very little about the private face of such a public figure.'' He shook his head. ''It was only a means to an end for him.''

''Why kidnap Brianne?'' Pierce asked.

Sabon looked at her with quiet, secretive eyes. ''Kurt was wavering in his support for my cause.

By hinting that I wished to marry Brianne, I appealed to his greed. All those millions in the family and he would never have to worry about money again, you see.'' He sighed. ''The only explanation I have is that he found out somehow that my claims to wealth were exaggerated. I must have left a loophole for him to find.'' He leaned forward, crossing his forearms over his knees and locking his long fingers together. ''It's ironic, you know. He would actually have seen a profit on the oil,'' he added. ''But not for some years. Perhaps he was too impatient. Gunrunning is, after all, a profitable profession with the potential for immediate capital.''

''He told me that his finances were desperate,'' Brianne mentioned.

''And I gather that he also saw through my offer of marriage.'' Sabon glanced at her and his smile was genuine.

''Saw through it?'' Pierce stared at the other man grimly.

Sabon met his hostile gaze. ''I can never marry,'' he said curtly. He got up from his seat and stretched. He looked around their surroundings with resignation. ''That it should end here, in such a way,'' he mused. "All my hopes for my people…''

"Fifty thousand dollars won't be enough to mount a counterrevolution," Pierce said.

Sabon turned. "Yes, it will," he argued. "These mercenaries are bloodthirsty and merciless. But they are no match for the sort that my men can hire across the border.''

"What sort?"

Sabon's eyes narrowed. "I think you already know."

Pierce grimaced. He searched the other man's cold eyes. "I don't like being a party to carnage.''

"Nor do I," the other man said with barely contained rage. "But I already have been. My house servant, Miriam, had been with me for ten years. They left her in the garden, in a condition that it hurts me to recall." He bit down hard and averted his eyes, trying to blank out the memory. He clenched his lean fists at his side. "I will have my country back," he said tightly. "And I will see to it that Brauer pays a very high price for his treachery." He glanced at Pierce. "Help me."

Pierce threw up his hands in defeat. "I can't believe this," he said with pure exasperation. He let out a heavy breath and stared hard at the other man. "I never thought I'd see the day when I lined up on the side of my worst living enemy."

"I was never your enemy," Sabon said simply. "I had no knowledge of the attack on your drilling platform or I would have warned you. Kurt appeared to be a rich foreign investor with contacts in the oil business. I never thought of myself before as politically naive, but perhaps my education was scanty in too many spots. I must rethink my ability to judge people."

"Kurt had a lot of people fooled," Brianne said softly. "Including my poor mother."

Sabon's eyes narrowed. "Fortunately, he will have little time for her at present. When he finishes here, one way or another, her life will be in jeopardy if she knows anything at all of his business dealings. He will not want to risk having too many witnesses around. Accidents can easily be arranged."

"Oh, my God," Brianne whispered.

"Don't borrow trouble," Pierce said gently. "We'll protect her."

"As soon as we get out of here, I'll get a message to my contact in Freeport," Tate said in a deep, quiet tone that was reassuring. "He'll get your mother and the child out of Nassau before Kurt gets home.''

"Thank you," Brianne said with heartfelt gratitude.

"So that was how you knew where to find Hutton and Brianne," Sabon mused, watching Tate. "I underestimated you right down the line, Mr. Winthrop."

"Most people do," Tate replied with a flash of white teeth.

"I think I hear something outside the ship," Pierce said, cutting into the conversation.

They listened, and the sound came abruptly: sirens. They grew louder and louder.

"The Coast Guard!" Brianne exclaimed.

"In the Persian Gulf?" Sabon asked with lifted eyebrows. "The Americans may think they own the area, but I assure you, they haven't taken possession yet!"

"It's the harbor patrol, at the very least," Tate murmured. He rushed to the porthole and looked out. A minute later, he let out the breath he was holding and turned back to the others. "They're boarding a ship. Not ours. We've almost cleared the harbor."

There were relieved sighs all around. If they

were discovered too soon, the captain might have no choice but to turn them over on demand. It would mean certain death if Brauer got to them before they reached sanctuary.

Pierce and Tate exchanged worried glances. They were a long way from home. They had connections and Pierce's sudden windfall, but if they used his credit cards, Brauer's men would trace any transaction immediately and close in. Even if they landed at Miami, they were going to have to outwit the henchmen who would certainly be on the lookout for them. They weren't even sure of passage out of St. Martin. If they were being watched, and that was possible, they might never make it aboard another westward-bound freighter.

Sabon stared at them with a pensive expression. "The captain is not going on to Miami, which is as well. If you did go all the way to Miami on this vessel, you'd be carried on shore in body bags," he said.

Three pairs of eyes turned toward him.

"We were planning on changing ships. This is as far as the captain can take us. But I have a contact in Miami," Tate said after a minute.

"Brauer will know who it is by now. Don't underestimate his intelligence network. I did, and you can see what it cost me," Sabon reminded him.

Tate exhaled roughly, and his thin lips compressed as he tried to think rationally.

"Have you a pen and paper?" Sabon asked after a minute.

"You want to write home?" Pierce murmured dryly, but he handed the man what he'd asked for.

Sabon scribbled a name and an address, added a note in Arabic and his signature, and pressed the ring on his little finger into the paper. He handed it to Pierce, along with the pen. His expression was somber.

"For all I know, this—" Pierce waved the paper at him "—could be our death warrants. I can't read Arabic."

"Unless I'm an even worse judge of character than I thought, he can read it," Sabon mused, nodding toward Tate.

"Can you?" Pierce asked his security chief.

Tate took the note, scanned it and handed it back to Pierce. His black eyes narrowed as he studied the tall Arab. He looked perplexed for a moment, and then he nodded, very slowly. "It's a legitimate request for the recipient to give us any aid possible." He didn't add what else the note said. But his gaze was eloquent.

Sabon also nodded. A look passed between the two men. Sabon spoke in quick, sharp Arabic. It was a question that neither of their companions could begin to understand.

Tate replied in the same language with equal fluency.

"What is this, charades?" Pierce asked curtly.

"Nothing that concerns anyone else," Tate assured him. "And nothing to do with the matter at hand."

He said nothing more, nor did Sabon. Night fell, and the four of them slept.

"St. Martin," Sabon said as he studied the approaching island. "And my destination." He pulled the hood of his robe over his head and paused to look back at his companions. "We Moors once had very strong Spanish connections. The gentleman whose name I gave you is Spanish, but he has a grandmother in my country. He will do what he can for you because I requested it and he owes me a favor. Trust him. But trust no one else. Your lives may depend on it."

"Why are you helping us?" Pierce asked shortly.

"Ask your comrade" came the quiet reply. He met the other man's eyes. "I will be here for three days, under an assumed identity. If you're still willing to help me, wire the money to Señor Alfredo Cantada in care of the Gardell Bank."

Pierce sighed. "God knows why I should. But I will. I don't make promises lightly."

"We'll erect a statue to you, as our benefactor," Sabon said with twinkling dark eyes.

Pierce didn't reply for a minute. "He may find you, if you stay here that long."

"His men won't recognize me," Sabon replied. "I have resources that I haven't used in years. He won't find me."

"Good luck, then," Pierce said.

"And to all of you. Including Mufti," he added with a secretive grin, "who has been trying desperately to avoid me since I came on board. Tell him that I did know who he was, and that he kept my secret, as I will keep his. There will be no reprisals against his family when my power is restored." He looked at Brianne long and poignantly. "By getting you out, he saved all his relatives."

Brianne was more touched than she wanted to be. She felt so sorry for the man, and even vaguely guilty for having so badly misjudged him. "Take care, Monsieur Sabon," Brianne said gently. "Good luck."

He smiled at her. "And *bon chance* to you as well, *chérie*," he replied in a soft tone. His eyes searched hers intensely. "I will mourn you for the rest of my life," he added in Arabic, with unexpected emotion.

He turned and went up to the deck very quickly, and without looking back.

"What did he say to you in Arabic?" Pierce asked Tate.

"Just that he wasn't selling us out," he replied evasively. "Interesting man."

"Damned interesting," Pierce agreed.

Tate glanced at Brianne and frowned curiously. "I don't suppose you know why he said that to you?"

"I don't speak Arabic," she reminded him. "What *did* he say?"

"Just that he was dying for love of you and, having lost you, he'll never be able to think of another woman," he said facetiously.

"Idiot," Pierce murmured, chuckling as he turned away.

But Tate Winthrop's dark eyes met hers and he wasn't smiling.

Brianne frowned curiously, but he didn't say a word. He turned back to Pierce and looked out the porthole as Sabon blended into the crowd.

"We'd better make a move, and quickly," Tate said after a minute. "We don't have long to find this ship Sabon mentioned and get aboard."

"If we aren't walking into a trap," Pierce said uneasily. He glanced at Brianne with a scowl. "I hope we know what we're doing."

"Don't know about you," Tate replied. "But I know exactly what I'm doing."

The three passengers stripped off their Arab robes and stashed them in the hold under some sacks of grain. They'd donned their European clothing the morning of their departure and they were still wearing them now. Mufti was wearing his headdress, but he borrowed a sweat suit from another sailor and shaved. He looked vaguely American when he was through.

Brianne's silk slacks were hopelessly crumpled, like her blouse and jacket. She knew her hair was a terrible mess and she wanted a bath until it was almost painful. But she was more worried about reaching the American coastline. Even with Sabon's dubious help, it was going to be very dangerous.

"I don't even have a gun," she murmured.

Pierce glanced at her. "What brought that on?"

"We may have to fight our way out," she said simply. "I do know a little karate."

Pierce nodded toward Tate. "Tenth degree black belt, tae kwon do," he told her.

She whistled through her teeth. "Not bad, Mr. Winthrop."

"What was your discipline?" he asked her.

She smiled ruefully. "Tai chi," she said. "I thought of the movements as ballet."

"They're graceful," he agreed. "But if you put speed behind those graceful movements, they can kill."

"I'd be better off with a tire tool, I'm afraid. I wish you had a spare gun."

"Can you shoot one?" he asked.

"I'm great with laser tag."

"These targets shoot back and they don't use blanks," he returned. "You'd better leave the shooting to us."

She wondered if she should mention the judo classes she'd taken. She decided not to. She already felt like a third leg on this trip.

Chapter Twelve

The four prospective passengers wandered down the marina and blended in nicely with the tourists in port, in their European clothing. It wasn't hard to find the vessel in the marina. It was another freighter, but cleaner than the one they'd just departed, with Spanish registration. Its wiry little captain read the note Sabon had scribbled, took a long look at Brianne and offered them the hospitality of his ship without any hesitation whatsoever.

They were taken below, and the ship started up at once in the marina where it was moored.

"What about customs when we get to Miami?"

Brianne asked worriedly. "What if Kurt has some of his men waiting there for us?"

"This isn't Hollywood," Pierce replied. "Little fish slip through big nets. We're fugitives, you know. We don't do this with passports and suitcases."

"Fugitives?" she exclaimed.

Pierce nodded. "If we come into the country in any legitimate way, we won't get to a car before we're cut down by Brauer's men. We have to sneak in."

"It's illegal," she groaned. "We could go to jail for circumventing customs!"

"She's catching on," Tate murmured dryly.

She shrugged back her inhibitions. One did, after all, have to roll with the punches. At least she'd have company in prison. "Okay. What do we do?"

"We avoid Miami altogether. This captain is sailing to Savannah. He's let me use his radio to get in touch with my people in the States. We'll get off where they won't be expecting us," Tate told her. "You'll like it. There's a candy factory right there next to the harbor where you can get the world's best pralines."

"Can we buy some without getting shot?" she wanted to know.

"Let's find out."

Pierce frowned. "I hope we can trust this captain."

"We can," Tate said with conviction.

"How can you be so certain?" Pierce asked.

Tate glanced at Brianne and away. "Never mind how. But I am."

"Then I suppose we'll have to trust your instincts."

"You're really going to wire Mr. Sabon the money he asked for?" Brianne murmured as they watched the coastline grow farther away through the porthole.

"God knows why, but I am," Pierce agreed.

"He's not a bad man," she persisted. "He only wants a better future for his people."

"He should leave that up to the sheikh who rules his little kingdom," Pierce muttered. "And speaking of the sheikh, instead of running for the border with his bodyguard and his harem, he should be out like a decent leader, trying to work on his country's behalf."

"He is," Tate replied without looking at him.

"How do you know that?"

Tate turned and looked at him. "Did you look closely at the signature on that slip of paper Sabon gave you?"

Puzzled, Pierce drew it out and studied it, with a curious Brianne peering over his muscular arm.

The scribble was all but undecipherable, except for an embossed impression near it that was only visible with the light on it in a certain way.

"You noticed the ring he wears on his little finger?" Tate persisted.

"No. I didn't."

"It contains an official seal," Tate said. "I saw him make the impression. You might notice the crest. It's the coat of arms of the Tatluk sheikhdom."

Pierce was really puzzled now. "So?"

"Who do you think Philippe Sabon really is?" Tate murmured with a dry smile.

Pierce was very still. "Not the sheikh himself."

Tate chuckled. "Not quite, but he will be one day. The ruling sheikh is his father, a rather rotund and aged gentleman in failing health. Philippe is the power behind the throne these days. So he did what his father couldn't; he disguised himself as a wealthy businessman and went out to attract investors to develop his country's untouched oil reserves and keep his treasury from going bankrupt.''

"Why not do it as himself, then?" Brianne asked, astonished.

"Too risky. If he were kidnapped, his country would be bankrupted even sooner trying to ransom him." Tate smiled. "Hell of an idea, wasn't it? And he almost accomplished his plan."

"No wonder he had so much pull in his government," Pierce agreed. "He *was* the government."

"He still is," Tate said. "And that group of soldiers he sent over the border is his personal guard, the elite of his father's military. They're on a level with the British SAS, and they'll recruit mercenaries to work for them, to help take their country away from Brauer."

"Not unless we can get to Washington in time to stop Brauer's plan from working, or American troops may bomb him out of existence, thinking they're stopping World War III," Pierce said grimly. "Can you get a message to D.C.?"

Tate nodded. "But who's going to listen to us without proof? We have to take Mufti to someone

high up in the secretary of state's office and let
him spill his guts. Then we have to wait while
the story is checked out. The wheels of progress
turn slowly at the diplomatic level.''

"Mufti?" Brianne realized suddenly that they
hadn't seen Mufti since they'd boarded the ship.
"Where is he?"

"He found a poker game down below," Tate
chuckled. "He hasn't anything to wager except
matchsticks, but if we can get him to Vegas, I
think he can break the bank. He's a natural.''

The mention of Las Vegas made Brianne uneasy. She didn't look at Pierce. She didn't like
remembering the quick, unemotional ceremony
that had joined them together. Her sad eyes went
to the gold band on her ring finger and she
touched it wistfully. If only he'd been able to love
her, just a little. When this adventure was over,
they were going their separate ways. She'd be a
divorcee long before she ever learned to be a wife.
Not that he'd care, she mused. He might enjoy
her in bed, but his inhibitions about being unfaith-
ful to Margo would always be there between
them.

She turned away and went to the porthole to
stare out at the sea.

"I think I'll go check on Mufti," Tate said. He went through the hatch and closed it gently behind him.

Pierce joined Brianne at the window. "One way or another, it's been a momentous few days," he remarked.

"I'll be glad when they're over." Her voice was strained as she spoke. She was lying through her teeth. She'd rather be in danger with Pierce than safe without him, but she had no choice left.

He stuck his hands in the pockets of his slacks and stared down at her bent head sadly. "I'm sorry about the other night," he said a little hesitantly. "I never meant it to happen."

She shrugged. "No harm done. I got my one night after all."

He caught her arm and turned her toward him. "Don't make it sound cheap," he said shortly. "It wasn't."

She searched his hard face quietly. "Go ahead, then. Tell me how you were thinking of me instead of Margo while you were making love to me."

His intake of breath was even louder than the throb of the engines. He stared at her with narrow, glittering eyes, so intently that she lowered her own quickly.

"Oh, damn, I'm sorry," she muttered tightly. "I'm sorry! But we both know you don't really want me, Pierce, except as a substitute. I'm too young and too unsophisticated, and we've already agreed that I'm bound to cling too much." She lifted her resigned face to his. "Let's just think of it as an exercise in mutual attraction and let it go at that," she added in a dull, lackluster tone. "I'm looking forward to college, you know," she said suddenly, forcing a smile to her face. "I'd like to go to the Sorbonne, if you don't mind."

He stuck his hands in his slacks pockets and stared blankly out the porthole. "Whatever you want."

"You can get a quiet divorce when we get home," she added, not looking directly at him.

"We'll fly back to Vegas for it," he said with a cold smile. "I believe it can be done in twenty-four hours. I'll make all the arrangements and let you know when I've got a free hour in my schedule. I expect to do a lot of traveling when this is over."

She'd have liked to do some herself, but she had to be content with Paris again. She felt a sudden chill and wrapped her arms around herself for comfort. It might have been better if she'd left him to that wallet-pinching lady of the evening in Paris, she mused silently. At least her own poor heart would have been spared its present state of misery.

He studied her silently, his dark eyes running from her disheveled blond hair to her small feet. She was pretty and sweet, and in bed she was all any man could ask. She loved him. He was throwing all that away for his ghost, so that he could go on pretending that Margo wasn't really dead, that she'd just gone away for a while and would come back.

Listening to his own thoughts startled him. Did he really believe that? Was he willing to be alone for the rest of his life because he couldn't face the reality of his loss?

He scowled as he looked at the slender young woman near him. How many men wouldn't go down on their knees to have such a pretty little thing love them unconditionally? Brianne had spirit and class, and a heart as big as the whole world. She'd go away to college and some bright, eager young man would discover all her assets. He'd want her. Perhaps he'd treat her as Pierce never had, tenderly, with constant attention, little presents of flowers and candy and trinkets, late-night phone calls and lazy lunches and late dinners. The opera, perhaps, and the theater and concerts.

He drew in a wounded breath. Brianne deserved that sort of attention. She was a rare and unusual girl. No, she was a rare and unusual woman, he reminded himself, and his body began to throb as he recalled her initiation at his hands. She was sweet heaven to love. Her skin was soft, like a petal warmed by the sun. Her body rippled when he touched it. She never held back or played games with him. He could do anything he liked to her, and she accepted him eagerly. But he was going to walk away from her because he couldn't accept the reality, the finality, of his beloved Margo's passing. Margo was dead. She wouldn't come back. He'd be alone forever.

Brianne sensed his pain and she turned, looking up at him with soft, curious green eyes that loved him.

He glared at her. Sabon had gone to this trouble, arranged this passage, for Brianne. Why? What had she given the man in return?

Jealousy, new and surprisingly fierce, surged

through him and left a faint blush across his high cheekbones.

"What did you do with Sabon?" he asked abruptly.

"I beg your pardon?"

"Why is he going to so much trouble on your account?" He shifted, his eyes narrowing. "What did you give him, Brianne?" he added in a dangerously soft tone.

"I—I gave him nothing," she stammered.

"Don't hand me that! His reputation can't be all conjecture and lies!"

She couldn't tell him about Sabon. It would be cruel and unfair, to permit him to be made a laughingstock, an object of pity in a world where masculinity was defined by capability. Pierce might one day mention it to someone. It would be devastating enough for a common man, but for someone who would one day rule a sheikhdom, in a very masculine part of the world, it was unthinkable.

She stared bravely into Pierce's angry eyes. "Believe what you like," she said finally. "If you think I'm devious enough to use my body as a bargaining tool, then you don't know me, anyway."

"Such a sweet body," he murmured, but his measured scrutiny of it was lewd and insulting. "Enough to make a man do anything, even go against his own principles. I imagine he enjoyed it."

"At least he wasn't thinking of another woman and calling me by her name!" she exclaimed, torn by the memory of Pierce doing just that.

His face paled. He couldn't even deny it. But what hit him hardest was her admission that she'd gone from him to Sabon. He clenched his fists in his pockets and fought down homicidal rage. He wouldn't give Sabon a penny to mount his counterrevolution. He'd kill him instead!

Brianne realized too late what she'd done to Sabon's chances for a loan. She didn't quite know how to repair it.

She folded her hands at her waist with a long sigh. "He wanted to, but I couldn't," she lied, averting her eyes to the floor. It was Philippe who couldn't, but no need to tell Pierce that.

"Why?"

"Because I'm married!" she shouted at him, livid and wounded by his sarcasm, by his willingness to believe that she could betray him. "Even if you don't consider yourself my husband, I'm not going to cheat on you with another man!''

He knew she was telling the truth, and he felt ashamed of his suspicions. Jealousy was new to him. He didn't like it.

''All right,'' he snapped, irritated by his own erratic behavior. ''I'm sorry.''

She shrugged and turned away. ''You can't help how you feel, Pierce,'' she said stiffly. ''I'm grateful for what you've done for me, especially since it seems the whole charade was unnecessary. Philippe only wanted to bring me to the island so that Kurt would think he was serious about marrying me. He was sure the prospect of all that money in the family would keep Kurt from backing out of the deal with his investment. He was wrong.''

''Why are you suddenly willing to credit him with noble motives?''

''Because we talked a little,'' she replied honestly. ''And his men talked about him. From the beginning he'd had his sights on me, as a means to get Kurt involved in the oil wells. He pretended an interest in me, and Kurt dangled me as bait to reel us both in, seeing a merger that would guarantee him financial security.'' She laughed. ''How stupid he must have felt when he discovered that it was all a farce, that Philippe wasn't a multimillionaire, that he only needed Kurt to approach the consortium and invest in his oil development.'' She shook her head. ''Kurt is a vindictive man,'' she added quietly. ''He'll kill Philippe if he can. He's lost his shirt. He may not even be able to buy guns on consignment to sell to people in the Middle East. If it gets out that he's hired men to invade and overthrow a sheikhdom, the international community will go after him. He can't afford to leave any witnesses around.''

''You're absolutely right,'' Pierce agreed. ''I'll do what I can for Sabon,'' he added reluctantly. ''But not because I want to. I just don't want Brauer to get away with it.''

''Neither do I.'' She turned and stared at him quietly. ''Philippe isn't at all what he seems. Despite his power and whatever wealth he realizes from his oil development, he has so little.''

''Tell me why,'' Pierce demanded.

She shook her head. ''It isn't my secret to tell.'' She walked away from him and sat down on a boxed crate nearby. ''How long will it take to get to Savannah?''

''I'm not sure,'' he replied, distracted. ''Why

don't you try to get some sleep? I'm going to find Tate and Mufti.''

She looked around. There were some old sacks nearby. She lay down on them and pillowed her cheek on her hand. She hadn't realized how tired she was.

''They won't get us, will they?'' she asked drowsily.

''No.'' He sounded supremely confident. She smiled and went to sleep.

The freighter pulled into Savannah harbor and the four passengers in the hold were suddenly confronted by men in dark suits.

The tallest of the three newcomers glanced from one tense face to another, then lingered on Tate's. A look passed between them.

''U.S. Customs,'' the tall, suited man said abruptly, and flashed open a wallet, showing a badge. He closed it before it could be seen clearly. ''Come with us, please.''

The four passengers were marched up on deck. Brianne felt for Pierce's hand and held on tight. She was seeing a lengthy trial while they tried to explain their predicament, followed by a jail sentence. She hated closed places. She'd never get to college. She'd never be a real wife and mother. She'd be a jailbird.

Once inside at the customs gate, they were stopped by other customs officials who listened to the curt explanation the tall man gave them. There was some difficulty, but it was quickly sorted out, and Brianne and her companions were hustled from the building and out into the humid heat of Savannah with its perfect squares and live oaks and secret gardens. Brianne longed to see it all, but she wasn't a tourist.

Their escorts led them down the side of the building, into two waiting stretch limousines. Black, of course.

"We've been captured by the 'men in black,'" Brianne moaned as they waited for the suits to get into the car. "We'll never be seen again!"

Tate chuckled. When the tall man was in the front seat and the car was moving, he opened the glass partition and leaned over the plush black leather seat.

"I damned near had to deck the customs guy," the tall man muttered. "Why couldn't you just fly into Miami?"

"We were expected there," Tate said. He held out a hand and the other man handed him an Uzi.

He slid it under his jacket. He glanced at his puzzled companions. "This is Marlboro," he introduced them. "He works for me," he added. "So do the other two."

"You're not customs officials?" Brianne burst out.

"No, but we did used to belong to the government," the tall man said sheepishly. "I'd tell you which part, but then I'd have to…"

"Shoot us," Brianne muttered. She sighed. "See? *Everybody* says that!" she told Pierce.

"That's true. But he isn't kidding, either," Tate murmured dryly.

Her eyes widened. "Really?"

The tall man grimaced. "I don't like shooting women."

Brianne actually gasped.

"It was only one woman, and she turned out to be a male foreign national with a pack of plastique hidden in her…his…well, never mind," Tate muttered. "Anyway, it was a matter of national security and the 'woman' drew first."

"Where do we go from here?" Pierce asked, confident that his security chief would get them where they were going in one piece.

"Straight to D.C.," Tate replied. "By way of a private airstrip."

Trust Tate to know someone everywhere he needed assistance, Pierce thought amusedly as the car pulled off on a dirt road and stopped, finally, at a deserted airstrip where a small jet was parked and waiting.

"Don't tell me," Pierce murmured as they climbed aboard the small, neat aircraft. "Someone owed you a favor."

"Well, he did," Tate said enigmatically, and grinned. "So did this pilot."

"Hiring you was the best thing ᵀ ever did," Pierce told him.

Tate chuckled. "I'm glad you noticed. I'll sit up front."

Brianne found herself sandwiched in between the two security men, with an irritated Pierce and a silent but amazed Mufti across the aisle from them.

"You married?" the taller man asked Brianne expectantly.

"Yes, she is," Pierce said tersely.

"Gee whiz, the best ones always are," the tall man said. "Guess your husband will be glad to see you back home and safe, huh?"

''Her husband is sitting across the aisle from you,'' Pierce said in a voice that was pleasant enough; it was his eyes that made threats.

The taller man unfastened his seat belt and got up at once, moving to a seat behind Brianne. ''Sorry, Mr. Hutton,'' he said in a strained voice.

''No harm done.'' Pierce didn't move to sit beside Brianne. He leaned back and closed his eyes.

Brianne glared at him. Some husband, she thought angrily. Dog in the manger, more like. She closed her own eyes and shut him out.

As they suspected, the plane didn't land in Washington, D.C. It landed on a palatial estate in Virginia, which Brianne learned later was owned by a shadowy figure with ties to the world of espionage. He, too, apparently owed Tate a favor.

A car was waiting for them, and three more suited men were standing around it, also wearing sunglasses, and carrying automatic weapons.

''Aren't automatic weapons illegal?'' Brianne asked worriedly.

''Of course,'' Tate assured her.

''I saw the Uzi you were given in the limousine,'' she remarked. ''These look just the same.''

He nodded. ''That's what they are, all right.''

She stared at him. His lean face drew into a smile.

"You aren't going to tell me anything, are you, Mr. Winthrop?" she asked.

He was still smiling.

"You might as well give up," Pierce told her. "When he smiles, you've already lost the advantage. The hell of it is that he almost never smiles, and on this trip he's done little else."

"I like tight escapes," Tate said with a shrug. "Life has been mostly boring in the oil industry...until a few days ago."

"Now that we're safely home," Pierce replied, "we need to find the under secretary of the State Department and let Mufti tell what he knows."

"No problem," Tate said. "I've already had my men phone him and brief him on what's been happening. There's a group of intelligence people waiting for us even as we speak. Let's get rolling."

"Brianne, you come with me," Pierce said when she hesitated about which of the two limousines to get into.

She joined him, noting that he barely touched her arm to let her get inside first. Their adventure was nearly over, and she had no idea what lay in store for them. All she knew was that very soon, Pierce was going to divorce her.

She spared a thought for her mother and half brother. She hoped that Tate could keep his promise about getting her family safely away before Kurt returned from the States. She also thought of Philippe. She hoped that he could retake his government. He might have a strange way of going about it, but he did care for his people.

She sat beside Pierce, aware of him, but not speaking as the big car ate up the miles heading north.

Chapter Thirteen

Apparently the mysterious Mr. Winthrop had covered his tracks very well, Brianne thought as the big car sped toward Washington, D.C. They weren't being followed, he said, and he must know, because he had all sorts of electronic gadgets up and working. She understood why Pierce had hired him. Very likely the government agency these men had belonged to was connected in some way to the CIA. For all she knew, it might have been the CIA. They were quiet, very professional, and looked capable of handling any eventuality.

The one concession Tate made to comfort was to stop in Charleston at a small pink building with wrought-iron balconies and palm trees and tropical vegetation all over the sandy lot surrounding it.

"Best seafood in Charleston," Tate said as the other occupants of the car disembarked. "Mills, check around the perimeter and make sure we're secure."

"Yes, sir," the other agent said at once, and went to do as he was told.

"It's a family business," Tate told them as they went up the wide steps into the restaurant. "I've known the owner for some years. He was with me overseas when... Well, never mind, he's a friend."

It was something of a shock to see that the owner of a conservative little Charleston seafood restaurant was another Native American, almost as tall as Tate, with sparkling black eyes and a ponytail.

The two men shook hands and spoke in a language Brianne had never heard.

"This is Mike Smith," Tate introduced them. "That's not his real name, but it's what he's gone by for several years. He and his wife and daughter run the restaurant."

"You're a long way from South Dakota," Pierce said with a grin as they shook hands.

"I like fish," he replied, chuckling. "Nobody else in my family eats it, but a seafood restaurant sounded like a good deal."

"He won it in a poker game," Tate said, tongue in cheek. "That's why it sounded like a good idea."

"Don't knock it," the other man replied dryly. "I make a good living."

Tate laughed, then changed the subject. "We need to get into D.C. unseen. Any ideas?"

The other man became somber and pensive. "Give me ten minutes. In the meantime, sit down and I'll have Maggie bring you a menu."

"Thanks," Tate said. "I'll owe you one."

"You already owe me three," Smith replied. "And when I collect, you'd better be in great shape."

"I'll do my best!"

They had a quick lunch. It was, indeed, some of the best seafood Brianne had ever tasted. She loved the setting. Through the picture window, she could see something of the charming old city from whose harbor the first shot of the Civil War was fired. There were Southern mansions and small houses, palm trees and sand. It was vaguely reminiscent of architectural styles in the Caribbean, and she said so.

"It is, isn't it," Pierce mused as he sipped his coffee. "A lot of South Carolina planters settled in the Caribbean after the war, to avoid taking the Oath of Allegiance to the Union. Some eventually returned here. In fact, there were several pirates from the Carolinas."

"I remember reading about them in school," Brianne replied.

It was a reminder of how young she was. Pierce turned his eyes toward her and studied her with quiet remorse. She should be dating boys her own age, having fun, learning about life and the world around her. Instead, she was married to a much older man and running for her very life from a gang of cutthroats, not unlike the pirates he'd just mentioned.

She caught his intense scrutiny and turned to look at him. "What's wrong?" she asked softly.

"I'm counting my regrets," he said. His black eyes narrowed. "You should never have been mixed up in this."

"Blame my mother," she returned. She grimaced. "She and I have had our differences, but

I do care about her and about Nicky, too. I expect she's scared to death."

"I asked Tate about her while you were freshening up in the ladies' room," he returned. "He said that his man in Freeport got her onto a ship, with the child, and they sailed for Jamaica. He's got family in Montego Bay. He'll hide her there until the threat's over."

"Oh, thank God!" she exclaimed, wiping away quick tears of relief.

"Tate's resourceful," he murmured. He glanced around him at the suited men at various tables and noticed that they had Pierce and Brianne completely enclosed without it being obvious. Nobody could threaten them without going through Tate's people.

"He is, indeed. He isn't married, is he?" she added, just to make conversation.

"No, he's not. There's a young lady in D.C. who'd give her right arm for him, but he won't let her near him," he mentioned. "He put her through school and still keeps a careful eye on her safety. If there's a woman in his life, it's Cecily, but you'd never get him to admit it. Strictly a platonic relationship, you see, on his side. Or so he says."

"Poor woman," she murmured, thinking privately that she and the shadowy Cecily had a lot in common.

"She's a forensic anthropologist, working on her doctorate at George Washington University," he murmured. "Does a lot of work for the FBI."

"How exciting!"

"I wouldn't call looking at dead bodies exciting," he said quietly. "She's often called upon to identify people from skeletal remains."

"I liked anthropology," she replied. "I only had one course in it." She pursed her lips. "Maybe I could study it in college."

His face closed up. "Maybe you could."

"But accounting is going to be my major," she said. "I love numbers."

"Learn it well and I'll give you a job."

She glanced at him with a wan smile. "No, thanks. I expect to find a job as far away from you as I can get."

He scowled. "Why?"

She put down her cup and wiped her mouth with the linen napkin. "Don't be dense, Pierce, it doesn't suit you," she replied. "I won't spend the rest of my life eating my heart out because you don't want me. That will be easier if I'm someplace where you aren't.''

He clenched his jaw hard. "It was infatuation, coupled with the fascination of your first sexual experience," he said bluntly. "That's all it was. You're very young. You'll get over it."

"Of course I will," she said, rising. "Just like you got over Margo."

She turned and went toward the rest room.

Tate came and sat down beside him the minute she left. "There's a complication," he said shortly. "Brauer has learned that we're in the States and he's got his men tracking us. It's just a matter of hours before they find us. Smith says he can smuggle us onto a shrimp boat in the harbor. It will be smelly, but we won't have to risk a gun battle—unless you want to."

"Not with Brianne in the line of fire," Pierce replied at once.

"That's what I expected. We'll go right to the boat. Smith's going to drive us there in his van. My men will get back into the stretch limos and continue to D.C."

"They might be attacked."

"They can handle themselves," Tate replied.

"And two of them don't belong to us. They're federal."

"*What?*"

"That's 'need to know.' You don't." He got up. "If Brauer's men jump them, they'll be on their way to prison immediately afterward."

"You're a strategic genius," Pierce murmured.

"That's what my drill sergeant in the Green Berets used to say," Tate grinned.

Pierce wiped his mouth and dropped the linen napkin to the table. "The food here really is first class."

"I told you. Smith has his moments."

"We won't be endangering his family?"

Tate looked around them and leaned closer. "The 'family' is his cover. He's not related to anyone here."

"Brauer won't know that."

"Never mind. If he sends goons in here, they'll come out looking like fresh sausage. And that's all I'll say on the matter. Let's go."

Pierce gave his surroundings another quick scrutiny. The waiters were tall and well built. The woman, Maggie, had short black hair and blue eyes and real muscles under that thin T-shirt. She was tall for a woman, too. In fact, she had a real military bearing. Something was mysterious here. Not unlike Tate himself.

But Pierce had no time for conjecture. He followed Tate to the door, where Brianne had just reappeared. Mike loaded them into the van and took off for the harbor. The men in suits didn't even wave. They got back into their cars and followed the van out onto the highway. But when Mike turned off toward the bay, the others continued north.

"No offense, but I'm really tired of ships," Brianne muttered as they sat in the hold of the shrimp vessel with the smell of its recent cargo all around them.

"I must confess that I am tired of them as well," Mufti, who'd kept his silence for most of the trip, replied. He sighed. "My poor people," he added quietly.

"Monsieur Sabon will protect them," she assured him.

"We are enemies," he protested. "He will want revenge because I spied on him in his household."

"He said he wouldn't," she reminded him.

He shrugged. "Things are unsettled. If the Americans come with their bombers, many will die. Even if my country is not blamed for the uprising, it will suffer.''

She put a gentle hand on his arm. ''Mufti, things happen the way they're supposed to. It may not be logical, but there it is. You have to accept what you can't change.''

He grimaced. ''A hard thing to do.''

''For all of us. But usually, we have little choice.''

He nodded.

She glanced toward the other end of the hold, where Pierce and Tate were speaking in hushed whispers. She wondered why none of Tate's men had come with them. Surely they'd be safer under armed guard. But perhaps he thought that it would be less conspicuous this way.

As they chugged up the coastline, Brianne went out on deck for some air. Two crewmen who were mending the huge nets that the ship used to catch shrimp were watching her stealthily. She glanced at them, puzzled because they didn't really look like fishermen. They had clean, neat hands with trimmed nails and no dirt beneath them. Their shoes, deck shoes, looked brand-new. They were both wearing lightweight dark jackets, and there were bulges under them. They lifted their heads and stared at her with that same unsmiling, serious gaze she'd come to expect from men like Tate Winthrop. And that was when it all clicked into place. This was no shrimp boat. It was a facsimile of a shrimp boat, but with a crew that probably came no closer to searching for fish than with a fork in a restaurant.

Her arm was grasped firmly by Pierce's big, lean hand, and she was led back down into the hold.

"We're within telescope distance of the coast, and helicopters can reach us here," he said firmly. "Don't go out on deck again."

She looked him straight in the eye. "This isn't a shrimp boat."

"Clever girl," he mused. "No, it isn't."

"Who is Smith?"

"A professional mercenary," he replied quietly. "And not one of those bloodthirsty assassins your stepfather hired. Smith only takes on a few jobs, and they have to meet a strict criteria. He's worked for our government a time or two." He put his finger against her lips. "You didn't hear that from me. You know nothing."

"I feel like a spy," she mused, enjoying the touch of his skin against her lips when she spoke.

"Do you?" He framed her face in his big hands and bent to take her mouth tenderly, gently, under his. "Try to stay out of trouble," he whispered into her open lips.

"Who, me?" she replied unsteadily. "I never go looking for it, it just seems to find me." She reached up with her arms. "Come back here," she murmured, tugging at his neck.

He sighed with resignation, smiled and lifted her up to his waiting mouth. It was a long, hungry kiss that never seemed to end. But before it became urgent, he set her back on her feet with a jolt.

"I'm divorcing you tomorrow," he said.

She searched his eyes, hoping for humor, but there wasn't any. He was serious.

"Are you sure?" she asked. "I could make it worth your while to keep me."

"Oh?"

She stared at his mouth, his chin, his thick wavy hair. She met his searching eyes squarely. "Pierce, don't you want a child?" she asked softly.

The reaction she got was unexpectedly violent. He jerked her hands down and pushed her away firmly. "No, I don't want a child," he said through his teeth. "Not ever!"

She was a little surprised by his vehemence. "Why not?"

His eyes were flashing danger signals. "Don't ask me that."

"I want to know," she persisted. "Why don't you want children?"

He turned away from her in an agony of grief and loss. He remembered the baby he and Margo had anticipated, the joy of her pregnancy, the dreams they'd shared. Her miscarriage and the subsequent knowledge that she could never bear another child had shattered both of them. He told Brianne of the loss, never meeting her eyes.

"Oh, now I see," she said in a resigned tone. "Margo lost hers, so you don't want one with anyone else."

He jammed his fists into his pockets. "Dreams die hard."

"Tell me about it," she returned harshly.

"A child would make a tie we couldn't break," he said, not giving an inch. "Divorce would be impossible."

"Why?" she asked. "Don't you think I could raise a baby on my own? I'm not helpless."

He turned slowly and looked at her. "There won't be a child, Brianne," he said. "I don't want one with you."

That was the hardest blow of all. He wasn't risking his heart again, either with a woman or a pregnancy. His emotions were going to hibernate. He'd already withdrawn from Brianne in most respects; now he was fortifying barriers. He didn't want anything that would bind them, least of all a child.

It was an interesting comment, when she knew quite well that she wasn't taking the pill and they'd been intimate at the very best time for a child to be conceived. Well, he didn't know that and he wouldn't know it. He didn't want a child with her, so if one happened, he'd be the last person in the world to know about it, she decided. It would be her baby. Hers alone.

"I'll remember that you said that," she replied quietly. She even smiled. She turned away with a long sigh. "Are we going straight to the Capitol?" she asked pleasantly.

He pondered her question, which temporarily diverted him. "Near enough. All we have to do is get to the Senate office building without being shot."

She laughed. "What a reassuring way to put it."

"Tate and these guys will get us there," he said.

"I hope you're right." She went to the porthole and looked out. There was only miles of ocean to see, but even that was preferable to having to look at her husband's closed face.

Pierce was feeling guilty about what he'd said to her. But it wouldn't have been fair to let her hope that anything was going to change. She'd go to college and he'd go back to work. A child would only...complicate things. His eyes narrowed as he looked at Brianne and had a sudden, shocking picture of her with a nursing baby at her breast. She'd be a perfect mother, he thought irritably. She'd do all the right things for it, cherish and love it. It would be a wanted child, a needed child. He closed his eyes. He couldn't afford to let himself think that way. She was too young to make that sort of commitment to a man, he was certain of it. He wasn't risking his heart on a gamble. He gave her one last, lingering look and went to find Tate.

The shrimp boat pulled into a little marina near the river inlet that led to Washington, D.C. A long black limousine was waiting for the three passengers who came up on deck when the boat docked.

A lean, dark man in a suit got out and approached the boat, flanked by two of Tate's men who'd met them in Savannah.

"Lane," Tate said, shaking hands with the newcomer, who was almost as tall as himself.

"Good to see you, boss," Colby Lane answered with a brief smile that was more like a grimace in Pierce's direction.

"You can drop the sweet talk," Pierce muttered. "My fist has almost healed."

Colby rubbed his jaw. "So has my jaw," he mused. "I won't make that mistake again!"

"See that you don't," Pierce replied pleasantly. "Have any trouble getting here?"

"A minor skirmish at the Maryland border," he replied. "Two of Brauer's men are now in federal custody."

"Good for you."

"Let's go," Colby said. "We're still being followed, but I think we can outrun them."

"Everybody inside," Tate said, motioning his companions into the car.

Mufti grimaced as he compared his sweats to

the dignified suits of the people with him. "I look not very convincing in such clothing," he murmured uneasily.

"You look quite convincing to me," Tate replied, and smiled at him. "Nobody is going to expect any of us to look bandbox fresh." He wrinkled his nose at the way they all smelled. "Good thing, too. We smell like a cheap shrimp dinner."

"And many days old, too," Brianne murmured with a subdued chuckle.

"We've tracked Senator Holden to his hot tub," Tate told them. "He'll smell better than we do, but he won't be as nicely dressed."

"Is that Brauer's friend?"

Tate shook his head. "We wouldn't risk approaching him, under the circumstances. Brauer's probably got him convinced that we're dangerous subversives. No, Holden is..." He hesitated and averted his eyes. "He's someone I know. Cocky as all hell, and hard to talk to, but he's honest and fair. He'll give us a hearing."

Something was suspicious there, but Pierce didn't push his security chief for information. It was hardly the time. He glanced at Brianne with renewed worry. Nothing was going the way he'd planned, lately, least of all his private life. He'd be glad when this was over and he could make decisions.

Chapter Fourteen

The ride through the capital was one Brianne wasn't likely to forget. Another black limousine picked them up as they headed into D.C., and shots were fired at them from behind. She didn't realize the car was armored and had bulletproof glass until she saw the lack of effect the bullets had.

"Pull into the next lane," Tate told the driver, pulling his automatic weapon from under his jacket. His friend Colby did the same.

"Don't get shot," Pierce muttered.

Tate looked shocked. "I'm bulletproof," he said haughtily.

"Me, too," Colby agreed.

"All right. But be careful."

The car stopped and the two men leaped out of the doors simultaneously, slamming them shut on the way out.

It was like ballet, Brianne mused, spellbound as she watched the action through the tinted windows.

The men in the car that had been following them jumped out of their own stopped vehicle and started firing nonstop. The gunfire was returned, but in short, sharp bursts.

"SAS style," Pierce mused.

"What?" Brianne asked.

"Two shots, pause, two shots."

"What's an SAS?"

"The British special forces."

"Oh, those guys!" she exclaimed. "I've read about them."

"Everybody's read about them, but Tate once served with them on a hush-hush mission in the Middle East in the early nineties."

"Is there anything he hasn't done?" she asked, aghast.

"Not much." He was watching the action, too. Suddenly, Pierce pulled Brianne to him and hid

her face in his shirt, holding her even when she
tried to draw away. "Stay there," he said curtly.

"Why?" she demanded, her voice muffled by
his shirt.

"You don't need to see this."

The gunfire had stopped. Seconds later, Tate
was back in the car, leaving Colby behind. Another of the suited men nodded toward Tate and
got out, slamming the door behind him.

"They'll phone the appropriate authorities and
clear this up," Tate said. "Get going," he told
the driver. He didn't say another word for two or
three minutes. "You can let her up now. They're
out of sight."

Pierce let Brianne lift her head. "I'm no lily,"
she muttered as she pushed back her disheveled
hair.

"You're no rock, either," Pierce told her
firmly. He caught her small hand in his and held
it warmly. He was going to miss her, he mused
sadly. She was the only reason he'd had to smile
in recent months. The smile faded as he tried to
picture his life when she wasn't in it. He didn't
like what he saw.

She drew her hand away with a mock glare.
"You don't have to hold my hand. I wouldn't hit

you,'' she said innocently. ''Well, not very hard.''
She glanced toward Tate, who looked unap-
proachable and taciturn as the car turned into a
long driveway that led to a Georgian mansion hidden behind some trees.

''I thought we were going into D.C.,'' Pierce
remarked.

''We are, when we get through here. The senator's had the flu and he's confined here for another day or two. Colby spoke to him. He thinks,
considering what we've just sustained, this is the
safest way to proceed.'' He checked his watch.
''Right on time, too.''

If Brianne was puzzled, so was Pierce. His security chief was one of the best in the business,
but the man was irritatingly taciturn sometimes
about his objectives and how he accomplished
them.

''You're sure Holden won't turn us in?'' Pierce
asked.

''Oh, I'm sure,'' Tate said. He didn't smile. If
anything, he looked tense and uneasy.

They got out of the car at the front door, and
with wary glances all around, they rushed into the
house that a butler was holding open for them.

''Senator Holden is in the library, sir,'' the man

told Tate, as if he knew him. "He's expecting all of you."

"Thanks." Tate avoided the man's searching gaze and strode ahead of the others into the walnut-paneled library, full of floor-to-ceiling bookcases and leather-covered furniture.

The man sitting in a thick bathrobe and pajamas before them came as a shock. He couldn't be Native American, Brianne surmised, but he certainly looked it. He had black eyes and straight black hair with more than a trace of silver threading through it. He was big and burly, more like a wrestler than a politician.

"Well, don't just stand there, sit down," he said in a gruff, husky voice, reminiscent of a soldier's commanding tones. He scowled at Tate. "Are these the people you had your cohort tell me about? You couldn't have spoken to me yourself, of course."

Tate seemed to grow taller. His black eyes flashed. When he scowled, he looked amazingly like their host. "There wasn't time, Senator," he said, fighting down his hostility. "My boss, Pierce Hutton, his wife, Brianne, and Mufti—our star witness against Brauer."

"I'm glad to meet you," the old man said

sharply. "This thing is very disturbing, very disturbing," he repeated. "I simply can't believe that any rational human being would bend so low. Starting a war and blaming it on an innocent nation—it's obscene!"

"Yes, it is," Pierce said. "But he thinks he can get away with it. He's tried every way he could think of to stop us, right down to attempted assassination."

"You made it. I knew you would," the senator replied, with a hostile glance toward Tate. "He's good. In fact, he's the very best at what he does—professionally."

It was a dig, and Pierce was surprised to see it register on his security chief's impassive face. Tate rarely showed deep emotion. He was feeling it now and Pierce wondered why.

"I want the whole story," the senator continued. He stared at Mufti. "Let's start with you."

Mufti was nervous at first, but the senator, despite his gruffness, quickly put the man at ease. After a few minutes, Mufti felt like an old and trusted friend. He told the man everything, from his attempts at spying on Sabon, to the sudden appearance of the mercenaries, to Sabon's flight.

"This man Sabon, he was in on it?" the senator asked.

"Only at first," Brianne said quickly, knowing that nobody else would defend Philippe. She explained who the man was and why he'd enticed Brauer to his country and used him to approach the oil cartel.

"Brauer's told his friend in the Senate that Sabon is the culprit," he replied. "That Sabon used the excuse for a military coup to take over his country, because he's really working for the revolutionaries in Salid."

"Philippe Sabon is the son of the ruling sheikh of Qawi," Brianne said. "Something that my stepfather doesn't know. Yet. It doesn't make sense that after going to so much trouble to attract investors and oilmen to his country, Philippe would sabotage the whole thing by staging a military coup that he doesn't need in order to gain power. He already has power."

"He wanted American intervention."

"Only to save his oil fields from Mufti's employers," Brianne said with an apologetic glance at Mufti, who was looking uncomfortable. "They're even poorer than Philippe's countrymen, and they were looking toward an assault on those oil fields, hoping to capture some of them. I'm sorry, Mufti, but he has to know the whole truth. A war will serve no one."

He seemed to slump. "Yes, I understand that."

"Third World nations," the senator said with a heavy sigh. "Most of them have economies that amount to less than my annual grocery bill. Starving people, starving economies, and the industrial nations just go right on letting it happen. Millions for arms and research to make better weapons, pennies to feed the hungry." He smiled ruefully as the others stared at him. "I'm a liberal," he said shortly. "You can't eat money."

Pierce chuckled. "No, but you can feed a lot of people if you can convince those who have it to use it wisely."

"You don't have to paint me any pictures, Hutton, I know how you use yours," he returned with a look of admiration. "You've done more for relief efforts than any other businessman I know."

Pierce shrugged, ignoring Brianne's surprise. "I do what I can." His eyes narrowed. "Brauer has to be stopped. We think if he knows how badly he's being beaten, he may order his mercenaries to set fire to the oil fields."

"What would be the point?"

"Revenge, plain and simple. He can throw suspicion on Sabon and even on Mufti's people. If he manages to start a war that way, couldn't the threat of an ecological disaster in the region provoke U.S. intervention?"

"It could," the senator said grimly. He ran a hand through his thick, straight hair. "Damn!"

"Can you get us in to see the under secretary of state?" Pierce asked.

Senator Holden was thinking. He didn't reply for a minute. "Brauer will have spiked your guns by the time you get there. I imagine he's got government agents looking for you right now."

"Then what can we do?" Brianne asked.

The senator studied the four people intensely. He pursed his lips and smiled. "I have a friend at the news station INN," he murmured.

He did, indeed, have several friends at the International News Network, and they came to his home, complete with reporter, cameras and sound equipment. In the senator's study, the whole terrifying plan that Kurt Brauer had evolved was laid out for the world community to hear. Mufti was eloquent in defense of his people and the way they were being used in Brauer's attempt to overthrow Sabon's little country. By the time they finished and the camera crew was on its way back to D.C., there were many busy people in the capital looking for Kurt Brauer.

He wasn't hard to find, once the breaking news story hit the airwaves. He was arrested right in the office of his friend the senator and taken away by federal officials. Some of his mercenaries were picked up in Florida, others in Georgia and near the coast of Virginia.

International police officers caught another batch in St. Martin just as they closed in on a dark European who'd just exited a local bank there, on the French side of the island.

Troops from a nation friendly to the United States, and working unofficially, went to support a contingent of Sabon's military over the border as they returned to launch a counterrevolution against Brauer's hired mercenaries. Many of Brauer's cohorts were killed in the firefight, many others were taken away to jail. In a matter of days, the ruling sheikh, returned from exile, was back in his seat of office. The oil fields were under guard now, and the oil consortium's officials and workers were free to return to their jobs there.

Kurt Brauer was held under a federal warrant

because the mercenaries he'd used were American nationals. He was accused of multiple crimes, one of which found him coming to the attention of the KGB under a warrant issued by the Russian government. His attempt to destroy an oil rig in the Caspian Sea was documented in a sworn and notarized statement by a man named Philippe Sabon. The Russians, it was said, were demanding Kurt's extradition to Moscow for trial. Tate seemed to think that the Americans might be relieved to have Brauer off their hands.

"Your mother is safe in Jamaica," Tate told Brianne, when all of them, including Mufti, had gathered in Pierce's Washington town house to discuss the future. "She can come home now. She'll be safe."

"Thank you," Brianne said with heartfelt gratitude.

He shrugged. "Thank Pierce," he mused, with a smile at his boss. "He gives the orders."

She turned to her husband. She noticed that he'd had a chance to shower and shave, because he looked fresh. She'd showered, too, but the days of uncertainty had left their mark on her. She was pale and she'd lost a little weight, even in the brief space of days since they'd been in the States, telling their story to one subcommittee after another.

"Thank you for saving my mother and the baby," she told him.

Pierce only smiled. "No problem. She'll have anything she wants when she returns. I've made arrangements for her to have a house on the ocean in Jacksonville. She'll like it."

"You don't have to do that," she began.

"I'm afraid I do. Brauer invested everything he had in the oil scheme. He didn't leave a penny unaccounted for." His dark eyes narrowed. "I can afford her, Brianne. She won't be able to live as extravagantly as she has, but she'll get by, she and the child."

Brianne still felt uncomfortable letting him keep her family, especially since she was shortly to be his ex-wife.

"Putting me through college is going to be expense enough," she said tightly.

"Pocket change," he said flatly. "Or didn't you realize that when people said I was rich, they weren't kidding?"

She averted her eyes. "Your money was never of much interest to me."

"I know that."

She turned away. "I'd better pack."

Pierce felt his heart kick hard against his ribs. "Pack?"

"Pack."

She kept going.

Tate studied his boss curiously. "Is she going somewhere?"

Pierce rammed his hands hard into his pockets. "To Las Vegas to get a divorce," he said through his teeth.

Tate pursed his lips. "Smart girl."

The look on the older man's face surprised his security chief. It wavered between homicide and shock.

Tate wasn't intimidated. He went to the piano and picked up a framed photo of Margo that still stood there. The glance he gave Pierce was eloquent.

Pierce's expression hardened. He knew what the other man was saying, even without words.

Tate put the photo down. "She must have been a unique and very special woman, to deserve such loyalty from you." His dark eyes narrowed. "But Brianne is unique and special herself."

"The years are wrong," Pierce said shortly.

The other man smiled sadly. "I've used the same argument myself. But in the early hours of the morning, when I'm alone, it's not much consolation."

Pierce couldn't detect a shadow of emotion in the other man's face, and he felt vaguely sorry for Cecily, who loved his security chief with so little hope of happiness.

"She loves you," Tate continued.

Pierce's face hardened. "She thinks she does."

Tate's broad shoulders rose and fell. "Suit yourself. Where is she going to school?"

"She wants to go to the Sorbonne, in Paris. I'd rather she went here, in D.C., so that you can keep tabs on her. Brauer may still have henchmen who owe him a favor."

"She'd be just as safe with you in Nassau," Tate returned. "And I don't need any more complications in my life right now than I've already got, especially female ones."

That was when Pierce was certain that something had gone very wrong for Tate Winthrop. "Can I help?" he asked sincerely.

Tate shook his head. "Personal problems, and they aren't easily resolved, even for the people involved."

"Cecily?" Pierce probed.

Tate's face closed immediately. "I can't think about Cecily right now. I won't."

That meant that she wasn't directly involved. He wondered what was.

"If I get in over my head, I'll let you know," Tate told him. "And thanks."

"What are friends for?" Pierce turned away. "All right, I'll let her go back to Paris. It isn't as if I've got much choice. Assign one of your agents with a current passport to go with her, and get him a visa. I'll also want one to keep an eye on Mrs. Brauer in Jacksonville. Hire more people if you have to. This is important to me."

"Will do. I'll send Marlowe with Brianne. He's young and handsome and sharp as a tack. She'll like him."

Pierce whirled, his eyes furious. He didn't have to say a word. That expression said it for him.

"So," Tate mused, smiling faintly. "Not as uninvolved as you pretend to be, hmmm?"

Pierce's big fists tightened at his side. He realized at that moment just how involved he was with Brianne, so involved that the mere thought of her with someone else was enough to make a madman of him.

Tate sobered. "Live your life as you please," he told his boss. "But if you let her go, you'll have to realize that she's young and pretty and full of fire. She won't be sitting around by herself."

The knowledge was painful. Of course she wouldn't. She'd be out dining and dancing, having fun with people her own age, enjoying her youth. Once Pierce was out of the picture, it wouldn't take long for some new man to step into it. He felt rage all the way to his toes as he considered that.

"Pity," Tate murmured, turning away.

"What's a pity?"

"The waste of all that wide-eyed wonder. Brianne isn't used to wealth. She isn't blasé about life in general." He shook his head. "She might have given you a new perspective on the world around you. But, as you say, it's just as well. She'll be happier with someone younger."

He went to find Mufti, to tell him about the arrangements they'd made to fly him back to Salid in style. At least things were working out for one member of their little party, he thought.

Chapter Fifteen

Tate took Mufti to the airport and sent him home to his native land.

"He'll be a hero," Pierce told Brianne when the others had gone and they were alone. "Of course, he'll also convey a warning about what can happen if his people decide to make a grab for Qawi's oil."

She glanced at the framed photo of Margo and wrapped her arms around herself. She felt a chill as she thought about the coming trip to Las Vegas. Margo had won again.

"When do we leave for Las Vegas?" she asked with her back to him.

He drew in a sharp breath. That trip had no

appeal to him whatsoever. He was worn-out from their captivity and escape, and it wounded him to think of throwing Brianne out of his life so quickly. She looked vulnerable in her soft oyster silk pantsuit, with her long blond hair wound in a braid around her head.

"Not today," he said shortly. "I have to get out to our platform in the Caspian Sea and check on my men's progress."

She glanced at him curiously. Shouldn't he be anxious to get it over with? Her eyes ate him up, from his powerful long legs in black slacks to his broad chest in an open-necked beige silk shirt. He looked bigger than ever, so attractive with his thick, wavy, silver-flecked black hair and black eyes and olive complexion. She ached for him all over again and hated herself for her vulnerability.

He moved closer to her as if drawn by invisible threads. The silence in the apartment was suddenly tense, alive.

He stopped, towering over her, his black eyes sliding with growing hunger over her lifted face.

His eyes narrowed. "Do you want me?" he asked in a tone she'd rarely ever heard him use.

Her heart jumped. "Wh-what?"

"You wanted one night," he reminded her. "Not a rushed encounter where interruptions were always a threat." He jerked his head toward the hall. "The bedroom is through there. It's a king-size bed," he added huskily.

She wanted to. She didn't have to put it into words. It was visible in her eyes, her face, her tense body.

"Do you…want to?" she whispered.

"Oh, yes," he said with bitter self-contempt. "More than anything in the world."

She lifted her arms, and he bent and swung her up off the floor, feeling a foot taller, ten years younger, as she burrowed close and buried her warm, soft mouth against his throat where thick hair peeked out of the opening of his shirt.

His arms contracted. He walked down the hall with her, into his bedroom. He kicked the door shut behind them and lightly tossed her onto the cream-and-brown striped coverlet. After he unplugged the telephone, he unbuttoned his shirt, standing over her prone body, his eyes smoldering as his hands dealt with the pearl buttons.

She watched him undress, her breath coming rapidly. It was broad daylight. The curtains were open. She could hear traffic in the street below, she could see the stripes the sun made as it filtered through the venetian blinds and onto the beige carpet of the room.

Her whole body was tense with delicious anticipation when he came to her, tall and fit and completely uninhibited about his nudity, and his arousal. He drew her up long enough to divest her of her own clothing.

His lean, warm hands slid over the softness of her body from her breasts down her flat belly and then to her hips and thighs. "You're trembling," he chided softly. "Surely you aren't afraid of me."

She arched a little under the electrifying sensations caused by his caressing hands. "I'm on fire for you," she whispered huskily.

He smiled gently. She was never coy or coquettish about this. He touched and she yielded completely. It made him proud, because he knew how cool she was with other men.

He drew her gently to him, enjoying her soft gasp as she felt his arousal against her so blatantly.

His mouth brushed against hers. He took his time, nibbling first her upper lip and then the lower one, toying with her mouth before he finally eased his own between it, and began to kiss her with slow insistence.

Her nails bit into the hard muscles of his upper arms, and she moved closer as the familiar throbbing ache settled in her lower stomach.

His hands eased between them to trace around her firm breasts. He touched her delicately, with fingers that barely brushed her, in circles that were lazy and sweet and arousing. She arched, but he ignored the invitation and kept his hands at a deliberate distance from her nipples.

Her nails bit harder into him. "Pierce!"

His hard mouth teased her soft lips while his hands continued their subtle play on her body. "Don't be impatient," he said quietly. "I'm going to take a long time with you."

She made an odd little sound in her throat. He covered her mouth with his own, and his hands moved ever closer to those hard, aching peaks. Finally, finally, when she was almost mad with hunger, his thumbs and forefingers took the nipples between them and contracted gently.

Her hoarse cry of pleasure was loud in the silence of the bedroom. Pierce's mouth on her lips became insistent as her headlong response kindled a roughness in him.

But he controlled it quickly. He lifted her onto the bed and held her between his hands while his mouth replaced his hands on her breasts. He suckled her in a silence that was alive with tense passion. She writhed helplessly under the torment of his warm lips as they moved from her breasts to her rib cage, to her soft, flat stomach and then down to the silky softness of her upper thighs.

Time seemed to go into permanent eclipse in the heated minutes that followed. He touched and tasted and nipped and teased, savoring her violent reaction, her soft little cries of delight as he pleasured her.

When he poised at the threshold of her womanhood, she caught his hips and tried to pull him down, but he wouldn't be moved.

He lifted his head and black eyes bit into hers at point-blank range. "No," he whispered. "Lie still."

"Pierce," she sobbed, shivering with torment.

"A breath at a time, Brianne," he whispered, moving gently as he looked into her eyes. She gasped and his hips withdrew, hesitated, and then came back to hers in a slow, seductive dance.

"I...can't..." she sobbed.

"You can." He caught both her hands in his and held them over her head on the coverlet. One long leg moved hers gently apart, and he eased down and then up again, repeating the teasing movement rhythmically, but never coming closer than that.

She tensed, shivering, as each movement of his powerful body sent thrills of pleasure up and down her spine. Her heart was racing madly. He seemed completely removed from what they were doing, his eyes watchful, in total command of himself and her.

He shifted sinuously, increasing the contact. She caught her breath and her body lifted to his helplessly.

He looked down the length of her body, enjoying its soft innocence, its wondrous response. He could smell her light perfume, the faint sweat that clung to her, the womanly smell of her.

Her eyes followed his, a little shocked at the intimacy of it, and then met his own again. There was delight in them, mingled with lingering traces of inhibition.

He bent and brushed his lips over hers. "You haven't looked before."

"It was too quick before," she said unsteadily.

"And now it isn't." He traced her upper lip with his tongue while his body rose and fell tenderly against hers. "I want to feel every pore of you as close to me as you can get," he breathed into her mouth. "When I have you, I want to possess you completely."

She caught her breath, aroused by the words as much as the rhythm of his body.

He shifted roughly to one side and then the other. The action was so arousing that she cried out.

He pushed down suddenly and lifted just as suddenly, feeling her body constrict with pleasure. He gasped, too, overwhelmed by the delicious stab of delight it gave him to feel her like that.

He moved again, slowly losing control. His mouth opened against hers and penetrated it in warm, soft thrusts that mirrored the movements of his body.

She arched up to him, tears wetting her eyes as the pleasure became unbearable. Her fingers grasped his feverishly as she shivered.

"It won't be enough," he said roughly. "Dear God…!"

He shifted her quickly, sitting up on the bed. His hands gripped her thighs and held her over him, his breath rasping in his throat as he let her ease down to possess him in one slow, achingly sweet motion.

She clenched onto his broad shoulders, feeling the thick hair on his chest tickle her breasts as he moved her against him.

He lifted her and then pulled her down, shifting her body sharply with each slow thrust, his black eyes looking straight into hers. He could barely keep his head. He felt the pleasure build and then flare like a fire with gas thrown on it. He watched her eyes mirror the fierce ecstasy she was giving him. His big hands contracted harshly, bruising her, as he began to build the rhythm.

She heard the box springs of the bed make alarming sounds as he moved her ever closer. She felt him in an intimacy that, despite their brief marriage, was beyond anything she'd ever known.

"I've never been this potent, Brianne," he whispered to her as his hands contracted again.

He grimaced and groaned as the fever burned in him. He shivered. "I can feel you..." His body shuddered. "I want to get...closer," he bit off, his blind eyes meeting hers in the grip of madness as his movements became violent. "I want to go...deeper...deeper...deeper!"

She felt her body suddenly open to him completely, felt the throbbing pleasure explode in waves of unbelievable ecstasy, felt her body convulse over his as the tension snapped and splintered into a scalding heat of satisfaction that made her cry out.

She knew he was looking at her, seeing her face, her wide, shocked, unseeing eyes as her body whipped against him.

The contractions spread from her body into his. He groaned harshly, his voice breaking as he gripped her hips and held her against him, riveted her to him, as the violent spasms lifted him straight up into the sun, into an oblivion so passionate that he felt himself throbbing for endless sweet seconds before the release came in a shattering rush.

She leaned her damp forehead against his equally damp chest, her whole body a sensitive instrument that registered delicious little explosions of pleasure in the aftermath of their loving.

He shivered, too, holding her close as he savored the delicious sensation of her body welded to his in such intimacy.

Her breasts were soft where they lay against his chest. He moved and felt her all around him, like warm, moist silk where she sheathed him.

He became aware slowly of the position they were in, and for an instant he felt staggering concern. "Brianne, did I hurt you?" he whispered urgently at her ear, his fingers slowly loosening their bruising grip on her hips.

"No," she whispered back, too shy to meet his eyes. Her lips touched his neck hesitantly. "We...never did it like this," she added.

"I've never done it like this," he replied in a deep, solemn tone. His hands moved up to caress her soft back. "I shouldn't have. I could have damaged you."

She looked up into his worried black eyes. "How?"

He looked down at where they were joined and swallowed hard. "You took all of me, baby," he said gently, lifting his eyes back to hers. "Are you sure I haven't hurt you?"

She shook her head and smiled tenderly. She touched his hard mouth with soft fingers. "It was incredible," she said, a little dazed.

His hands framed her face and he touched his mouth tenderly to her eyes. "Incredible," he agreed huskily. "I couldn't get close enough," he added, sounding as dazed as she felt. "I've never had it like this, never felt it like this." He drew in a shaky breath and shifted. As he did, his body reacted suddenly and violently and he gasped.

She felt the reaction with awe. "The books say that men can't, so soon afterward," she whispered shyly.

"That part of me can't read." He moved, easing her down onto the mattress. He positioned her gently, so that they were curled together with her legs over his, his knees on either side of her body. He held her face in his hands as he moved tenderly, watching her eyes register the fierce pleasure he gave her. It occurred to him at that moment, in the grip of the most sweeping tenderness he'd ever shared with any woman, that he wanted most desperately to make her pregnant.

He loved her as if he could, as if the exquisite

union would produce a child. Ridiculous, of course. She was on the pill and he was going to divorce her. But he could pretend. And he did. He made love to her in such a way that when the contractions came, they were the most poignant and profound pleasure he'd felt in his life. She felt it, too. He knew without the rushed, whispered words that were torn from her throat as the ecstasy shot through her like sweet fire.

They lay like that for a long time, unmoving. He never wanted to pull away. He wanted to stay in her arms like this. He wanted to stay with her.

The sweetness of it drained him of strength. He felt the world blurring around them. He slept, and she slept, intimately joined to him on the cover of the big bed.

Sometime during the night he awoke and pulled her under the covers with him, cradling her in his arms as they slept again.

But with morning came sanity and shock and disbelief. He looked at her pretty nude body on the white sheets and his head spun with memories of what she'd given him so generously.

He'd never felt more confused or more afraid. She was sweet and young and she loved him. He could stay with her. He could give her a child. They could live together forever....

He turned away and jerked clothes from drawers and the closet before he went to shower away the scent of her from his skin.

An hour later he let himself out of the apartment, leaving a brief, terse note behind to explain that he was making all the arrangements for her to go to Paris before he left for the Caspian Sea. They could discuss the divorce at some later time. He signed it with his initials and had to fight not to go back into his bedroom and look at the exquisite sight of his young wife in bed.

He'd shared that bed with his beloved Margo, and he felt like a traitor, an adulterer. Margo was dead, and he was alive. He realized that he had to face the future, but he couldn't do it now, in the shadow of that exquisite experience with Brianne. He had to get away, to think, to reason it out. He had to!

Brianne woke and found the note. It didn't surprise her. He was feeling guilty again. She went to the piano and looked at the smiling face in the photo.

"I love him, too," she told it. "What am I going to do?"

As she spoke the words from a breaking heart, she realized that there was only one thing she could do. She had to go to Paris and give Pierce enough time to make a decision about their future. She hoped and prayed that he made the right one, for both their sakes. In the meantime, she hugged the sweet memory to herself and thought that, if she had to, she could live on last night for the rest of her life.

Chapter Sixteen

Eve Brauer and her young son Nicholas set up housekeeping in a nice stucco house outside Jacksonville, near the Atlantic shoreline. Brianne spent a few days with her mother and Nicholas before she left for Paris. Eve and Brianne had entered into a tentative new relationship, a little strained on both sides. Eve was devastated to find herself with a husband facing a stiff prison sentence and also with no money to support herself.

The following week, one of Tate Winthrop's men went to Paris with Brianne: an older agent with a wife in the military. She almost grinned at the idea that Pierce had done that deliberately, to remove any chance of her getting too chummy with her bodyguard. But if he'd been jealous, she reasoned, he'd have gone to Paris with her. He hadn't phoned or written since his abrupt departure from the apartment. Oddly, she drew comfort from that. If he'd been able to be indifferent or cool about it, surely it wouldn't have bothered him to get in touch with her. The fact that he hadn't gave her hope.

He did go out to the drilling platform in the Caspian Sea and stayed there for several weeks, without a single word to his absent wife. He ached for her night after lonely night, despite his determination to forget what had happened.

Brianne enrolled at the Sorbonne, surprised to find that her application had already been accepted and her classes assigned. Fortunately, her French was adequate for her course of study, most of which involved numbers, anyway. She buckled down and buried her broken heart in hard work.

About the fourth week since their return from the Middle East, she started losing her breakfast. The following week, she fainted at the sight of a cut finger in her biology lab during a dissecting experiment. The sixth week, she stopped hiding her head in the sand and went to see a physician.

It seemed there was a reason for all her symptoms, and it wasn't strain or overwork.

Coincidentally, she had an unexpected visitor on the one day she was ill enough to skip classes and stay home in her luxurious Paris apartment.

The apartment building had perfect security, of course; Pierce wouldn't have let her stay anywhere else. So the buzzer in the apartment sounded when the security guard downstairs was asked where she could be found.

"There is a gentleman down here asking for you, *madame*" came the softly accented voice. "He wishes to impart news of a Monsieur Sabon...."

"Oh, please, send him right up!" Brianne said without hesitation. She'd wondered where her captor was since his return to his own country. Apparently things were settling down there, because the defeat of the mercenaries and the return of the ruling sheikh, as well as the oil consortium's discovery of enormous oil reserves, had become front page news.

She brushed her long hair and pulled a gold-and-white caftan over her nightgown to meet her visitor. It wasn't a revealing garment; it looked much more like a lounge dress than a bathrobe.

When the door buzzer sounded, she opened the door at once, expecting a dignitary from Sabon's country. Instead, there was Philippe Sabon himself, in a gray Italian suit that looked as if every thread in it was placed with the utmost care.

He smiled at her surprise, pulling the scars on his cheek tight, so that they were white and noticeable against his swarthy complexion. He produced a bouquet of white roses and baby's breath and handed it to her.

"I may not be welcome, but I had to come, to see for myself how you are," he commented, not revealing the joy it had given him to hear her voice excited at the prospect of news about him.

"You're very welcome," she said with a smile, cradling the roses. "Do come in and sit down. Would you like coffee?"

He held up a hand. "I wish to put you to no trouble...."

"It won't be. Therese!" she called, and the young maid came out and was given instructions. "And slice some pound cake, Therese. Our guest may be hungry."

"I am, indeed," Philippe replied as he studied her drawn face with a narrow, clinical gaze.

"You look pale, and I am sure you have lost weight."

"A little, perhaps," she said noncommittally.

He leaned forward, with mischief in his dark eyes. "Come home with me and live in my harem," he challenged. "I will have the servants feed you sweetmeats and marzipan until you are a proper size!"

She laughed delightedly. "That's the best offer I've had in weeks," she said.

He smiled, too, less abrasive about his limitations than most men would have been. He studied her with soft eyes. "Would that it were so," he said on a gentle breath. "But a harem would bring constant danger of discovery, would it not? Something I would never dare risk."

"You're the son of the reigning sheikh," she reminded him. "Won't you have to have an heir?"

"Certainly." He crossed one long leg over the other and studied her quietly, drinking in her radiant beauty. "Your firstborn will be my heir."

"That's not funny."

"It wasn't meant to be," he said nonchalantly. "My father knows how it is with me, Brianne," he added. "It is a great sorrow for us both. But your husband is dark and the child is likely to be so, as well, with Greek blood in his veins. A kingdom, even a small kingdom, is nothing to turn your pretty nose up at, *chérie.*"

She was stunned. "But why?"

He just stared at her, for a long time. "I think you know why."

She was still absorbing that when the maid came with a tray of coffee and condiments, and a plate of sliced cake. She put a glass of milk in front of Brianne, who made a face.

"It is good for you," the maid, a widow with three grown children, said firmly. "You drink it."

Philippe eyed the milk with a chuckle. "Does he know?" he asked pointedly.

She sipped the milk with a militant glare. "No, he does not," she said through her teeth. "He doesn't want a child, so there won't be one. God has spoken!"

He burst out laughing. "It amazes me that you could keep it from him," he said, studying her. "You look mysterious and content."

"How would he know? He's sitting out in the middle of the Caspian Sea playing with his oil well."

He put cream in his coffee and sat back on the sofa to sip it. "You should call and tell him to come home."

"As if he would," she scoffed.

"You underestimate your charms," he replied.

She was remembering something that she'd almost let slip away. "When you left us, you said something in Arabic to Tate Winthrop. What was it?"

"Ask him."

"I have no idea where he is," she replied. "Tell me yourself."

He shook his head. "Some secrets should be kept, don't you think?" He finished his coffee. "I came to give you this for your husband," he said, producing a sealed envelope that she took and placed on the side table. "The repayment of his loan," he explained. "And also I came to ask both of you to attend my coronation."

Her heart skipped. "Is your father...?"

"No, he's not dead," he said at once. "But he realizes that his health makes it impossible for him to continue as head of state. A sheikhdom is not the same as a kingdom, you understand, but it is a sovereign nation just the same. Now that we will have access to oil money, from our first very successful wells, we must move into the twentieth century. This will not be easy for the various nomadic tribes that make up my nation. It will not be easy for me, either, since my blood is mixed. But these days, such things matter less than the authority and strength of the leader. I hope to be equal to the task.''

"Certainly you will,'' she said without hesitation. She studied his lean, dark face with faint sadness.

"Don't pity me,'' he said starkly. "I have more than many men. Allah decides these things. One must never fight that which is fated.''

"Now you sound Arabian.''

He smiled. "As I should, yes?'' He put the empty cup down. "Will you come, with your husband, of course, to see me invested? It is a very ancient ceremony, full of ritual and color.''

"I'd like to.''

"And Pierce?''

She shrugged. "I'll ask him. When is it?''

"In the spring. Six months from now.'' He glanced at the flowing caftan under which her child lay. "That might be an awkward time, but if it isn't, I'll make sure all the arrangements are made for you. All three of you, if necessary," he added with a grin.

"We wouldn't have escaped so easily without your help," she told him.

"You wouldn't have been in danger if I hadn't done such an insane thing. At the time, it seemed quite logical."

"Most things look clearer in hindsight," she agreed.

He stood up and so did she. He took both her slender hands in his, and kissed them lightly, before dropping them again. "Keep well. I meant what I told you. If ever you need help, in any way, I am yours to command."

"Thanks," she said sincerely. "But I'll muddle through."

"And take good care of my heir," he added with a smile in the direction of her belly.

After he was gone, she went out to the balcony overlooking the city and stood in the faint breeze, letting it ruffle her hair. She felt sorry for Philippe and sorrier for herself. She was pregnant and alone. Pierce wouldn't even write or call her. It was as if he'd shut her completely out of his life, at the very worst time. She wondered if she was going to see him before their child was born.

* * *

She wouldn't have wondered if she'd seen his face two hours later, when a telephone call interrupted his conference with his drill rigger on the drilling platform in the Caspian Sea.

"She *what?*" he burst out, his black eyes exploding with rage.

He listened again for a few seconds, cursed and broke the connection. "Get the helicopter pilot up here," he said shortly. "I'm flying out."

"But, sir, there's a gale...."

"I don't give a damn if there's a hurricane. Get him up here!"

Ten minutes later, they were airborne and on the way to the mainland.

It was dark, and Brianne was watching a French news broadcast when the front door of the apartment swung open and Pierce stalked in.

She sat up on the sofa where she'd been lounging, still in the pretty white-and-gold caftan, and gaped at him. He was disheveled, his shirt unbuttoned, his tie draped loosely around his neck under his jacket. He looked absolutely dangerous.

"Where is he?" he demanded fiercely.

"He?"

"Sabon! Don't deny that he's been here, I've already checked with the desk!"

She could barely find words. He was eaten up with jealousy. It absolutely oozed from every pore, and the delight she felt almost choked her. She forced words out. "Yes, he came to pay back the loan," she said, and moved to produce the envelope with Pierce's name on it.

He didn't even look at it. He was too preoccupied. "What else did he want?"

"To—to invite us to watch his father hand over control of the government to him," she stammered. "His father is stepping down."

"I don't care to watch him become king or sheikh or whatever the hell it is," he said shortly. "I want to know what he was doing here! He could have mailed the check and sent a message."

"Why are you so angry?" she asked with a wicked little smile.

"Because he told Tate Winthrop that you were the only thing on earth worth losing a kingdom for, that's why!"

So that was it. The mystery. She studied her furious husband with fascination. "Why should you care what he said?" she asked innocently.

"You went off to the Caspian Sea to forget about me. I live alone, I go to school alone, I do everything alone. Why shouldn't I have company if I want it?"

"You're married!"

She held up her ringless finger. "No, I'm not," she said. She'd just taken the ring off earlier to wash her hands.

His cheeks went ruddy with temper. His big fists clenched at his side. "Put the ring back on."

"I took it off and dropped it in the sand back in Qawi. I have no idea where it is," she informed him.

His jaw looked as if he were grinding his teeth. "I'll buy you a new one."

"I won't wear it, if its only purpose is going to be for show," she replied. "Speaking of weddings, when do I get my divorce?" she probed deliberately.

The strain in his face grew worse. "Why? Has Sabon proposed?"

"He would if I asked him to," she said confidently.

"You're married to me. I'm not giving you a divorce."

That was surprising, and absolutely delightful.

She stared at him with deliberate hauteur. "Dog in the manger, Pierce?" she taunted.

She saw, actually saw, his control snap. He went toward her like an avalanche, never pausing to count the cost. He tossed her down on the cushions and followed her down. She barely had a second to get her breath before his hard, warm mouth moved onto hers.

He was heavy, but the weight of him was welcome. She reached around his neck and gave in to the ardent fury. It was like coming home. She laughed softly under the crush of his mouth and wrapped herself around him, glorying in his anger, his jealousy, his headlong passion.

"Oh, Pierce, you idiot," she moaned into his hard mouth. "As if I could ever...*ever*...look at another man after you!"

He heard that, but he couldn't stop kissing her to analyze it. His body was on fire for her. He groaned as the kiss grew to a climax, and he felt himself going rigid with aching hunger for her.

Brianne was feeling just as hungry. But even through the unbridled delight, she felt the increasingly familiar discomfort rising into her throat. It was always worse lying flat. She squirmed, fighting nausea, and drew her mouth from under his.

"Damn!" she whispered miserably, swallowing hard. "You have to let me up, darling. I think I'm going to...oh, Lord!"

She pushed at him, surprising him into shifting. She was up and running for the bathroom. She barely made it in time.

He found her at the front of the toilet and suddenly everything made sense. He realized immediately what was wrong with her, and his face paled. All he could think of was that night with her in D.C., and his hunger to make her pregnant. But this was too sudden for him to think rationally.

"You said you were taking the pill," he ground out. "You promised me that you were protected! You lied!"

She couldn't answer him. She lifted a shaking hand and waved him away, resting her head on her forearm.

He contained himself long enough to jerk a washcloth from the rack and wet it. He handed it to her, watching as she began to relax. A minute later, she flushed the toilet and managed to drag herself to the sink, to bathe her face and rinse her mouth.

She tried to go around him, because his bulk was blocking the doorway, but he swung her up and carried her into the bedroom, depositing her gingerly on the bedspread, where she lay clutching the cloth to her eyes. He looked like thunder and lightning, and she knew that news of his approaching fatherhood had hit him hard. Very hard. They were right back to square one.

"Okay, you're right, it's all my fault. Why don't you go back to your oil platform?" she said in a ghostly tone. "Therese is here to look after me. I don't need you!"

He didn't speak. He couldn't manage words. He was torn between indignation and terror. She was pregnant. She was carrying his child. It was a complication he'd been determined to avoid. She hadn't even told him. Was she even planning to?

She moved the washcloth to her dry lips and stared up at him with resignation. The fury in his dark eyes told her how she felt. She didn't need to ask.

She put the cloth back over her eyes. Its cool

moisture took the nausea away and soothed the beginnings of a headache.

"You're pregnant," he said flatly.

"Give that man a cigar."

"Were you going to tell me?"

"No," she said at once. "I assumed that your first question would be who its father was."

Her flat accusation made him uneasy. "I wouldn't ask such a stupid question," he muttered.

"Imagine that!"

"Don't make jokes. It isn't funny."

"I won't contest a divorce," she said through the folds of the cloth. "Go ahead and start the proceedings."

"I can see us now in court, with you in a maternity dress, petitioning for an annulment."

She took away the cloth and glared at him. It surprised her to find him not mocking or sardonic, but actually smiling. And smiling tenderly, at that!

"I didn't say an annulment," she clarified. "I said a divorce."

"Who gets custody of the child if we divorce?"

"Since I'm carrying it..."

"I put it there," he reminded her.

"How long have you had the nausea?" he added gently. "I remember that Margo never suffered with it...."

She threw the washcloth at him with an expression that told him she wished it were a brick bat. "Get out!" she raged at him. "Get out of my apartment, out of Paris, out of my life! I hate you!" She sobbed with mingled fury and grief. "I don't want to hear about Margo!"

He winced. He didn't know what to say, but he certainly hadn't meant to say that.

She rolled over on the bed and buried her hot face in the pillow. "Leave me alone," she said in a hoarse whisper.

He hesitated, but he didn't want to make matters worse, if that was even possible. He looked at her small figure curled up in the voluminous caftan and wondered at the fragility of it. She seemed so strong, so capable normally, that it was a shock to see her vulnerable.

In the end, he did go out of the bedroom, though not out of the apartment. He went into the kitchen and had Therese make some hot herbal tea for Brianne. When it was ready he took it, with a small packet of unsalted biscuits, in to her on a tray.

She was sitting up in bed with red eyes and wet cheeks. He put the tray down on the bedside table and sat beside her on the bed.

"Here," he said gruffly, handing her the delicate china cup. "Therese says you like this. It's chamomile."

She took it reluctantly. "It helps settle my stomach," she murmured, sipping it.

He watched her drink it while he thought about what he was going to say.

"Las Vegas is that way," she pointed out the window. "You can divorce me by yourself, can't you?"

"Try to be reasonable," he said calmly. "A man just doesn't divorce a pregnant woman."

"You don't want it," she accused, staring into her tea. "You were a fanatic about birth control." She looked up angrily. "I keep my pills in my bedside table, which wasn't included in our impromptu trip to Philippe's island!" She lowered her eyes again quickly. "Afterward, there didn't seem much point in taking them at all anymore."

"Of course not. I was trying to save you from

Sabon.'' His eyes narrowed and he studied her face thoroughly. ''Rumors and gossip aside, Tate did some checking. It's hinted that Sabon isn't capable of fathering a child, and I don't think it's a question of sterility.''

She stared at her husband with a stark expression that involuntarily confirmed his suspicions.

''Don't worry,'' he said quietly. ''I don't intend to advertise what I know. Rather, what Tate found out for me. It was the only explanation I could find for Sabon's strange attitude toward you, and the fact that once we were kidnapped, you weren't afraid of him.''

She shifted uncomfortably and sipped more tea. ''I promised I wouldn't tell anyone.''

''It's nice to know that,'' he mused, watching her closely. ''I can tell you my own secrets and not have to worry that they're being repeated.''

She glared at him. ''You never tell me anything. Not that I care.''

He traced a pattern on the caftan over her softly rounded belly. ''You have an obstetrician?''

''No, I thought I'd let the stork do the delivery…. Of course I have an obstetrician, I'm not stupid!''

He sighed. "You mean to keep it, then."

The glare became pronounced. "Accident or not, I want the baby," she said shortly. "If you don't like it, that's just tough!"

He looked straight into her eyes as his big hand flattened over his child. He hadn't done much thinking about being a parent, but all sorts of outrageous events fixed themselves in his mind. A little child with dark wavy hair and Brianne's soft green eyes whom he could teach about the oil business and the world of high finance. A child to cuddle in the evenings when he came home from work. He and Brianne could take it to the museum and the opera, later, when it was older....

"I said, why did you come back?" she asked.

He lifted his eyes to her face. "Because your bodyguard phoned me on the drilling platform and asked if he should keep an eye on your Arab visitor."

Chapter Seventeen

Brianne grinned. "So that's why you rushed here."

She looked smug. Well, why not, she deserved to. He smiled sheepishly, and his broad shoulders rose and fell. "I suppose it was inevitable from that first day in Paris," he said absently as he studied her with a tender smile, "when you drew me out of the shell I was hiding my heart in." He caught her small hand in his and smoothed over it. "I was trying to get back to Margo, but there was nothing I could do short of suicide to accomplish it." He looked at her evenly. "The years are still wrong, but the baby is my guarantee that you won't dash off with the first younger man who catches your eye," he added with a mocking smile.

Why, he was jealous of her, she thought dazedly. And not only jealous; frightened as well, that he wouldn't be able to hold her.

"I love you," she said bluntly. "Why should I want to run off with anyone else, younger or not?"

She felt his fingers contract painfully around hers.

"What did you say?" he asked in a husky whisper.

"That I love you desperately, Pierce," she replied matter-of-factly. She searched his black eyes with a sigh. "Didn't you know?"

His gaze fell to her soft hand, engulfed in both of his. He released the pressure. "Not really," he said, his voice stark and flat. "I haven't given you much reason to love me lately." He eased his fingers between hers and scowled as he looked at them.

"Why else would I stay with a man who's still married to his late wife?" she asked a little sadly. "Any woman with good sense would have run the other way while there was still time."

His fingers curled closer into hers. "I loved

Margo,'' he agreed. ''It took a long time to let go of her.'' He lifted his face. ''But Tate was right. He said that you had the same qualities Margo had, and that I was a fool to let you go.'' He smiled halfheartedly. ''I wouldn't listen, of course. I went to the Caspian Sea and became my men's worst nightmare. I imagine they're all drunk with joy by now, having waved me off in the helicopter in virtual droves.''

She smiled back. ''Really?''

''I was looking forward to knocking Sabon through the window,'' he continued with a shrug. ''I guess we don't always get everything we want.'' He glared at her. ''From now on, he comes to see you only if I'm at home. Period.''

''You possessive chauvinist,'' she accused.

He lifted her small hand to his mouth and kissed it gently. ''I'm not sharing you, not even with the head of a foreign government.'' He glanced at the envelope. ''I didn't expect him to pay back the loan at all, much less this soon.''

''He's drowning in oil,'' she reminded him. ''I suppose his country is going to have a new lease on life.''

''He can stay in it, with my blessing,'' he said shortly.

She decided that it wasn't a politic time to tell him about Philippe's other promise, about their child.

"You have to go back, I suppose," she fished.

He drew her hand to his broad thigh and held it there. "I'm the boss," he told her. "I don't have to go anywhere unless it pleases me."

Her heart jumped. "You're staying?"

His black eyes slid over her slender body in the pretty caftan and he smiled. "For a few years, I guess. Fifty or so."

She didn't feel her breath whispering inside her at all. "Fifty...years?"

He nodded. His hand moved back to her rounded belly. "I'm not leaving you to go through a pregnancy with my baby alone. My baby," he said again, his voice full of wonder and hesitant delight. "I never thought about babies."

"You need to come to the Sorbonne with me and study biology," she told him.

He glared at her. "I know what causes them."

She chuckled shyly. "I noticed."

He smiled gently. "I'll take good care of you," he said quietly. "All my life." The smile faded as he traced her face with tenderness. "I'll give you anything you want."

She felt a thickness in her throat. "I only want you. But I'll take care of you, too, my darling."

His indrawn breath was audible. He looked at her with such poignant tenderness that she blushed. He bent and kissed her soft eyes with fierce gentleness. "Brianne!" he whispered. He drew in another steadying breath and looked at her hungrily for a long time before he spoke.

"What's wrong?" she asked softly.

His fingers touched her soft mouth and he stared at it, struggling with words he didn't want to say. "I can't...lose you," he whispered. "Dear God, Brianne, I can't lose you...!" Incredibly, his voice broke on the words.

"My darling!" She reached up and drew him hungrily down to her, kissing him everywhere she could reach, cradling him, overwhelmed with the wonder of his love for her. She felt his broad, warm face at her throat, felt the unashamed wetness against it as she murmured softly and kissed him with breathless tenderness. "I'll do my best to live as long as you do, but you can't leave me, either!" she whispered on a watery chuckle. Her arms contracted hungrily around him. "Oh, Pierce, I do love you so much!"

His arms became almost bruising as he reacted to the passion in her voice and the love for her that knocked the breath out of him. She felt his mouth at her ear. "I love you, Brianne," he whispered back. *"Je t'aime si beaucoup!"*

Not only did he love her, he told her he loved her in two languages, she mused, dazed with wonder and joy. She held him closer, and closed her own very wet eyes to savor the sound of it. Pierce loved her, and there was going to be a child. They had a lifetime ahead of them to share. It was the happiest moment of her life.

Margo's image didn't fade immediately, but over the months it became less a part of their lives as she grew large with the baby, and Pierce discovered the unadulterated joy of approaching fatherhood. She had two closets full of baby toys and a nursery already equipped with every modern convenience known to man. Pierce chose a new wedding band, with her, and he wore it now, instead of the ring Margo had given him.

Everyone knew that she was pregnant, because long before she began wearing smart maternity clothing, Pierce was announcing it with beaming pride to anyone willing to listen.

The baby was born on the very day that Philippe Sabon became regent of his country, so there was no question of them being able to attend the ceremony. But despite the importance of the day in Sabon's life, he still managed a bouquet of white roses for Brianne and a word of congratulations to the Huttons on the birth of their young son, Edward Laurence.

A weary Brianne kissed her exuberant husband while he gazed with awe and fascination at the tiny child in her arms, feeding hungrily at her breast.

"Thank you for not fussing about the roses," she whispered with a tired smile.

He chuckled. "Oh, I can forgive a rose or two, since he's an ocean away from us," he murmured. "God, Brianne, isn't he beautiful?" he exclaimed, watching the child.

"Very beautiful indeed," she agreed. She searched her husband's dark face and smiled.

The baby's fingers curled around one of his and he smiled, too.

"And you thought I was too young," she chided.

He chuckled. "That was before I realized how young you were going to make me. What a present," he murmured, bending to kiss his son's little head. "I can't think of anything of equal value to give you."

"He's mine, too," she reminded him. She reached up and touched his hard mouth gently. "We might give each other a daughter next time."

He pursed his lips and gave her a rakish grin. "Okay."

She laughed. Life was so sweet. She spared a thought for poor Philippe, who would never know the glory of holding his child in his arms. But it was only the one thought. The rest were centered wholly on the two most beloved males in the world, in her arms.

Take 2 of "The Best of the Best™" Novels FREE

Plus get a FREE surprise gift!

Special Limited-Time Offer

Mail to The Best of the Best™

3010 Walden Avenue
P.O. Box 1867
Buffalo, N.Y. 14240-1867

YES! Please send me 2 free novels and my free surprise gift. Then send me 3 of "The Best of the Best™" novels each month. I'll receive the best books by the world's hottest romance authors. Bill me at the low price of $4.24 each plus 25¢ delivery per book and applicable sales tax, if any.* That's the complete price, and a saving of over 20% off the cover prices—quite a bargain! I understand that accepting the books and gift places me under no obligation ever to buy any books. I can always return a shipment and cancel at any time. Even if I never buy another book, the 2 free books and the surprise gift are mine to keep forever.

183 MEN CH74

Name	(PLEASE PRINT)

Address	Apt. No.

City	State	Zip

This offer is limited to one order per household and not valid to current subscribers.
*Terms and prices are subject to change without notice. Sales tax applicable in N.Y.
All orders subject to approval.

UBOB-98   ©1996 MIRA BOOKS